Trailer Trash

Other books by Denise Grover Swank:

Magnolia Steele Mystery
Center Stage
Act Two
Call Back
Curtain Call (October 2017)

Rose Gardner Investigations
Family Jewels
Trailer Trash
For the Birds

Rose Gardner Mystery
Twenty-Eight and a Half Wishes
Twenty-Nine and a Half Reasons
Thirty and a Half Excuses
Falling to Pieces (novella)
Thirty-One and a Half Regrets
Thirty-Two and a Half Complications
Picking up the Pieces (novella)
Thirty-Three and a Half Shenanigans
Rose and Helena Save Christmas (novella)
Ripple of Secrets (novella)
Thirty-Four and a Half Predicaments
Thirty-Four and a Half Predicaments Bonus Chapters
Thirty-Five and a Half Conspiracies
Thirty-Six and a Half Motives
Sins of the Father (novella)

The Wedding Pact
The Substitute
The Player
The Gambler
The Valentine (short story)

Bachelor Brotherhood
Only You
Until You

denisegroverswank.com

Trailer Trash

A Neely Kate Mystery
Book One

Denise Grover Swank

Copyright 2017 by Denise Grover Swank

Cover art and design: Damonza
Developmental Editor: Angela Polidoro
Copy editor: Shannon Page
Proofreaders: Carolina Valedez Miller
All rights reserved.

Dear Reader:

When I decided to give you a peek inside Neely Kate's past, I had planned on making it a novella. I love giving you insights into the other characters' pasts, and I was dying to tell Neely Kate's story. But soon after I started writing, I realized her story was an actual book, not a novella.

So then began a new dilemma: I was releasing this book under the series title Rose Gardner Exposed Novellas, since my original plan had been to tell my readers about the other characters' "secrets." But then I started to realize this wasn't the end of Neely Kate's voice. She's a strong, interesting character who deserves a voice of her own. So, after a short discussion with my editor, Angela, we decided to give Neely Kate her own series—the Neely Kate Mystery series.

Here's what you don't have to worry about: Neely Kate is not leaving Rose's world. They are too perfect together, and I couldn't imagine splitting them up. (I would mourn that breakup.) But I could let Neely Kate have adventures of her own.

I can tell you that there will be a future Neely Kate book. I can not tell you when it will be. It might follow For the Birds, or it might follow the third Rose Gardner Investigation book, In High Cotton. Just know that I have a semi-plot of Neely Kate's second book in my head—I just need to figure out where it fits in the Rose Gardner world.

When you finish Trailer Trash, please read the Jed bonus chapter at the end. (There's another note about that chapter at the end, because apparently I'm really chatty with this book.)

Denise

Chapter One

My worst nightmare had just shown up at my front door. Well, the front door of RBW Landscaping, to be precise. Miss Dorie had brought it in with the morning mail.

I wasn't alone, but I was the only employee present. While RBW Landscaping now had six employees, everyone else was out working. Besides me, the person who spent the most time in the office was Rose. She was technically my boss, but if you ranked the complexities of our relationship, it would be:

1) Best friends
2) Housemates
3) Boss/employee
4) Co-investigators (although I suspect she wouldn't include this one)

Rose was out this morning, but my brother Joe, the chief deputy sheriff of Fenton County, had stopped by on his day off to bring over my current favorite drink (vanilla caramel latte with almond milk, sprinkled with nutmeg), using the drink delivery as a pretense for a chat. He'd been doing that a lot lately, ever since we found out the truth about my soon-to-be ex-husband. That he wasn't dead. That he'd turned tail and run off with some other woman.

But Joe knew me better than to up and mention that. He'd settled in on the edge of my desk, sipping his coffee while talking about his plans for his kitchen. He'd been remodeling a rental farmhouse, exchanging labor for rent. I'd seen Joe's work; his landlord was getting the better deal, but the more I got to know my newly discovered half brother, the more I realized the work he was doing was helping him with his demons.

I had plenty of my own demons, most of which Joe had no inkling of, and as soon as I saw the look on my mail lady's face, I knew one of them was about to claw to the surface.

The bell on the door chimed as Miss Dorie came in, carrying a stack of envelopes, but her eyes were wide with excitement. "Neely Kate, I have another one of your *mystery* envelopes."

Crap. Sometimes I hated being right.

Miss Dorie saw Joe on my desk and did a double take. "Deputy Simmons. I heard you were taking a day off."

I had to hand it to observant postal workers. Sometimes they knew more about what was going on in Henryetta than I did, and I made it my business to know things.

"It is," he said in his easy, laid-back tone, offering no other information.

Miss Dorie approached, handing me the stack of mail as she took stock of Joe's jeans and T-shirt, realizing he was lazing around my office, draped on my desk in a casual manner while we drank our coffees together. Alone. Her eyes flew wide open. "Are you two secretly *married?*"

Oh, my stars and garters. It would have been funny if it weren't so disturbing.

Joe spat out his coffee and started to cough.

I dropped the stack on my desk, jumping out of my chair to pat his back.

I wasn't surprised by her question. Now that Joe had decided to be part of my life, he'd taken to it with gusto. I suspected he only hung around so much because he was lonely, but I latched onto his attention like a woman dying of thirst, leaving her open mouth under a slow dripping faucet to catch every drop. I couldn't imagine why he'd be so interested in me otherwise.

Joe Simmons had grown up in a fancy house with servants and more money in his allowance than I'd earned in a year at my old job at the county courthouse. I'd grown up in trailer parks. I was trailer trash and I knew it, no matter how hard I tried to prove otherwise. Sometimes I watched Joe, prepared for the moment when he'd finally let me in on the joke, pointing and shouting, "Gotcha!" I didn't want to be caught off guard.

But now I was watching him closely for another reason. While I was whacking him on the back, he was eyeing the mail—more specifically, the white legal-sized envelope with the jack-o'-lantern stamp. It was addressed to Neely Kate Simmons with no return address.

Legally, my name was still Neely Kate Colson. I wanted to start using my maiden name of Rivers, but since no one could track down my renegade husband to serve him divorce papers, I was stuck. Not from any lack of trying on Joe's part. He'd tracked Ronnie down in New Orleans two weeks ago, only to watch my ex board a bus to Memphis.

And that's where his trail had run cold.

While we'd found out I was Joe's sister back in February, hardly anyone else knew about our new family dynamics. Who could blame Miss Dorie for jumping to conclusions?

Joe leaned forward and picked up the envelope.

"My word," Miss Dorie exclaimed, growing more and more excited over her scoop. "At first I thought the name was a mistake. Remember me asking if it was a mistake?" she continued, starting to dance in place. "I sure as Pete never put it together."

"We're not married, Miss Dorie," I said, trying to sound grumpy and not breathless from nerves. Joe could *not* see what was in that envelope, and if he figured out I was anxious, he'd insist on taking a peek.

"Then why do you keep gettin' mail delivered to Neely Kate Simmons?" she asked with a hand on her hip. "And the same dang stamp every time too. Who sends a Halloween stamp in the summer?"

Joe turned the envelope over to examine the back. Sure enough, there was nothing on there. Just like the last four. He stared at me, waiting for an explanation, while I debated my best course of action: should I refuse to discuss it or flat-out lie?

The look on his face told me he'd never let it go.

Lie it was.

I snatched it out of his hand. "It's my cousin's bad idea of a joke," I said with a grimace. "I think she's not-so-secretly jealous."

"Jealous of what?" Miss Dorie asked.

I opened my mouth to tell her the truth, but Joe said, "A Rivers family inside joke." He shot Miss Dorie a sympathetic grin. "Neely Kate tried to explain it to me, but I never got it."

"Huh," Miss Dorie said with narrowed eyes.

Huh, indeed.

"Have you had any more trouble with those teenagers egging your house?" Joe asked her.

"Nope," she said. "You seemed to put the fear of God into 'em."

"If you have any more trouble, you be sure to let me know."

"I will, Deputy Simmons." She headed out the door, none the wiser that Joe had hijacked some grade A gossip from her.

As soon as she left, Joe crossed his arms over his chest. "Who are the letters really from?"

I gave him a look that suggested his question was ridiculous. "I told you. My cousin."

"And since when did you have cousins in Little Rock?"

How did he know where it was from? The dang postmark.

I tried to hide my reaction by scrunching up my mouth in irritation. "Who said I didn't? You don't know everything about my family, just like I don't know everything about yours."

"That's for your own protection, Neely Kate."

"Like you lied to Miss Dorie about me being your sister?"

His face paled.

"Are you ashamed of me, Joe?"

His mouth flopped open like a hinge. "How can you ask me that?"

"Because you went to great lengths to make sure Miss Dorie didn't find out we're related."

His face softened. "It's better this way," Joe said. "And we've never gone out of our way to tell people."

"But we haven't hidden it either."

He paused and seemed to weigh his words before he said them. "Maybe we should."

He couldn't have hurt me more if he'd shot an arrow into my heart. "So you *are* ashamed of me."

"Neely Kate," he soothed as he stood and reached for my upper arms. "Don't take it like that."

I noticed he didn't deny it. "How am I supposed to take it, Joe?"

"Can't you see I'm trying to protect you?"

"You keep saying that, but you never explain what you mean. Protect me from *what?*"

He dropped his hold and took a step back, running his hand through his short hair. "My father isn't the only dangerous Simmons."

As if he needed to tell me that . . .

"Maybe you're confusing me with Rose because we're best friends, but I'm not as naïve as her." Even as I said the words, I felt like a traitor. While I had plenty of experience with lowlifes and two-bit criminals—unbeknownst to anyone around here—Rose had experience with the upper elite of the Fenton County crime world. I wasn't sure either of us would want to list that sort of thing on our résumés, but Rose wasn't one bit naïve. Not anymore.

"I know you're more worldly than Rose. Hell, most kids are more worldly than the woman I met a year ago."

"She's changed," I said, getting frustrated that I'd headed the conversation down this path. "But that's beside the point. The point is that I've lived with a lot of crap in my life, Joe. You know that. So why are you shielding me from this?"

He cupped the side of my face and gave me a pained smile. "Maybe I want to protect you because of everything you *have* been through."

It was a pretty story, but I wasn't about to fall for it. If I had a nickel for every pretty story I'd been told, I'd be living in a mansion. No, people told me pretty stories for a host of reasons, none of which ever seemed to benefit *me*. "Is this about Kate?"

His body froze; then he dropped his hand. "Why do you ask?"

Because she keeps sending me letters. There's one in my hand right now.

I set it down like it had burned me.

"You've babied me ever since we went to visit her."

"How could I not?" he said in exasperation. "I willingly took you to see our psycho sister, then sat there while she tormented you by withholding information about your mother. She was purposely cruel, and she hurt you. I felt responsible, Neely Kate." A smile lifted the corners of his mouth. "I've missed out on a lot of years of watching over you. Just makin' up for lost time."

"Well, quit. I'm a grown woman. I face my problems head-on." Which was an outright lie. Otherwise, I would have done something about the letters. Rose had practically begged me to tell Joe about them, but I couldn't bring myself to do it. I'd spent five years trying to bury the misdeeds of my past. Now they were rearing their ugly heads, and I was starting to panic. I'd finally gotten everything I'd ever wanted—a family who loved me and a pastime that fascinated me, no matter how many times Rose told me we weren't real detectives— and I was close to having it all snatched away because of my half sister's schemes.

Joe grabbed my shoulders and stooped to look me in the eyes. "I'm not ashamed of you. You're the least reprehensible of the three Simmons siblings. Hell, you'd be canonized as a saint if people held us up side by side."

No, there'd be no chance of that happening. Not if people found out what I'd done.

My cell phone rang on my desk, and I broke from Joe's hold to check the number. *Rose.*

"I have to take this. She's probably calling about an order mixup we're dealing with."

"Okay . . ." He looked reluctant to leave. "You're right. I'm trying to protect you from Kate. I have no proof that she's up to something, but I can just *feel* it." He shook his head. "I didn't want to tell you because it sounds paranoid. Kate is locked up tight for years, yet I'm scared to death she's going to find a way to hurt you," he said. "I know it sounds crazy, and like I'm being overprotective, but I've learned to trust my gut, and my gut tells me she's going to hurt you."

His gut was right.

I wrapped my arms around his neck and hugged him, burying my face into his chest. I had no idea how long it would be before he turned away from me, so I was going to savor every moment I could.

"Hey," he said gently, leaning back to study my face. "This is exactly why I didn't want to tell you. Now you're scared."

I swatted his chest. "That's not why I'm hugging you, you idiot. I'm hugging you because I'm overwhelmed by how sweet you are."

The phone stopped ringing, but neither of us commented on it.

A huge grin spread across his face. "So now would probably be a bad time to tell you the real reason I stopped by."

I playfully lifted an eyebrow. "And what's that?"

"I need to run to Magnolia to look for kitchen cabinets. I wanted you to come."

"But I'm working."

"After you get off. We can grab dinner too."

"Just you and me?"

He hesitated. "Were you wanting Rose to come too?"

"No, she has plans," I said before I thought about it. She used to have standing Tuesday night plans, but she'd missed them the past three weeks.

"Just the two of us." He looked relieved, not that I could blame him. It had to be hard on him that his newly discovered half sister was so close with the woman he'd claimed to be the love of his life, even months after their breakup. "I'll pick you up from the office at five."

"See you then."

Chapter Two

I knew I should call Rose back, but that damn envelope was burning a hole in my mind. I had to find out what my psycho sister had sent me this time.

I sat at my desk and slowly opened the flap. A sweet floral and clove smell hit my nose. The envelopes before had all carried the same scent, but not this strong. I pulled out the white paper and several white flowers fell out. I didn't have Rose's expertise, but I definitely knew what these were.

Azaleas.

Fear slithered in my gut. What did Kate know?

I placed the flowers on the desk and then opened the letter—handwritten, just like the others before it. Each of her hateful notes had started the same way, *Dear sister*, and each parceled out a little more information about her meeting with my mother. The first one had been a tease, telling me little other than that my mother had been wearing a blue shirt. In the next, Kate had said my mother looked like she was in her late fifties and not her actual age of forty-two. *Let's hope you age like a Simmons, sis!*

Sometimes the threats were subtle; other times they hit me center mass. Kate had made one thing perfectly clear: when the time was right, she would make sure Joe knew what I had done. The *what I had done* part was vague enough that it could mean anything, except for the drawing she'd included in the last two letters— something that looked like an upside-down frying pan. Anyone else might have been confused, but I knew what it meant.

She was hinting that my mother had told her stories about our lives in Oklahoma.

But the azaleas . . . that was nothing my mother would have known about.

This note was longer than the rest. My pulse spiked. Usually I read Kate's notes hoping for information about my mother, even though I knew deep down there was little chance she'd tell me anything about the woman who'd dumped me at my granny's house when I was twelve. No. Now that this longer letter sat in front of me, I suspected she'd been toying with me these past months, working up to this moment.

Fear gnawed at my gut, but I took a deep breath and started to read.

Dear sister,

I hope this letter finds you squirming. How is our brother? I hear you and Joe are spending a lot of time together. He even went to the church picnic with you. How plebeian of him. How did you ever manage THAT? Joe's allergic to anything religious, and he never gave me the time of day, so why is he spending time with trailer trash like you? Perhaps I wouldn't be so judgmental if I weren't also jealous. Why don't you ever spend time with me, Neely Kate? After everything I've done for you . . . I'm beginning to think you love Joe more than me.

That won't do at all . . .

I've been thinking a lot about your mother—what a hard life she's had and how you were the cause of it. Do you ever think she wishes she'd gotten rid of you before you were born? Do you think the world would be a better place without you?

I bet Beasley thinks so. ☺

You and I are so much alike . . . so many secrets. Have you ever had a secret so big that you were sure it would burst out of you? No, I suspect not. You're such a great secret keeper. Me . . . not so much. You'll need to tell me your secret for holding them in the next time you visit.

Don't wait too long.

Your loving sister,

Kate

By the time I finished reading, I was close to hyperventilating. I'd hoped she was bluffing about what she knew—or at least exaggerating—but the azaleas and her mention of Beasley suggested otherwise. But *how?* It was all ancient history, buried deeply in my past. Or so I had thought.

And how did she know about Joe spending time with me and going to the church picnic? Did she have spies watching me?

The front door bell chimed, and Rose walked in with a coffee cup in hand. Since she was working outside today, she was wearing capris and a sleeveless shirt, her hair pulled back in a messy ponytail bun. I knew she had multiple consultation appointments scheduled throughout the day—it was why she'd left her little dog, Muffy, at home—but she'd started off by going to see a client about a mixup. The phone call . . .

I shook myself out of my distress. "Oh, my stars and garters. Joe was here when you called, and I forgot to call you back."

"That's okay," she said in a cheerful tone. "I was calling to see if you wanted coffee, but I see that Joe must have already brought you some."

"It came with strings," I said, folding the letter and trying to nonchalantly slip it in my purse in the desk drawer. While Rose knew Kate had written to me, she didn't know much else about it. "He wants me to go up to Magnolia with him after work to look at kitchen cabinets."

"Oh, is he remodeling his kitchen now?" she asked, eyeing the stack of mail on my desk. "Did the Pearson check arrive in the mail? I might have to pay them a visit to get their final payment."

She moved closer. As she picked up the envelopes, she noticed the flowers scattered across my desk. Picking one up, she turned it over to examine it. "Azaleas? At the end of June?" Her gaze lifted to me. "Where did these come from?"

"A customer," I lied. "A man came in and said he wanted some of those planted in his yard."

"Where'd he get them? All the azaleas died out by the end of May."

"Beats me." I shrugged.

"That's so strange . . . Did you set up a consult?"

"No. Turned out he wanted to buy the plants and do it himself. I told him to head over to the nursery."

Rose lifted it up and breathed in. "This is a deciduous azalea. Their scent is stronger." She set it back on my desk. "No wonder you kept them. They smell wonderful."

I would have loved nothing more than to burn them to a crisp. But right now, I had a ton of questions that I couldn't hope to answer myself, and if Rose was here, she could cover for me. "Do you plan to be here long?"

Her eyebrows lifted. "About forty-five minutes."

"I need to run a quick errand. Can you cover?"

"Yeah . . . of course . . . How'd your car do coming in?"

"It sputtered along." But we both knew it was on life support. I'd be better served to put the money toward a new one instead of fixing this one piecemeal. While Rose and I usually rode together, now that we were deep into summer, she was busy with consults while her business partner, Bruce Wayne, kept having to hire additional crew to keep up with the demand. She couldn't worry about carting me around.

"Do you want me to drive you?" she asked. "We've been so busy this last week we haven't had a chance for a good chat."

I couldn't help wondering if part of her wanted to come see what I was up to. I'd been anxious lately, kicking Rose's mothering instinct into high gear, but she respected my privacy too much to outright ask.

Lord knew we both had secrets, some more obvious than others. I considered lying about where I was going, but I was tired of lying to her. Besides, if I really had to leave Henryetta for good—and I was beginning to think it might come to that—I wanted her to remember the good things about me, not a pack of lies.

"You stay here," I said with a wave that suggested her offer was ridiculous. "There's no sense in you wasting valuable work time to pick up some toilet paper at Walmart. Let's plan a *Grey's Anatomy* marathon this weekend."

It wasn't a lie if I actually did it. Or so I told myself.

She frowned as she studied me, worry filling her eyes. She would never push too hard, but I knew she would be there for me if I changed my mind and asked for help. This was what unconditional love looked like, although it had taken me a while to figure it out. Still . . . everyone had limits. A line they would refuse to cross.

What was Rose's line?

I needed to get out from under her worried gaze. I grabbed my purse and hopped out of my seat, heading for the door. "I should be back in a half hour."

"Neely Kate."

I spun around to face her.

She paused and lowered her voice. "Have you gotten any more letters from Kate?"

Had she linked the azaleas to Kate? *No.* She was just worried. She'd probably been stewing about the letters and my refusal to tell Joe about them. "Nope. She must have realized she was barking up the wrong tree."

"Huh." I could see she had serious doubts. Especially since I hadn't seemed quite like myself lately.

I'd regretted mentioning Kate's letters to her as soon as the words had spilled out of me a couple of weeks ago. But I sure wasn't telling her anything now.

If she found out what I'd done . . .

She wouldn't find out. I'd make damn sure of it.

That's why I was about to swallow my pride and pay a visit to Skeeter Malcolm, the king of the Fenton County crime world. Even if I was currently on his shit list.

Chapter Three

My car was coughing and blowing out noxious fumes by the time I pulled into the parking lot of Skeeter's pool hall. I prayed the stupid thing would start and get me back to the town square after I finished my task here. I might have to break down and ask Joe for help after all, and that stuck in my craw. I'd vowed never to ask my brother for money.

Dammit. I felt like my world was imploding.

I was taking plenty of risks by showing up here at ten thirty on a Tuesday morning, the biggest one being that he might not be here yet. The pool hall wasn't his only business, but he spent most of his time here. Besides, it seemed more likely he'd be here on a weekday morning than at his strip club, the Bunny Ranch. Then again, rumor had it that Skeeter had spent several nights there last week, so maybe I should have started my search there after all. But I was here now, and I had serious doubts my car would make it to the Bunny Ranch, which was located about ten miles southwest of town, and then back to the town square. I was already here. I might as well check.

But Skeeter's availability wasn't my only concern. After our last encounter, I wasn't sure how he'd receive my impromptu visit.

Last winter Skeeter and Rose had formed an unlikely symbiotic—yet secret—arrangement. She'd used her visions of the future to help him ferret out the turncoats in his newly acquired kingdom. In turn, he'd helped her protect her then-boyfriend Mason, the county's assistant DA, from death threats. They'd saved Mason (who had, rather ungratefully, broken up with Rose and moved to Little Rock) and toppled a mutual enemy—my father, J.R. Simmons—thereby saving Skeeter's kingdom.

Only, that hadn't been the end of Rose's relationship with Skeeter.

She'd taken to meeting him on Tuesday nights, even if she hadn't told me. It fell under our *don't ask, don't tell* unspoken rule. I'd worried Skeeter would take advantage of her emotionally vulnerable state.

Everything came to a head a few weeks ago when Rose and I started looking for a necklace for a man I knew from high school. What had appeared to be a simple investigation had landed Rose and me smack-dab in the middle of Skeeter Malcolm's crime world. Rose had helped avert a turf war by holding a parley between Skeeter and a new challenger, the real owner of the necklace.

The meeting might have saved the county plenty of trouble, but it had created a rift between Skeeter and Rose. She was angry because he hadn't been truthful with her about how he'd planned to handle the situation; he was pissed because he'd wanted the necklace she'd returned to his challenger. As far as I knew, they hadn't spoken to each other since the meeting two weeks ago. And since I was the one who'd stolen the necklace from

Skeeter's right-hand man, Jed, I was pretty sure he wasn't too happy with me.

There was only one way to find out.

Lifting my chin, I marched inside the empty pool hall, a little surprised the door was unlocked since the sign said it was closed.

I stopped in the middle of the place, feeling on edge in the darkened room. The upended stools on the tables gave it a deserted and creepy look.

I headed toward the back, intending to make a beeline to the office, but a beefy guy appeared in the doorway to the hall, blocking my way. I recognized him as one of Skeeter's trusted men, but *I* didn't trust him one iota.

"Get out of my way, Merv," I said in a voice that suggested I wasn't taking crap. "I need to speak to Skeeter."

He crossed his arms over his bulky chest. "He's not here. Now get the hell out."

I narrowed my eyes and held my ground. "Then you won't mind if I see for myself before I leave." I tried to get around him, but he was quick for a man who could double as a prize-winning bull.

"Leave. *Now.*"

The look in his eyes told me he wasn't playing, and I knew I had no right to even be here, but desperation was clawing at my insides. I needed help, and the fact that I was here in the first place meant I'd obviously resorted to begging for it, but I sure as shinola wasn't begging for help from *him.*

My jaw clenched. "Get out of my way, Merv."

"You need to leave."

I took two steps back, pretending to retreat while I came up with a plan. Merv was big, but he was clumsy.

If I managed to draw him out to the main room, I could bolt for the hall and make it to the office.

Backing up to a table close to the bar, I grinned as I shoved a stool to the floor. "Oops."

"Pick it up," he barked.

I moved sideways to another table, keeping my eyes on him as I pushed another stool to the floor. "Oops again."

He took two steps into the room. That wasn't enough. I need a clearer shot.

I turned my back to him, fully aware that he was hulking behind me. Choosing a table closer to the front door, I pushed all four stools to the floor in a big sweep. Then I turned to give him a defiant look. I knew he had a temper. I was counting on drawing it out.

I was a little too successful.

Merv charged for me on my left. I zigged right, skirting around the tables and aiming for the hall.

While I was running between the tables, Merv acted like the bull he resembled and plowed through tables, heading right for me. Apparently his problem wasn't with the mess I'd made so much as the fact that I was the one who'd made it. Stools and tables went flying everywhere. I would have made it to the opening if a stool hadn't flown into my path. It slowed me down enough to give Merv an advantage. He gave me a hard shove, slamming me with enough force the back of my head hit the wall, sending stars across my vision and momentarily stunning me.

The hall was mere feet away, but Merv stood at an equal distance, heading straight for me with dark, dangerous eyes. I bolted for the hall but barely made it a few inches before Merv's meaty arm reached up. His fingers wrapped around my throat as he slammed me back against the wall.

"Get your goddamned hands off her," said a deep, menacing voice I recognized. "*Now.*"

Merv's eyes narrowed, his hand still on my neck. "I'm taking care of the trash, Carlisle."

"What part of that order *did you not understand?*"

Merv's hold tightened, cutting off my air supply. "Don't overstep your bounds, Carlisle."

Jed stepped out of the hallway, looking like he was about to murder his associate. "The way you're clearly overstepping yours?"

Great. They were having a contest of manliness while I was being choked to death. To hell with this nonsense.

I lifted my arm in front of Merv and then brought it down hard on his forearm, breaking his hold as I lifted my knee hard into his crotch.

He grunted as he bent over.

I was free, but I was pissed to the point of rage. I might be a five-foot-four blonde woman who often came across as flighty, but dammit, I was tired of taking shit.

I elbowed his nose as I swung to the side. He grunted, reaching for me, but I kicked him on the inside of his elbow with the heel of my shoe. Losing his balance, he fell face-forward like a toppled tree. His left hand was splayed on the floor, and I stomped on it, putting all my weight on my heel.

He cried out in pain, then reached for my ankle. "I'm going to kill you!"

I took a step backward as I pulled my gun out of my purse and pointed it at his face, which was now covered in blood. "Go ahead and try."

If looks could kill, I would have been blown into a million pieces.

Jed stepped between us, my gun now pointed at his back.

"This is done, Chapman," he said in a guttural voice that rebuked the challenge Merv had laid out. "Let it go."

There was no way in Hades Merv was going to let this go, and maybe Jed knew it because the next thing I knew, Jed was wrapping his arm around my back and pushing me into the hall.

I pointed my gun to the floor, jerking out of his grasp, and walked into the open office. Skeeter wasn't sitting at his desk.

"Where's Skeeter?" I asked, spinning around to face Jed.

He shut the door behind him and flipped the deadbolt on the door. "Out."

"I need to see Skeeter."

Without responding, he disappeared behind a door—a half bath, judging from the sound of running water—and returned with a wet towel.

I put my gun back in my purse and was about to ask him what he was doing, but he grabbed my upper arm and dragged me over to Skeeter's desk. He tossed the towel onto an empty part of the surface, then slid his hands under my arms and lifted me until my butt was scooted onto the edge of the wood.

I fought against his hold. "Let me go."

"Quit fighting, Neely Kate. You're bleeding. Let me look."

Quit fighting. That was an order I'd been rebelling against for as long as I could remember, but I suddenly realized he was right—the back of my head and shirt were covered in blood.

His phone rang, and he pulled it out of his pocket with a grim look. He didn't say hello when he answered, leading instead with: "There's a situation." There was a several-second pause before he said, "Got it."

As if something had been settled, he hung up and pocketed the phone.

"Man of few words," I said out of nervousness. I was used to men's attention. Shoot, a lifetime ago, I'd used it to get what I wanted more times than I could count. But no man had ever set my nerves on edge like the man in front of me did. Not even my husband.

Jed didn't respond, thereby proving my point. He gently swept my hair away from my shoulder before lifting his hands to the back of my head. His fingers prodded my scalp until I cried out as pain shot through my head.

He lifted the towel and patted at the spot as I clasped the edges of the desk beneath me to keep from crying out again.

Jed moved to my side, searching my face. "You need stitches."

I tried to slide off the desk, but he grabbed my arm and kept me in place.

"You need stitches. It's not up for debate. You have two options. I can take you to the ER, or I can have someone here within a half hour."

"You have someone who makes house calls?"

His mouth twitched and he looked like he was about to smile. Almost. "Skeeter."

He said his name as though that explained everything, but I supposed in most instances it did.

"I don't have time to go to the ER, and I sure as shooting wouldn't know how to explain it. But I told Rose I'd be back in a half hour."

"She doesn't know you're here?"

"No, and regardless of what you probably believe, it's not about her. I'm here for me."

He didn't say anything, just grabbed my hand and lifted it to the towel he had pressed against my head. Then he pulled out his phone and sent a text, pocketed it again, and returned to the half bath. He came back with another wet towel.

He cleaned my neck with gentle swipes, and something about the way he took care of me brought tears to my eyes. Soon they were streaming down my face.

"I'm sorry," Jed said so quietly I barely heard him.

"I'm not crying because my head hurts."

He set the bloody towel on the desk and then lifted my chin so I was looking in his eyes. "I know."

"Why are you being so nice to me after I pushed you into all that mud and pig shit?"

He grinned. "Oh, yeah. I forgot about that."

"Liar."

His grin spread and I marveled at it. Jed Carlisle was this big, tough guy—Skeeter's right-hand man and Rose's badass bodyguard. But several times now, I'd seen a different side to him, softer and more accessible.

I heard pounding on the office door, quickly followed by Skeeter's voice. "What the hell's goin' on? Why am I locked out of my own goddamned office?"

Jed's eyes turned hard as he dropped his hand and stalked toward the door. After he unfastened the deadbolt, he flung the door open and blocked the opening with his wall of a body.

"What the hell's goin' on, Jed?" Skeeter demanded again. "Merv's out there nursin' a broken nose and a busted hand. Was it Wagner's men?"

"Where's Merv?" Jed grunted.

"Have you lost your damn mind? I already told you he's in the bar. I just called Mindy."

"She was already on her way. And she's coming in here first." His voice took on a harsh edge. "And if the *fucker* comes anywhere near her again . . ."

"*Her?*" Skeeter asked in alarm.

Jed stepped out of the way, letting Skeeter get a good look at me sitting on his desk.

Several emotions swept over his face. Disappointment, followed by relief, and then admiration. I had no doubt the first two were related to the fact that I wasn't the woman he really wanted to see draped on his desk. But I'd take the third any day of the week.

"This is *your* doin'?" he asked as he walked inside and shut the door behind him.

"He had it comin'," I said in a defiant tone.

"He has a helluva lot more comin' than that," Jed said through gritted teeth. "Which I'll see to shortly."

Skeeter held his hand up to quiet Jed, studying me as though seeing me for the first time. A huge grin spread across his face.

"Who the hell are you, Neely K

Chapter Four

I saw no point in beating around the bush. I suspected time wasn't on my side. "That's why I'm here."

He quirked an eyebrow. "Go on."

"First I need to know that what I tell you won't leave this room."

He held his hands out from his sides. "Who am I going to tell?"

"Rose," Jed said behind him. "She wants to keep it from Rose."

Skeeter's face hardened. "That shouldn't be a problem since she and I are no longer working together. Not to mention I don't go around gossiping like busybodies at that damn bingo hall you go to with your granny." He grinned at my look of surprise. "You should know I know everything about you." A smirk lit up his eyes. "Or I thought I did."

"I need your help, but I don't have any money to pay you."

"Maybe we can work out a barter."

That was what I was equally counting on and fearing.

I reached into my purse and pulled out the envelope. "Kate Simmons has been sending me letters."

"Like pen pals?"

I gave him a dark look. "I've never responded, so no. It didn't seem like a good idea."

He nodded.

"The first few started out vague, suggesting she knows about my past, threatening to tell about it, but her latest . . . I need to know what she knows." I handed him the letter. "And I need to know how she knows it."

He took it from me, but he settled into the chair behind his desk before he opened the envelope. He glanced up at me for several seconds before he said, "Why not tell your brother?"

"I don't want him to know about my past either."

Skeeter leaned back in his chair. He examined the letter, shooting glances at me every few seconds.

I could see why Rose was drawn to him, although she'd never admit it out loud in a million years. James "Skeeter" Malcolm was a man who demanded attention. His over six-foot frame and bulky arms and chest, not to mention the tattoos peeking out under the sleeves of his short-sleeve shirt and at his neckline, made him an imposing presence. His dark good looks only added to the effect. But it was his confidence that held sway over most people—a cockiness that bordered on arrogance yet assured that he could deliver on a promise.

I was counting on that last trait now.

He lifted the paper to his nose. "Perfume?"

"Azaleas. The others have smelled of them, only I didn't recognize the scent until today. She sent actual flowers with this one." I paused. "Rose says azaleas are out of bloom. They all died out by the end of May."

"Do you know why Kate sent you azaleas?"

I hesitated. "Yes."

He paused. "Rose knows about the letters?"

"I mentioned them in a moment of weakness a couple of weeks ago, but she doesn't know specifics. She found the azaleas on my desk after I got the latest letter this morning. I told her a customer had brought them in."

"And you don't want her to know about what Kate's referring to?"

"No."

He looked surprised. "You really think what you've done will turn her from you?"

"I'm not taking that risk with her *or* Joe."

"Do you plan to meet her?" he asked.

"Kate? Yes."

He nodded. "I think this goes without saying, yet it bears repeating: What we tell each other in this room stays with the three of us."

I nodded and winced when the motion sent a spike of pain through my head.

Jed was still standing in front of the door with his arms folded across his chest, looking like a sentry, except his full attention was on me. His face tightened when he saw my visible show of pain.

Skeeter handed me the paper. "I have someone watching Kate Simmons."

I gasped. "For how long?"

"Since she arrived in town this past winter."

"Then why didn't you figure out what she was up to before she sprang it on us?"

He grimaced. "Because she gave my guy the slip a few times. And she was barely a blip on my radar. No one ever took Kate Simmons seriously. Obviously she used that to her advantage."

"I'll say," I grumbled. "If you've had her watched, you should be able to figure out how she got the letters out, right?"

"Yeah, and I'll help you, but it comes at a price."

Here it was. "What is it?"

"When you meet with Kate, I want you to bring Jed with you."

I shot a glance to Jed to gauge his reaction. While he'd gone out of his way to protect me this morning, I'd learned from the way he always watched over Rose that protecting people was in his blood . . . just like seeing the good in people was in Rose's. But taking a road trip to see my crazy sister was something else entirely.

Jed stared at me with his usual poker face, those strong arms still folded across his chest, giving me absolutely nothing. After all the grief I'd given him over the last couple of months, there was no way he wanted to do this, but he would do it anyway because Skeeter would order it.

That was the last thing I needed.

"No way." Then I thought of a reason to leave him behind. "They record who comes to visit, Skeeter. And they may not even let me in without Joe."

"They'll let you in, and I'm well aware of the visitor list. I'm also aware of who's been recorded and who hasn't been."

"You're saying people have visited her without making it on that list?"

He remained silent.

There went my excuse. I had known Skeeter Malcolm's help wouldn't come for free. I should have realized it would cost me what remained of my pride, even if Skeeter had no idea about my conflict with his second-in-command. "So I go see Kate, and Jed tags along and does what? Spies on me?"

The look on his face told me I was close to crossing a line. "I have questions of my own. If Jed comes with you as your protection on a family visit, it will look less suspicious."

"I can't risk Joe finding out I took Jed to see her."

"Don't you worry about that part," Jed said. "I've got it covered."

My eyes narrowed. "You knew I'd come to you?"

Skeeter laughed. "Hell, no. But this isn't the first conversation we've had in regard to Kate Simmons. Let's just say it's fortuitous."

"Okay . . . when?"

There was a knock on the door, and Skeeter got to his feet. "Tomorrow."

"Tomorrow?"

His brows rose in an expression that dared me to question him. Usually I'd take him up on that dare, but I needed him too much to pose a challenge.

"I'm going to have a hard time explaining why I'm gone to Rose."

"Figure it out." He opened the door, revealing a middle-aged woman holding a leather bag.

"Another brawl, Malcolm?" she asked in a surly tone.

"You could say that," he said as he motioned her in.

She took one look at me and hesitated. "And who do we have here?"

"Mindy, the only thing you need to know is that she's the one who whooped Merv's ass."

"Mr. Chapman's having a rough year," the woman said. "Between his gunshot wounds and this, you're going to have to start giving him hazard pay."

Jed's dark look suggested he thought otherwise.

"Jed," Skeeter barked. "She's in capable hands. Time to have a chat with Merv."

After the two men left, Mindy set her bag on the desk.

"Lover's spat?" she asked, giving me a shrewd look as she rummaged through the bag.

I snorted. "Hardly. There's no love lost between me and Merv."

She stopped what she was doing and stared into my face. "Did he attack you?"

"I handled it."

She shook her head and pulled out a plastic container and set it on the desk. "Honey, this isn't a world any sane woman wants to get mixed up in."

"That's not why I'm here."

"Uh-huh," she said, obviously not buying it. "That's what they all say, sweetie."

"Seriously. I need help is all, and Skeeter Malcolm has the resources to give it to me."

"That comes at a cost, sugar." She poured something into the plastic dish—iodine, from the smell—then pulled out a giant sponge from her Mary Poppins bag and started dabbing my head.

I saw no point in arguing with her. Not when I'd already come to that conclusion on my own.

Jed and Skeeter returned about five minutes later, with Merv in tow. His face was now wiped clean, but he had cotton stuffed in his nostrils, and he was cradling his hand to his chest. Mindy had already deadened the back of my head and started stitching.

The moment I saw Merv, I stiffened.

"Merv has something he would like to say," Jed said, his eyes glittering with the promise of danger.

Merv looked like he wanted to strangle Jed. "I regret my overly aggressive behavior." He dragged out each word, as if the apology pained him worse than a dozen beatings—by a girl. "I will pay for any damages."

"Seems to me you're the one sportin' all the damages," I retorted.

Skeeter laughed, looking like he was loving every minute of this.

"I will be happy to pay to replace your clothes," Merv choked out.

Crap. I hadn't thought of that. I was going to need to change before I headed back to the office. Not to mention all the blood in my hair. "Fine. One hundred dollars should cover it."

"One hundred dollars?" Merv protested. "Hell, you can buy a new shirt for ten bucks at Walmart."

"Actually, add an additional one hundred for my pain and suffering. Two hundred."

"You'll have it before you leave," Skeeter said as Merv staggered out of the room. "And I offer you my guarantee this won't happen again."

"Well, *I* can't guarantee it won't happen again," I said, flinching as the woman tugged on a stitch. "If I'm attacked again, I'll do the same or worse."

Skeeter raised his brows, a slight smile still playing on his lips. "I would expect nothing less."

I could practically feel Mindy staring at the back of my head. "Jed will pick you up at noon tomorrow," Skeeter continued. "Text him where you'll be." He headed out the door. "Now I have actual important things to do . . ."

Jed stayed behind, watching the woman work.

"Well, that was a decent gash. You got four stitches," Mindy said, pulling away. I watched as she

36

wrapped up the kit she'd used and stuffed it into a small red trash bag. She checked my eyes, looking for signs of a concussion, then deemed me fit as a fiddle. "You can wash the blood out of your hair, but try to keep your scalp dry. You won't be able to use a bandage, so it might seep onto your pillow for the next few nights."

"Thanks."

"You can get your stitches out in a week. Have Malcolm call me, and I'll take care of it."

"Okay."

She stole a glance at Jed before returning her focus to me. "Remember what I said." Then she turned to Jed. "Where's Mr. Chapman? Am I taking care of him in the pool hall?"

"No. Skeeter wanted to keep him away from her."

She nodded. "Then send him in if he's ready."

Jed moved toward me, gesturing toward the door. He followed me out to the pool hall, and when Merv shot me a glare from his chair—probably one of the ones I'd knocked over—Jed slid in between us. A silent warning. Merv got up, slapped some money on the table, then headed to the back.

I kept on going. Jed snatched it up and followed me.

"Neely Kate," he said as I reached the front door, but the worry in his voice told me I needed to get out of there quick before I lost it.

Ignoring him, I headed out into the summer heat, temporarily blinded by the sunshine.

He followed me to my car, pushing the door closed when I tried to open it.

"Get away from my car, Jed, or I'll give Mindy something else to do before she leaves."

Typical Jed, he didn't say a word, just grabbed my arms, startling me when he gently pulled me to his chest and wrapped his arms around me.

"I'm sorry." His words were muffled in my hair, but they burned a mark into my heart.

I gave myself several seconds before I jerked out of his hold. Looking away so he wouldn't see, I wiped at an escaping tear. "I've handled worse."

His eyes found mine. "From whatever it is you're running from?"

I hesitated, then nodded.

"I should have gotten to you sooner."

I shook my head, thankful my skin was still numb. "I can't do this."

I opened the door, and Jed didn't stop me this time. Instead, he handed me the money he'd picked up and closed the door once I was inside.

Just my luck, the damn car didn't start. I whacked the steering wheel with my fist. Why couldn't I escape this man?

Jed didn't say anything—he opened my door, calm as could be, and then reached in and popped open the hood. I told myself to stop him, that accepting help from Jed Carlisle was not to be taken lightly. Of course, I could say the same for Skeeter, but the risk seemed greater with Jed.

He lifted the hood and told me to turn it over again. After several tries, the car started running. He closed the hood and walked around, leaning in the window, which was open because my air conditioning had been one of the first things to go. "That will get you to the square but probably not back to the farmhouse."

"I'll take my chances."

But I'd been taking them my whole life, and my marker was finally getting called.

Because of my car, I didn't dare stop by Walmart for a change of clothes, let alone the toilet paper I'd used as an excuse. Besides, while I'd seen a lot of oddities at the supercenter, walking around in a blood-drenched shirt seemed like a bad idea. So I sucked it up and drove back to the office, racking my brain to come up with a feasible explanation. Nothing came to mind, but a somewhat frantic search of my car yielded a cardigan to cover the blood down the back of my shirt, and a floppy sun hat hid the rest. I pulled on both of them, tucking my hair into the hat. Later I could sneak away for a few minutes and buy a shirt at the new clothing store on the other side of the square.

I hadn't been gone that long given everything that had happened, but Rose was packing her tote bag with her laptop and notepad when I walked in the door.

"Sorry I was gone so long," I said.

"That's okay," she said, slinging the bag over her shoulder. She looked up and gave me a strange look. "It's got to be at least eight-five degrees outside already. Why are you wearing a sweater?"

"I got cold."

"The air conditioner is out in your car."

I shrugged.

She moved closer and put her hand to my forehead. "Are you coming down with something?"

"No," I said with a soft smile, hoping Jed had cleaned most of the blood off my neck. "I didn't eat breakfast, so maybe that latte didn't sit well."

"Why are you wearing a hat?"

I realized I could use this illness excuse to my advantage. "The sun was hurting my eyes. Maybe I *am* coming down with something."

"Do you want to go home?" she asked, looking worried.

"No. I'm feeling okay right now. It'll probably blow over."

"Maybe you should cancel tonight with Joe."

I'd considered that too, but I wanted to see him one last time before my visit with Kate. I wouldn't be coming back to Henryetta tomorrow afternoon.

I'd be catching a bus to Oklahoma. And if things went as badly as I feared, I wouldn't be coming back at all.

Chapter Five

I told Jed to pick me up from the farmhouse the next day.

Since I'd told Rose I wasn't feeling well, she'd left her dog, Muffy, to keep me company. I'd spent the entire hour before Jed showed up taking her outside for a walk—partly out of guilt, partly because Muffy had a way of making me feel better. She was such a happy dog, so full of love. As silly as it sounded, she gave me hope.

I felt like a snake oil salesman, sneaking off like this, but I knew she'd never let me go alone, and there was no way in Hades I'd let her anywhere near my past. Still, I couldn't take off without a word and worry her half to death, so I had left her a note on the kitchen counter saying I needed to take care of a few things and I'd be back when I could.

I expected to hear from her early this evening when she found it . . . probably sooner if I stopped responding to her calls and texts.

When Jed's car pulled up to the house, I scooped up Muffy and headed into the house, but she started to whine as soon as we crossed the threshold.

I rubbed her head and looked into her eyes, and I could tell she knew I was *leaving*.

"I'll come back when I sort this out," I whispered as I rubbed behind her ears. "I promise. Take care of Rose until I get back."

She licked my nose. I hugged her before lowering her to the floor. My heart gave a little pang as I shut the door and locked her inside.

I picked up my duffel bag and my purse from the wicker chair on the front porch and walked down the steps to Jed's car. He was leaning against the closed driver's door, his sunglasses hiding what he was thinking.

Who was I kidding? I rarely knew what Jed was thinking, sunglasses or not.

He was dressed in his usual jeans and a gray T-shirt that was tight on his arms, showing off his biceps.

Right or wrong, I was glad that I was wearing my blue and white summer dress and my white strappy sandals. My makeup was minimal, giving me a wholesome look, and my hair was down—putting it up hurt the back of my head too much, even after the over-the-counter medication I'd taken a few hours ago. I knew I looked good. I was counting on that for later.

He stepped away from the car and met me in front of the hood.

"What's with the bag?"

I gave him a lazy shrug. "I like to cart a lot of things around. You should have seen me when I was pregnant. You wouldn't believe what I had in my huge purse . . . and that was just here in Fenton County. *We're* heading up to Little Rock."

"It's a six-hour round trip, tops."

"Hey, you wear T-shirts that show off every bulging muscle," I said, flicking his bicep.

"I can cart a bag with me to Little Rock. If we start questioning each other's every decision now, it's gonna be a long trip."

He grinned, an honest-to-God happy grin. "Okay."

His smile caught me off guard. "Well . . . okay. Let's go then."

I headed toward the passenger side door. Jed followed me and grabbed the door handle before I could reach it.

"I can open my own door, Jed," I said, trying not to sound breathless. For some reason, he was affecting me more than usual. Maybe because I knew I'd be spending the next few hours within a couple of feet of him. Or maybe it was because we'd been at odds more often than not over the last month or two, but I had to admit that *I* was the one who'd made it that way. How would I handle being trapped in a car with him?

He took my bag from my hand, holding my gaze as he said, "I need you to know I'll make sure nothing happens to you today."

"Jed. You're not responsible for what Merv did."

He didn't respond, just opened the door wider, leaving me to wonder—yet again—what was going on in his mind.

I knew Jed was attracted to me. He'd pretty much told me so a few months before, but Jed worked for Skeeter Malcolm. If I could ignore the fact that I wasn't divorced yet, it would be absolutely insane for me to hook up with a guy who had his feet so firmly entrenched in the criminal world. Especially since I was trying so hard to escape my own past.

Jed was quiet as he pulled out onto the highway and headed north, not that his silence was unusual, but he seemed tense.

"Is everything okay?" I asked, turning to look at him.

"Fine." But his tight grip on the steering wheel suggested otherwise. His scraped knuckles caught my attention.

I considered asking how he got them, but I didn't want him to confirm my suspicions. I couldn't afford to have someone fight my battles for me. The only person I could rely on was myself. My husband Ronnie had driven that point home. But that wasn't entirely true. I could count on Rose, but I didn't want her fighting my battles. Especially not this one.

I'd chosen Ronnie Colson because he'd seemed uncomplicated. Hardworking. Devoted. Trustworthy. Easy. But somehow, unbeknownst to me, he'd gotten mixed up in the crime world, something I'd only figured out *after* he disappeared.

I'd presumed Ronnie was dead—why else would the man who had acted like the sun rose and set on me disappear? But Joe had seen him boarding that bus in New Orleans, and he had the photographic evidence to prove it. That alone had kicked me in the teeth—worse, Ronnie had been with another woman. And he had been wearing a wedding ring on his hand. A ring *I* hadn't given him.

If I couldn't count on Ronnie Colson, no man was trustworthy. I'd do best to stay away from all of them, and from Jed in particular.

But after ten minutes, the silence started driving me batty.

I turned sideways in my seat. "What kind of music do you listen to?" I lifted my hands. "No. Wait. Don't tell me. You're a Dolly Parton guy."

He turned and grinned, and I realized how much I liked his smiles.

That was a bad, bad thing. But I was stuck in this car with him for at least the next two hours. I could be a bitch out of self-preservation—which in all honesty was why we'd been at odds—or I could allow myself to enjoy these next couple of hours in a decent car with a handsome man. Fool that I was, I decided on the latter.

"Okay . . . no Dolly Parton. No. I would guess you're not a country music guy. Am I right?"

He gave me a hesitant look, not that I could blame him. Lately I'd jumped down his throat every time we were near each other. "Correct."

"Okay. Let me think . . . You're a simple man . . . I don't think I've ever seen you in anything other than jeans and T-shirts and Henleys . . . Oh, my stars and garters, please tell me you're not into Nirvana."

He laughed. "Do you want me to tell you?"

"Where's the fun in that?" But I didn't want to guess anymore either. That required me to think about what made Jed Carlisle tick, and I wasn't ready to dig too much deeper beneath the surface. "How about we turn on the radio?"

"That works."

We spent the rest of our time without conversation while I sang top twenty country songs and played the alphabet game in my head. But my good mood began to erode the closer we got to Little Rock. I was about to confront my half sister—without Joe's support this time—and I suspected she would make mincemeat out of me.

I turned down the volume. "Skeeter suggested you would be an undocumented visitor. How will you manage that?"

"We've made a connection with a nurse. She'll be there today to let us in."

"Us?"

"After some discussion, we don't think you should be on the record either. This way she can claim you were there with me, but if there's no record of it, they can chalk it up to her lunacy."

I nodded. "That's a good idea." I turned to him. "So the nurse in Skeeter's pocket has been watching Kate?"

"Yeah. There haven't been any unusual visitors, but the nurse says she thinks she has something, so we'll have a chat with her before we go in to see Kate." He paused, then added, "It sounds like Kate has someone on the inside too, but we've checked her bank accounts. We haven't seen any transfers."

"Wasn't her money frozen when her father's estate and Joe's money was frozen?"

"No. Joe's personal money wasn't frozen, just the estate's, so neither was Kate's. Maybe she was saving her monthly allowances or doing some creative investing. Either way, she has quite a bit of money, but she's hidden it pretty well."

"Not well enough, if you managed to find it." When he didn't answer, I asked, "Could money be coming from somewhere else?"

"Possibly. Or she might be offering something other than money."

"Like what?"

"That's what I'm hoping to find out."

"Why didn't you come talk to her before now?"

"She doesn't know me from Adam. She's far less likely to talk to me alone."

"You think you'll have a better chance because she'll be distracted by tormenting me." If they had someone on the inside watching her . . . "You knew she was sending me letters."

"No, Neely Kate. I promise we didn't."

"Did you know she was sending out mail?"

"No. We suspected she was up to something, but we also think it's bigger than you."

I let that sink in. *Bigger than me.* Even my own personal nightmare was insignificant to the big picture.

Jed shot me a questioning glance, but in typical fashion, he didn't press me.

The back of my head began to throb, so I grabbed my purse off the floor and pulled out a bottle of water and a bottle of ibuprofen.

Worry filled Jed's eyes when he heard me shake out two tablets. "Are you feeling bad?"

"A small headache. I've had it all day. Just keepin' it at bay."

I expected him to comment, but he turned his attention forward, his eyes on the road. Still, he seemed tenser than before.

As he pulled into the parking lot, I realized I hadn't worked out a plan to get the answers to my questions, but was there really any planning when it came to Kate? I'd be lucky to get anything out of her other than taunting and vague hints. But I also knew that Jed was going to hear whatever Kate told me. I shouldn't care . . . yet I did.

When Jed parked, I reached into the back seat and grabbed my bag. I suspected this was where I'd be parting ways with Jed. He just didn't know it yet.

"Why don't you leave the bag in the car?" he asked.

"What would be the point of bringing it just to leave it in the car?" I asked, hauling it onto my lap.

"Exactly. What was the point of bringing it?"

I released a sound of frustration. "And what's the point of wearing sexy T-shirts?"

"That's twice now that you've mentioned my shirt," he said with a satisfied grin.

"And that's twice now that you've mentioned my bag. What's your point?"

He just watched me with a cocky look, and I felt my resolve weaken.

Dang it. What was it about this man that got under my skin? I pushed the door open, my usual irritation around him resurfacing. "Let's get this over with."

I started toward the hospital entrance with Jed on my heels. I was getting hit with anxiety from all fronts—facing Kate, especially with Jed at my side, was worry number one. But after our visit, I needed to figure out how to ditch Jed and get to the bus stop. I'd mapped the route from a nearby bus stop to the Greyhound station. But on top of all that, I was beginning to worry about how Rose would react when she found the note. How would she take me leaving? Would it hurt her feelings? Would she try to find me?

One worry at a time.

Jed's long legs helped him catch up to me in seconds. By the time we were in the hospital, he was leading the way. He even knew which floor to push on the elevator.

When we reached the psych floor, he pulled out his phone and sent a text. Then he ushered me down a hall and away from the entrance. Less than a minute later, a door opened and a young woman's head popped out.

Jed saw her as soon as I did. He put his hand at the small of my back and hurried me through the door.

"Did you get it worked out?" Jed asked as the door shut behind us, enclosing us in a short hallway.

The woman smiled at him. "Yeah. I'm going to take you to the room before I bring her in."

Jed nodded. "Did you find out anything about the letters?"

"Not specifically about the letters, but I think I know how she's getting them out."

Jed gave her a look that suggested she should go on.

"There's an environmental services employee who started working this unit about a month ago." She glanced up at Jed. "You said that was when mail started arriving from her?"

"Close enough. I'm going to need a name and any information you have on him."

Her hand slipped into her pocket and pulled out a piece of paper. "Already done."

She was pretty—a dark complexion with dark hair and eyes. I shouldn't have been surprised by the look of appreciation that filled Jed's eyes as he took the sheet and opened it, but jealousy burned through my veins anyway. I quickly stomped it down. Even if I was interested in Jed, I wasn't stupid enough to think it would be more than a fling. Jealousy was . . . unwise, to say the least.

"Can we just get this over with?" Irritation seeped into my words.

Jed narrowed his eyes, but he folded the paper and stuffed it into his pocket. "Show us to the room."

It was showtime.

Chapter Six

The nurse checked the door opposite the one we'd used to enter the small space, then motioned for us to follow.

We slipped out the door and into a longer hallway, moving away from the waiting room. She opened a door and motioned for us to go in. As soon as we did, she shut us inside, and I couldn't help but feel trapped.

We were in an office. A desk sat in front of the window, and a wall of bookcases lined the wall to the left. Several diplomas lined the wall to the right. I took a closer look—Kristy Anne Tilton was a psychologist with a PhD from the University of Arkansas.

Jed motioned to the desk. "Take a seat."

"Behind the desk?"

"We're here for you."

That wasn't entirely true, but I supposed he wouldn't be there without the excuse of accompanying me.

I tossed my bag behind the desk and had barely gotten settled in the chair when the door opened and Kate appeared. Just like the last time I'd seen her, she was wearing yoga pants and a fitted T-shirt. Her eyes widened when she saw us, and a rough laugh escaped her.

"This is a surprise, and those are so few and far between these days."

Jed stood behind me as though he was my bodyguard. "Come in and have a seat, Kate."

She looked amused by Jed's command, but she walked in and let the door close behind her. Flopping down in one of the chairs across from the desk, she gave me a smirk. "Got yourself a new beau, Neely Kate?"

I kept my emotions hidden. "You wanted me here, so I'm here."

"But not in the waiting room . . . I told you that we're alike. Much more alike than you and Joe."

I saw no reason to beat around the bush. "What do you know about Beasley?"

She laughed, a hysterical sound that bent her forward at the waist, making her look downright crazy. My back tensed as I waited for her to calm down. "Have you ever heard of small talk, sis?"

"I don't see the point in making small talk about the weather. Especially since you only get to see it through a window."

"Good one." Her smirk spread. "How about girl talk? What do sisters normally chat about?"

"I have no idea," I said, piercing her with my gaze. "I don't have a sister."

She covered her chest with her palm. "Ouch, Neely Kate, and here I thought we were bonding."

"Bonding?" I spat in disgust. "This is not bonding. Sisters build a relationship based on love and trust. We have neither."

"We could have love, *little sister*," she said, her eyes lighting up with excitement. "But you refuse to love me. I love *you*."

"You don't love me. I suspect you're incapable of love, let alone unconditional love."

Her mouth scrunched into a mock frown, but her eyes twinkled. "Poor, poor Neely Kate. You of all people should have learned that unconditional love doesn't exist."

"What do you know about Beasley?"

She flung her arm wide and rested it on the arm of the chair. "The real question is what do *you* know about Beasley."

Banging my hand on the desk, I lifted my butt out of my chair as I leaned forward. "Enough with the circular talk. What the hell do you want?"

A triumphant grin spread across her face, and I knew I'd messed up.

"Glad to see you finally realized who's in control here," she said.

I sat down and stayed silent.

"Good girl," Kate said as though I were a disobedient dog. She waited several seconds before speaking, no doubt to get her point across. "I have to hand it to you, Neely Kate. You were good at covering everything up, *very* good, but you misjudged Beasley."

I tasted bile on my tongue.

"Go ahead and ask me, Neely Kate."

"Ask you what?"

"Ask me how Beasley got out of jail."

Beasley was out of jail? *How?* "What do you want, Kate?"

"I want you to be a better sister. I want you to visit me more often." She glanced up at Jed and licked her upper lip. "Mmm . . . and bring him back with you."

"You're doin' this because you want me to come *visit?*"

"And tell me about Joe. How's he doing? I haven't seen him since you both came together."

"I'm not spying on Joe for you."

"Spying? What are you talking about? He's our brother. I want to hear about his life. Is he dating anyone?"

I shook my head in disgust.

"Is that a 'no, he's not dating anyone'?"

"How did you know about the azaleas?"

She leaned closer and tapped the desk with her index fingernail. "That was a tough one, I'll give you that. And you have no idea how hard it was to get those flowers out of season." She gave me a patronizing smile. "See what a good sister I am?"

"You dragged me up here to tell me you want me to visit you more often?"

"Is that a problem?"

"You couldn't tell me in a letter?"

"What would the fun be in that?"

I wasn't getting anything, but then again, why was I surprised? She loved the smell of fear and desperation, and right now I reeked of it.

"I want weekly visits," Kate said, examining her nail beds. "Bring fire-engine red nail polish and paint my nails next time. That's something sisters do, right?"

I didn't answer.

"And I want Joe to know about the visits, but he can't come. Just you and me." She flicked her finger toward Jed. "But you can bring him. *He's* a pretty picture." She got to her feet and slowly glided toward him. "If you make your weekly meetings, then the letters will stop and your secret will be safe."

"Until you change the rules," I said.

"Rules are always changing, sis." She stopped in front of Jed and ran her fingers from his shoulder to the crook of his elbow. "You should have learned that lesson by now too."

I wasn't about to admit she was right.

Kate looked up into Jed's face. "Do you have a name, handsome?"

To his credit, his expression of disinterest could have been carved from granite. "What do you know about the Murray portfolio?" he asked.

Her eyes flew wide and she burst out into gleeful laughter. "Oh, you *are* a surprise. I suppose meeting in this office was *your* doing?"

Jed didn't respond.

"And what makes you think I know anything about the Murray portfolio?" Kate asked.

He remained silent.

"Does Neely Kate know about the Murray portfolio?" She glanced toward me. "No, I don't think you do. But does your man know about Beasley?"

Panic demanded I *do something*, but there was nothing I *could* do. I was at her mercy, and we both knew it.

Kate ran her finger over Jed's jaw. I wanted to snap it. "Did she tell you about Beasley?"

Jed didn't say anything.

"So . . . you're a man of few words. You must be a man of *action*." Her finger brushed over his lip. "Maybe we can work out a deal. It's very *lonely* in here."

I expected Jed to shake her off like a flea, but he just stood there and let her touch him.

"So, you're here to find out more about the Murray portfolio, are you? Since you're here with Neely Kate, and my sister has befriended that terrible woman, Rose, I bet you work for James Malcolm."

I was surprised she knew Skeeter's real first name. No one but Rose used it.

"Tell Mr. Malcolm," she continued, "I have needs that aren't being met here. If he can help supply resources to fulfill those needs, I think we can work out an exchange."

He glanced down at the desk. "Make a list, and I'll let him know."

She shook her head with a sly grin. "I couldn't possibly come up with a list in so little time. Come back next week, and I'll give it to you. Bring my sister with you." She reached up on her tiptoes and placed a kiss on Jed's chin. "See you two next week."

Then she sashayed out of the room.

"Okay," Jed said as though she hadn't nearly sexually assaulted him. "Let's go."

I stared up at him in disbelief.

"She's not coming back, and the less time we're here, the less likely we are to get caught."

What he said made total sense, yet something was irritating the crap out of me. I told myself it wasn't because Kate had come on to him so strong. It *definitely* wasn't because I was pissed that he hadn't shrugged her off.

I almost believed it.

I got out of the chair and started around the desk before realizing Jed wasn't following me. I turned around and found him still standing behind the desk, holding my bag in his hand.

"What do you have in here anyway?" he asked, hefting it up and down.

The room suddenly felt like it was too hot and tight.

"None of your business." I marched back and snatched the bag from him. "Let's go."

I stormed out, bolting back the way we'd come. When I made it to the elevator, I repeatedly jabbed the down button, hoping I could make my escape before Jed showed up.

I should have known better.

"I know you're disappointed," he said quietly.

"Is that what you think I am?" I snapped. What the hell was wrong with me? I'd come to get answers and barely gotten anything other than the demand I come back every week and the news that Beasley was out of jail.

How was Beasley out of jail?

But I hadn't expected any real answers. Kate only spoke in riddles. This was just a last-ditch effort to find out what I could before I left.

The elevator doors opened. I entered the empty space with Jed on my heels, and he pressed the button for the lobby.

When the doors closed, he turned to me. "Who is Beasley?"

"None of your business."

"Did you ever think maybe I could help you?"

"Why?" I looked up at him and demanded, "*Why* would you help me?"

He hesitated, then said, "Because you're Rose's friend."

His answer made sense and my fluctuating emotions made none, yet I was still hurt to the core. I gave a knowing nod. "Because of Rose."

"Neely Kate."

I shook my head. "I'm not doing this. I'm not going to be Kate's little puppet."

"What does that mean?"

"If you think I'm going to come back here with you week after week and watch you two make out or worse, you have another think coming!"

Surprise filled his eyes and he leaned closer, lowering his voice. "What part of watching us make out would bother you?"

Me and my stupid mouth.

I backed up until the wall stopped me, but Jed advanced until he was only inches away. He leaned down, his face so close he would barely have to move to kiss me. "I don't want to make out with Kate Simmons."

"Well, I guess you have *some* standards," I conceded dryly.

To my surprise, he laughed.

"We can't do this, Jed," I said, more to convince myself than him.

His amusement vanished, but he didn't back out of my personal space. "We have to come back here, NK."

I shook my head. "Maybe you do, but I don't."

The elevator door opened, and I gave Jed a shove as I walked out of the elevator. An elderly woman gave us a questioning look before she got on.

I needed to ditch Jed, but he was attached to me like a tick to a coon dog, and I had no doubt I'd lose a foot race. These sandals weren't designed for running.

"We have a two-hour drive ahead," I said. "I need to go to the bathroom."

"Let's get something to eat. You can go to the bathroom there."

"I need to go now."

"Okay." He pointed to a restroom sign. "They're that way. Let's go."

"What? Am I five years old? Wait in the lobby. I'll be right back."

He gave me a long look. "I'm not your enemy, Neely Kate."

"I never said you were."

"But you never said I wasn't. I know you're ashamed of—"

"Let's continue this conversation when I get back."

Disappointment washed over his face, but he nodded.

I spun on my heels and hurried away from him before I could change my mind. When I reached the restroom, I looked over my shoulder to make sure Jed wasn't watching, then bolted down the hall and never looked back.

Chapter Seven

I knew my escape had been too easy.

I'd slipped out the back door and walked to the nearby bus stop just as a bus was pulling up. I wasn't sure it was the bus I needed, but I couldn't risk Jed finding me, so I hopped on. Luck was on my side—I only had to switch buses once—and I was at the Greyhound station within forty-five minutes. I had exactly twenty minutes before my bus to Texarkana left. If I missed this one, I'd be taking the red-eye. I was standing in line when I heard an all-too-familiar voice behind me.

"I know a faster way to Oklahoma."

Well, crap on a stick.

I spun around, expecting to see Jed wearing a satisfied smirk, but his expression was as unreadable as usual. "I'm not going back to Henryetta."

"And I believe I offered you a ride to Oklahoma, not Henryetta."

"No, thanks." I turned back around to face the front of the line, and Jed moved in place behind me. How had he figured out I was going to Oklahoma?

That was the thing about Jed. He didn't say a whole lot most of the time, but he was sharp as a thumbtack.

I steeled my back. "I'm not gonna change my mind."

"I never expected you to."

"Then what are you still doin' here?" I asked, still facing the front.

"Buying a bus ticket, same as you."

I twisted at the waist to look back at him. "Why on God's green earth would you do that when you have a perfectly good car?"

He searched my face. "One could ask why you would take a ten-hour bus ride when the trip would be a little over five hours—and a lot more comfortable—if you took me up on my offer."

I sighed. "Look, I appreciate the offer, but I need to do this on my own."

He leaned closer and lowered his voice. "Why? I know you think you're going to lose Rose and Joe if they find out about your past, but you can't scare me off with the big bad things you've supposedly done. I guarantee I've done worse."

"There's no supposedly about it, Jed."

"Fine, then you've done some bad shit. So have I. Let's go face it together."

I was tempted for a lot of right reasons, but some wrong ones too.

I shook my head and turned back around. I expected Jed to try to convince me, but he was his typical quiet self. I reached the window and told the booth attendant I wanted a one-way ticket to Ardmore, Oklahoma.

"Make that two," Jed said, putting two one-hundred-dollar bills through the window.

I glanced back at him. "What in the Sam Hill are you doin', Jed Carlisle?"

"I'm buying our tickets to Ardmore."

"Why on earth would you buy a ticket when your car's parked right over there?" I pointed to the parking lot.

The attendant paid no mind to our conversation, but instead slid the two tickets and Jed's change through the window. "Platform two. Your bus is already here and pulls out in ten minutes."

Jed grabbed my bag from me and headed to the loading platforms.

"What the hell are you *doin*?"

He turned to face me, walking backward as a boyish smile lit up his face. "I'm getting on the bus. I hear they have tight schedules."

"Are you insane?"

He looked me up and down. "Probably."

A wave of lust washed through my body, nearly making me stumble. But Jed had already turned around and was heading for the bus. I followed along like he was the Pied Piper. I told myself it was because he had not only my ticket but also my bag.

I knew better.

He boarded, making sure I'd caught up before he showed the driver our tickets.

The bus was half full and he headed toward the back, continuing down the aisle until he found two open seats together. He glanced back at me. "This good?"

I looked at him, waiting for him to tell me "gotcha."

I'd spent most of my life waiting for the rug to be pulled out from under me when good things happened. My mother had taught me by experience that they were often a trick—a fleeting one at that. For the life of me, I couldn't see Jed making a ten-hour bus ride to appease me. At any moment, he was going to find some way to get me off—either physical manhandling or some kind of threat. But at the moment, he was simply expecting an answer.

"Uh . . . yeah."

He lifted my bag to the overhead bin. "Window or aisle?"

"Uh . . . window."

"Good," he said. "I prefer the aisle, but lady's choice."

I slid in and took my seat. He sat next to me, our legs touching. Heat seeped through my body where his denim-covered leg touched my bare one.

Good God. I was going to have to travel ten hours like this. I suspected I'd be jumping him in the bathroom when we changed buses in Texarkana. And we only had a fifteen-minute layover.

He tried to stretch out his long legs, but there was nowhere for them to go. His knees were bent at an awkward angle, and I had a hunch there was no position he could contort himself into that would be comfortable. He moved his arm so his right hand rested partially on his leg, but partially on mine.

I closed my eyes and sucked in a breath. *Sweet Mother of Mercy.*

He leaned into my ear and whispered, his breath fanning my neck and sending a shiver down my back. "You comfortable?"

My eyes flew open, and I gave him a look that suggested he'd just asked the most ridiculous question in the world. But any comment I'd thought to make got stuck in my throat when I realized our faces were only inches apart.

His eyes darkened, and I was sure he was going to kiss me, but then he shifted, moving back a few inches, making it look totally natural.

"You're not," I said, trying to slow down my rapid breathing.

"This isn't about me," he said, watching my expression. "This is about you."

"Why are you doin' this, Jed?" I asked, irritated my voice sounded so husky.

"Because I know in my gut you need someone with you on this trip. And while I recognize and appreciate that you feel like you need to do this alone, I'm going to be there behind you, giving you the support and backup you need."

"Why? Because of Rose?"

He met my gaze and held it. "No. I promise you it's not because of Rose."

I released a short laugh despite myself.

He lifted a hand and softly brushed a stray hair from my face. "Is it so hard to believe someone could care enough to be that person for you?"

"Yes."

Sadness filled his eyes. "Then you need me even more than I thought."

Someone started coughing behind us, and the driver announced that the bus was about to pull out of the station. I realized the sacrifice he was making for me, accompanying me on this trip he didn't really understand, sitting on this horrible bus for endless hours. Maybe, just maybe, Jed actually did want to do it *for me*, but part of me couldn't help thinking it was because Skeeter wanted him to keep an eye on me—for personal gain, not necessarily for my protection. After all, Skeeter had insisted Jed come with me to Little Rock. And yet .

. . that had been about Kate—what could either of them possibly hope to find in Ardmore?

Still, if Beasley really was out of prison—and Kate hadn't lied to me yet—I supposed it didn't matter what Jed's motivations were. There was a chance I'd need backup.

"Okay. You can go with me," I said, even though I knew this was a terrible idea. "But let's get off this bus and take your car."

"Are you sure?"

"Yeah." I gave him a shove. "Hurry or we'll be stuck on here until we get to Texarkana."

"Thank God," he groaned, but he tempered it with a wink.

He slid out of his seat and grabbed my bag in one fell swoop, then reached a hand down to help me up.

I took his hand, trying to ignore the tingles that immediately shot through me.

The driver closed the door, and Jed kept hold of my hand, dragging me down the aisle. "We're getting off."

The driver gave us a scathing look, but he opened the door—probably because of Jed's imposing stare. Jed hopped off, tugging me with him.

I landed on the pavement, and gravity pulled me forward. I ended up with my chest pressed to his. I took some satisfaction from knowing he was just as affected by the contact as I was—his dilated pupils and parted mouth were a telltale clue—but I had to set some ground rules or this trip would quickly become a disaster.

"Are you coming with me because you want to sleep with me?" I asked, bold as I pleased.

There was that grin again—it was like the man had saved up all his smiles from the past decade and was now using them indiscriminately—and his arm slipped around my back, holding me in place. I could feel the evidence that I might be on the right track, but fool that I was, I didn't pull away.

"We can't sleep together, Jed."

"Your trip. Your rules."

I narrowed my eyes. "Okay. So *this* is probably a bad idea."

"What?"

"Me plastered against you."

"You're free to step away at any time."

I stepped back, taking a breath and trying to get myself together. "We're not sleeping together."

"You already said that," he said, his voice laced with humor.

"I just want to make sure it's clear." But the fact that he wasn't protesting made me second-guess myself. "You don't want to sleep with me?"

"Neely Kate, I've gotten where I am today because I'm a patient man. I know when to bide my time."

Another wave of lust washed through me, and I told myself to calm down. Jed was a good-looking man—a dangerously good-looking man—and he was tossing bread crumbs of attention my way. It had been a while since a man had pursued me. That was all.

But I knew that was a lie.

Carter Hale had made no secret of his desire to hook up with me, but the sad truth was that I'd be another conquest for someone like Carter. For Jed too. They saw through the walls I'd stacked so carefully in my pathetic attempt to be worthy of someone's love, but it was like slapping paint on a pig—it didn't disguise that deep down I was nothing but a whore.

Until Ronnie, none of the guys in my life had seen me as anything more than a hookup or a possession.

Ronnie had been looking for forever, and I'd grabbed ahold of the bright shiny and hadn't let go. How ironic that I had thought I was the one settling for the commitment I desperately craved. For a man who would never leave me.

The joke was on me.

So why was I doing a fool thing like falling for Jed Carlisle? Because nothing but misery waited for me at the end of *that* road. Worse yet, I knew it, and I was letting myself fall for him like a pyromaniac drawn to a three-alarm fire.

Jed frowned as though he noticed the change in my demeanor. "Let's get out of the heat."

He put his hand at the small of my back and led me to the parking lot. Using his keyless remote, he started the engine before opening the trunk. He moved to open my passenger door, and I tried to push his hand away. What was he trying to prove?

"We're not on a date, Jed."

He leaned close. "Let's make this perfectly clear," he said in a low voice. "If you are riding in my car, I'm opening the door. Got it?"

I stared up at him with an expression that suggested I thought he'd lost his damn mind, but I let him open the door all the same.

We were silent as we took off, and I felt a sense of impending doom like I'd never experienced before. Not only was I about to lose the life I'd built in Henryetta, but I was handing Jed my heart on a silver platter.

And I was powerless to stop any of it.

Chapter Eight

We'd been on the road for ten minutes when I got another text from Rose. She'd sent the first one while we were still on the road to Little Rock.

Are you feeling better?

I tossed the phone into my lap. She'd see the note soon enough; I couldn't bear to answer. Tears stung my eyes, but I refused to cry. Crying never solved a thing.

Jed sent me a questioning look. It would seem he was back to his silent ways—he hadn't said a word since we'd climbed into the car. He'd just plotted a course on the map app on his phone and started driving.

A few minutes later, Jed's phone vibrated, and he turned it off without looking at the screen.

"Don't you need to get that?"

He stared at me for a long moment—longer than was prudent while driving seventy-five miles an hour on a highway lined with eighteen-wheelers. But then he turned back to the road and clutched the steering wheel so tightly I was surprised he didn't snap it in two.

Had he changed his mind? Sure, it was one thing to offer to go with me in the heat of the moment, but maybe he was having buyer's remorse? "Jed?"

"No."

"Are you sure?"

He didn't answer, making me more nervous. Maybe I should give him an out when we stopped for gas.

The car was chilly, but I sure wasn't going to complain given that the alternative was riding on a hot, smelly bus. I reached into the back and rummaged around in my bag until I found my denim jacket.

"What did you tell Rose?"

I stalled by starting to put my jacket on. How much should I tell him? I knew Rose had him on her speed dial—they weren't only protector and protectee, they were friends—but I found myself wanting to be honest with him nevertheless. This was a good place to start. "I just told her I had to take care of some things, and I didn't know when I'd be back."

"And she was good with that?"

I made a face as I slipped into my other sleeve. "I left a note. I expect her to be calling in another couple of hours. Or sooner, since I haven't answered the texts she's sent this afternoon." I glanced at him. "I told her I was sick and stayed home from work."

He studied me for a moment before he turned back to face the road. "You can trust her, Neely Kate. Rose is one of the most nonjudgmental people I know."

"I know . . ." I shifted and tucked my feet under me, staring down at my lap. "But if she found out . . . she'd never look at me the same."

"Rose has done some bad things herself. She's killed two men."

"In self-defense." I glanced up at him. "How many men have you killed?"

His jaw tightened. "Enough to damn my soul."

I turned my back to the door and gave him my full attention. "Do you really mean that?"

His gaze met mine. "Yeah."

The sadness and regret in his eyes caught me by surprise. This was the most real I'd ever seen him, and the rawness on his face touched something deep inside me. I grabbed his hand and sandwiched it between both of mine.

He seemed surprised, but he didn't let go. "How many people have you killed, Neely Kate?"

"Let's just say your damned soul has company." And every mile that brought us closer to Ardmore also brought me closer to the things I'd done.

He was silent for several heavy seconds. "Is that what you're trying to hide?"

Tears stung my eyes. Part of me thought I should answer, but I couldn't bring myself to admit to my sins just yet, let alone relive them myself. "Just because you're coming with me doesn't mean you're getting my life story."

"Fair enough. But I'm pretty much an open book. Ask anything you like, and I'll answer if I can."

Jed wasn't an open book by any means, but his offer piqued my interest. Would he actually answer? "How'd you get hooked up with Skeeter?"

A tight smile stretched his face. "I suspect you know most of that story."

"You grew up together."

He nodded. "The thing you have to understand about Skeeter is that he's loyal . . . sometimes to a fault. We were thick as thieves when we were kids . . .

hardscrabble kids. Skeeter and his brother were older than me, but Skeeter always included me and my sister Daisy, along with our friend Pete."

That caught me by surprise. "I didn't know you have a sister."

"Had." He paused, and I was sure that was all he planned to say, but then he added, "She drowned when we were kids."

I sucked in a breath. I could see he was still hurting. "How old was she?"

"Five."

"How old were you?"

"Eight, but she and I were close. I protected her from our parents. Only, I didn't protect her that day." A dark look filled his eyes.

"What happened?"

"We were fishing and Scooter caught a big fish. While we were helping him reel it in, I turned my back on my sister. When I checked on her, she was already dead, floating in the water."

I was still holding his hand, and I squeezed it hard. "Jed. I'm so sorry."

"We tried to save her. Skeeter was older, so he took over. He was a leader, even back then. He gave her CPR for a few minutes, and when that didn't work, he picked her up and ran to the house." He took a breath. "He took it almost as hard as I did. He considered us family and felt responsible for us. Even back then."

"So you two have always been close?"

"We were good friends, but after that, he took me under his wing. He knew Daisy was all I had." His voice broke.

When I spoke, I had to push the words out past the lump in my throat, indulging myself with a momentary lapse into self-pity. "At least you had her for a little while. I had no one."

He turned to me. "No brothers or sisters?"

"No, but it sounds like we both had crap parents . . . only mine was just my mom." Then I added in a snide tone, "You know who my father is."

"You're nothing like him, Neely Kate."

"I'm not so sure about that. I suspect Kate's right, and I'm more like my half sister than I care to admit. And she's a lot like our father." It scared the bejiggers out of me.

"If I ever have kids, I'll make sure they know I love them. They'll never be scared of me, and they'll never go to bed hungry."

"That's what I wanted for my babies." To my embarrassment, my voice cracked.

"I know. I'm sorry."

I had to give him credit for not telling me a bunch of platitudes like I was young and it was God's will.

He tried to grab my hand, but I shifted it out of reach and turned to look out the window. "Do you believe in divine providence, Jed?"

He hesitated. "Are you asking if I believe in fate? No. I think we make our own fate."

"So you don't believe in karma? Cosmic justice?"

"I know there's absolutely nothing you could have done to justify what happened to your babies, Neely Kate."

If he only knew everything . . . And I suspected he *would* know before this was all said and done. He certainly wouldn't be giving me compassionate looks then. "You don't know . . . you don't know."

"So tell me," he said quietly.

No. I wasn't ready to lose him yet.

We reached Texarkana an hour later, and Jed said he needed to stop for gas. When he pulled in front of a gas pump at a truck stop, I told him I had to go to the bathroom. He watched me get out but didn't say anything.

I headed inside, casting a glance over my shoulder. I couldn't figure out why he was here. It didn't make sense. Jed was one of the best-looking men I had ever seen, so I couldn't believe he was in this just to sleep with me. At the same time, I couldn't let myself think he actually *cared*. I'd been fooled by men before, which was what had gotten me into this desperate situation in the first place.

Rose texted again while I was peeing, but I ignored it. Pretending I didn't see her texts would only make her more anxious. I *knew* that. Even so, I wasn't ready to deal with her, and I wasn't sure I ever would be. The guilt was already as thick and choking as toxic smoke. Rose had done everything she could to show me that she wouldn't judge me. While I didn't disbelieve her, exactly, I simply couldn't live with the alternative.

Chapter Nine

Jed had been in the middle of a heated phone call when I'd left the building, but he'd hung up before I reached him. From the way he was leaning on the top of the car, it hadn't ended well. He looked like he was pissed.

"Are you okay?" I asked as a gust of wind kicked up my dress and blew my hair into my face.

Jed straightened, his gaze landing on my face, and he gave me a soft smile. "I am now."

I half-expected him to say it with a leer, not that he'd ever looked at me that way before, but his smile was genuine. It melted the frost of my earlier despair. Maybe having Jed with me was a good thing. I gave him a playful grin in return. "What's that supposed to mean?"

He hung the gas nozzle back on the pump and walked around the back of the car toward me. "It means I'm starving, and now that you're back, we can get something to eat. What are you hungry for?"

I pointed at the truck stop behind me. "They have pizza inside."

He shook his head. "I want real food. Are you up for stopping somewhere?"

"It depends," I said slowly. "I can't go anywhere too expensive. I have money, but I don't know how long I'll be gone . . . I need to make it last." Then I remembered the bus stop. "Not to mention I owe you for your bus ticket and mine."

He put his arm around my back, a gesture that felt more comforting than it probably should have, and steered me toward the passenger door. "We'll work out all the details as we go," he said as he opened the door for me yet again.

I climbed inside, and he shut the door behind me.

"Who were you talking to earlier?" I asked as soon as he got into the driver's seat.

He turned on the car and steered us back onto the highway. "It's not important."

I decided to push it. "It looked important."

He turned to glance at me. "It was Skeeter. We didn't see eye to eye about something, but you don't need to worry about it."

"Was it about me?" Had Skeeter told him to spy on me?

He reached over and grabbed my hand, linking our fingers together. "No. In the grand scheme of things, it was about me, and it was a long time coming." He shot me a look. "Mexican? Chinese? Steak?"

I was still in shock that he was holding my hand. This time he didn't just squeeze it and pull away; he held it like it was something precious. This was by far the most intimate touch we'd ever shared. It suggested familiarity and fondness, not lust and desire. This was dangerous ground.

He mistook my silence and said, "Or we can get pizza, if you'd prefer."

Should I remove my hand from his? For better or worse, I liked it. "Well, we *are* in Texas now. Maybe we should get Tex-Mex."

"Tex-Mex it is."

It didn't take us long to find a restaurant, and it was early enough for dinner that we didn't have to wait for a table.

After we ordered our food, Jed sobered. "How are you doin' after talking to Kate?"

"Better now," I said. It felt like we'd made our visit to the psych ward several days ago, not earlier that afternoon. "I was stupid to think she would tell me anything, but I had to try."

"Do you think she knows everything, or is there a chance she's guessing?"

I considered ignoring his question, but I didn't get the impression he was trying to fit the puzzle pieces of my life together. More like he was asking out of concern for me. "She definitely knows more than I would like. If she went to Ardmore and started snooping into my life, Beasley wouldn't be too difficult to figure out."

"Is he one of the people you need to talk to about the azaleas?"

My eyes narrowed. "Why do you think I need to talk to anyone about the azaleas?"

"Because you're ashamed of what it signifies. You need to know what Kate knows so you can do damage control. The best way to do that is to figure out who she—or the person she hired to look into you—talked to."

"Why are you helping me?"

He gave me a half-shrug and half-grin. "I needed a vacation."

"I'm serious, Jed," I said, leaning forward. "Why are you doing this?"

He shifted in his seat. "The honest to God truth, Neely Kate, is that I don't know. I've been asking myself that very question since I bought those tickets and got on the bus with you."

"Did Skeeter tell you to tag along with me?"

He released a bitter laugh. "No. The opposite, in fact."

My eyebrows shot up. "He wants you to come back? What about me?"

"The conversation devolved before we got around to you."

"What happened?"

He looked like he was weighing his words before he said, "I suspect people have fed you bullshit most of your life, and I don't want to be one of those people, so I'll tell you even at the risk of scaring you off."

My pulse picked up. "Okay."

"Skeeter gave me an ultimatum. Either turn around and go back or not come back at all."

"He fired you?" I asked in dismay and disbelief.

"Yeah."

"You got fired for helping me, and you don't even know why you're doing it?" He was right. It sounded fishy as hell.

"He'll change his mind," he said, sounding bitter. "He always does."

I blinked in surprise. "How many times has he fired you?"

"Maybe one too many."

That answer worried me, prompting me to say, "You still haven't explained why you risked Skeeter's wrath to help me."

He picked up a sugar packet and began to turn it in his hand. "Let's say I really wanted that vacation."

"A permanent one."

He shrugged. "I've never had a vacation before. Maybe we should head to Florida when we finish in Ardmore."

"We?"

"Why not? You're not sure if you're going back to Fenton County—"

"I never said that."

He gave me a no-nonsense look. "You didn't have to, Neely Kate. It wasn't hard to figure out, just like I figured out that you were heading to the bus station."

"You knew I was coming to Oklahoma." It was a statement, not a question. I still hadn't figured out the how of it.

"Before you took your first step down the porch."

In hindsight, that duffel bag was a pretty obvious tell. "But how'd you know I was taking the bus?"

He put the sugar packet down on the table. "That part was a gamble, actually. I knew you were headed to Oklahoma, but I also know you don't have a lot of money. We both know your car would never make it to Little Rock, let alone another state. If you were considering not returning to Fenton County, you would want to make the money last. The cheapest way to get to Oklahoma would be to ask a stranger for a ride, but I was hoping you wouldn't resort to something so dangerous. The fact that you escaped the hospital by bus was additional evidence."

I shook my head. "You saw me."

"I almost didn't. By the time I figured out your escape plan, you'd already run out the back door. I'd just gotten outside when I saw you getting on the bus."

"How'd you know it was me?"

There was that grin again. "I'd recognize those sexy legs anywhere."

I sucked in a breath, surprised he wasn't hiding his interest.

He rested his forearm on the table, a nonchalant pose that didn't quite match the hungry look in his eyes. "You made it painfully clear at the bus station that you don't want to sleep with me—and I suspect I made it painfully obvious to you, when you were plastered against me, that I am very interested in sleeping with you. That being said, I respect your choice, Neely Kate. You are in *full control* of what happens on this trip. I'm not going to try anything, so you don't need to be on edge. You have enough to be anxious about without worrying about fending off advances from me. Nevertheless . . ." He smiled at me again, and this time it was full of promise. "I'm a red-blooded man who has the eyes God gave him, and as long as I'm not being lecherous, I see no reason to hide my attraction to you."

My body flushed. "And if I change my mind?" I asked before I could stop myself.

"Then you're in control of that too."

My mouth parted in shock, but the timely arrival of our food saved me from having to respond. When the waiter left, I picked up my fork, ready to dive into my enchilada.

This time the interruption wasn't so timely. My phone rang before I could take a bite.

"Do you think that's Rose?" Jed asked.

"Yeah." I could feel my heart pounding in my ears.

"Do you want me to go outside or to the bar so you can get that?"

I'd considered continuing my evasive maneuvers, but she deserved better, and if Jed was taking a no-secrets policy, I could at least be open with this. "No. Stay."

I grabbed my phone out of my purse, answering the call seconds before it went to voice mail. "Hey, Rose."

"Thank God." She sounded like she was about to cry. "Where are you?"

"I'm safe."

"And I'm grateful for that, but where is that?"

"Rose . . ."

"You said you're taking care of things. What exactly does that mean? Does this have to do with Kate? Are you in Little Rock?"

I gave Jed a defeated look, but I couldn't bear to hold his gaze, so I glanced down at my plate. "Yes, I saw Kate, but there are some other things I need to see to."

"This has to do with your past, doesn't it?" Her voice was teary again. "What is Kate holding over you? I'll tell Joe, and the three of us can deal with it together."

"No! Don't call Joe!" I said in a panic. I hadn't even considered the possibility that she would, which was pure carelessness on my part. I'd convinced myself well and good that I'd managed to outrun everything . . . so much so I'd lost my survival instincts. It was a wonder it had taken so long for my past to bite back. "He won't understand."

"Because he's in law enforcement?" She paused. "I know you think we'll turn away from you once we find out your deep dark secrets, but we won't, Neely Kate. We love you. No conditions. No strings. Just come home, and we'll face it together."

"I can't come home, Rose."

"*Ever?*" She sounded panicked.

That was a good question. If things were as bad as I feared, I'd have more to worry about than how Rose and Joe would take the truth. I'd be evading a warrant for my arrest. "I don't know."

"You come home right now, Neely Kate Rivers!" she demanded in a voice so sweet it was almost comical. "You come home, and we'll come up with a plan together. You can't do this alone."

"I'm not alone."

She hesitated. "Who's with you? Witt?"

I could see why she might think I'd turn to my cousin, but Witt didn't know any more than she did. "No. Not Witt."

"Then who?"

I looked up at the man across from me, and he nodded.

"Jed."

Rose was silent for a second. "*Jed?* How did Jed end up with you?"

"It's a long story, Rose, and I'll tell you later. Once this is taken care of."

"Come home, Neely Kate."

It hurt not to tell her yes, especially since I loved the sound of that—*home*—but I knew I couldn't give her what she wanted. Not yet. "I love you, Rose."

"You let me speak to Jed *right now!*"

I held the phone down. "She wants to talk to you."

He grimaced, but his lips were tipped up in a slight smile. "I heard." He reached out and took the phone. "Rose."

I heard her voice, although I couldn't make out all the words, but it was obvious she was giving him an earful.

Finally, he said, "Rose. I'm watching out for her, and if you have any doubts, just remember how I watched over you."

She was silent for about five seconds; then I heard her say something else, something much too quiet for me to hear.

He said, "I promise," then handed the phone back to me.

"Rose," I said when I returned the phone to my ear, "I know you don't understand, but this is something I have to do."

"I know." Her voice broke and she sniffed. "Do you have any idea how much I love you?"

I started to cry. "Yes."

"No," she said insistently. "I don't think you do; otherwise, you wouldn't have run off without me. But you listen here: if you're not back by next Sunday night, I will come to Oklahoma and find you and bring you back myself."

"I never said I was in Oklahoma."

"I'm no fool, Neely Kate Rivers. I will come find you. Do you understand?"

I laughed through my tears. "Yeah. I understand."

"Promise me that you'll stick with Jed."

I glanced up at him. "I promise."

"Good, because I can't think of any other man I would trust you with besides Joe. So do what you need to do and come home."

"I will." Then I remembered one other issue. "What are you going to tell Joe?"

"What do you want me to tell him?"

I knew she wouldn't want to lie. "Just tell him I had to go take care of some Rivers family business . . . which is true. Say that I took off and you didn't know I was leaving until after I left."

"He'll probably call you."

"I know. I'll talk to him."

"Good. He cares about you too."

"I know. Now I have to go."

I hung up and put the phone on the table.

"You okay?" Jed asked.

I nodded and picked up my fork.

Silence hung over the table for several minutes before Jed broke it with a question. "How long did you live in Ardmore?"

This seemed harmless enough to answer. "I'm not sure about the first time. We probably moved there when I was five or six and stayed until I went to live with my grandmother when I was twelve. The second time . . . nearly two years."

"You moved back after you graduated from high school?"

I nodded.

"Why?"

I considered not answering, but in the scheme of things, this one seemed harmless enough too. "I kind of got lost with the whole Rivers family. They're this big, loud, overwhelming group, and I felt like I could never get my footing. I needed to go somewhere I felt like me."

"And you went to find your mother."

I nodded. "But she was gone, of course."

"Yet you stayed."

I wasn't sure how to explain. "You've lived in the same place your entire life. You know what it's like to feel like you belong somewhere. I've never had that. Not until Rose."

"Not even with Ronnie?"

I shook my head. "No."

We fell into silence again and finished our dinner. Jed flagged down the waiter so we could pay our bill. I insisted on paying for my half of the meal. It was bad enough he'd put his life on hold—and gotten fired to boot. I didn't really understand why he was doing so much for me, but I didn't want to owe him any more than I already did.

We walked across the parking lot, and when we reached his car, I turned to face him before he could open the door for me. "I'm still trying to figure out why you're here with me."

"I told you."

"No. Not really." I wasn't buying that he didn't know. I suspected he was still hoping to get laid. "Are you coming with me in the hopes I'll change my mind? You'll exchange . . . what? Support? Driving me around? Paying for my bus ticket for sex?"

His eyes darkened. "Let's get something clear right now." His voice was so hard I nearly jumped.

"*What?*" I asked with a defiant look.

"You are not a whore. You will not be bought, by me or anyone else. Have I made myself clear?"

I stared at him in disbelief, and damned if tears didn't burn my eyes. "You don't know my past."

"And it might be better if I don't know, seein' as we're about to muck around in it. I might have to beat a few faces in, and I'm not sure you have enough money to bail me out."

I smiled in spite of my tears. "Why are you so nice to me?"

"Because you're worth being nice to. I don't think you see what I see, Neely Kate."

"And what's that?" I asked against my better judgment.

"I see a woman so fierce she'd take on a man twice her size without a second thought. I see a woman who is willing to risk anything and everything to help her best friend. I see a woman so desperate to hold on to the few people who love her she's willing to risk her life to keep them." He gave me a sad smile. "I see a woman who deserves love more than anyone I know. I'm irredeemable, but I can help you."

I stared at this man who felt as lost and hopeless as I did. I slipped my arms around his back and pressed the side of my head to his chest. "You're not irredeemable, Jed."

His arms tightened around me, but this embrace was different than the one at the train station. This one was about comfort and strength.

Maybe we could save ourselves together.

Chapter Ten

We arrived in Ardmore around ten p.m. Jed suggested we get a motel room and start in the morning, but I shook my head. It was time to start my investigation. Maybe all my investigations with Rose had been practice for this.

"We need to go to Slick Willy's."

His brows lifted and he asked in a dry tone, "Slick Willy's?"

"It's a strip club west of Ardmore. Just outside of Wilson."

He gave me a long look, then said, "Tell me how to get there."

I gave him directions, and about fifteen minutes later, he pulled into the half-full parking lot. My stomach was in knots, but I knew I didn't have a choice.

"Are you looking for someone in particular here?" Jed asked.

Pulling down the visor, I checked my appearance in the mirror. I grabbed my lip gloss and swiped my lips. "No. I just thought you might enjoy the show. You know . . . compare it to the Bunny Ranch. Maybe get a lap dance. My treat in exchange for the bus tickets."

His eyes narrowed.

I closed the tube, dropped it in my purse, and then fluffed my hair, careful to not disturb my stitches. I knew he deserved the truth, but he'd figure it out on his own soon enough. Of all my friends and family, Jed was the person I would probably feel most comfortable bringing here with me.

Rose and I had gone searching for my cousin at Gems, the other strip club in Fenton County (until it burned down), and there'd been no mistaking the look of horror on Rose's face the entire time we were in the club. That look had told me she couldn't know the truth about how I'd learned to dance on the pole. I'd come up with a lie about my cousin teaching me in her garage, when in truth, *I'd* been the one to teach *her.*

But picking a companion to come here with me felt a whole lot like picking a body part where I wanted to be shot. Any location would hurt like hell, but some were less fatal.

I stuffed my phone and some cash in my jacket pocket and got out of the car, leaving Jed to follow.

"I take it you've been here before," Jed said in a dry tone.

"A time or two."

"What should I expect inside?"

"It's Wednesday night, so it will be pretty tame. The church crowd."

I half-expected a response to that, but one, he had experience with Skeeter's strip club, and two, I suspected people were pretty much the same wherever you went.

We were greeted in the small foyer by a bouncer, a guy who tried to look tough but shrank a bit when he saw Jed. I didn't recognize him, not that I was surprised. Turnover was understandably high. I slipped him a twenty to cover both of us, then headed inside before Jed could protest.

A couple of men were at the bar, but several more were sitting at the tables in front of the stage. On the far side of the room, a man and a woman sat facing the door. They were both well-dressed and totally out of the league of everyone else in the room. Interesting. But I'd temporarily caught the eye of the unaccompanied men, and they were practically ignoring the dancer gyrating to a Lady Gaga song. Her bra was already off, and there were several bills stuffed into her G-string.

I felt Jed's chest press against my back and left shoulder, and it occurred to me that he was crowding close to broadcast that I was off-limits. I practically rolled my eyes before I headed toward the bar.

I was safe here. Probably.

The bartender had his back to me when I sat on one of the stools, but I recognized him nonetheless. Jed slid onto the seat to my right, slowly scanning the room. He seemed tense, but I supposed that was my fault for springing this on him without any warning.

Time to rip that Band-Aid right off.

The bartender—who was also the owner—turned around and did a double take when he saw me. "Kitty?"

"Hey, Stan," I said, trying not to cringe.

"Oh, my God! I haven't seen you in years! Not since . . . well, all that shit went down."

"Yeah. I left right after."

"How are you? What are you doin' here?" His gaze landed on Jed and he looked equally impressed and intimidated. "Got yourself a man."

"No," I said, but Jed's harsh "Yes" was louder.

I shot him a look, wondering what the hell he was doing, but in this conversation, I didn't think it would matter.

"I'm back in town for a visit, so I figured I'd drop by. Any of the old girls still here?"

He shook his head. "Most are gone, but a few are left."

"Who?"

"Raven. Maddie."

"Carla?" I asked.

"Yeah . . . I forgot she started working right around the time you left."

"Does she happen to be working tonight?"

He shook his head. "Nope, but she's on tomorrow night."

"Thanks." I'd had a feeling I'd have to come back, but it didn't mean I was happy about it. How did I handle the next part without drawing suspicion? I decided to just go for it. "Heard anything about Beasley?"

He froze, a tell if ever I'd seen one, then picked up a bar rag and started to wipe the counter. "I don't know nothin' about it, Kitty."

"Forget I asked."

His shoulders relaxed and he set two glasses on the table.

"How about a drink for old times' sake?" He glanced at Jed and set out another tumbler before he picked up a whiskey bottle and gave us each a generous pour.

That made me suspicious. Stan's ass was so tight he shit out ribbons in the mornings.

He handed out the drinks, then held up his tumbler. "To old friends returning to the fold."

I clinked my glass with his, but Jed simply picked up his glass and took a drink. The scowl on his face suggested he was in no mood to chitchat. Surely he'd figured out my dirty little secret by now. Maybe he was reexamining his decision to come with me.

I couldn't handle his derision, so I avoided looking him in the eye.

My gaze flitted to the bottle as I took a sip. Looked like Stan had broken out the good stuff, or what passed for good stuff in this place. Now I was really on edge.

"So . . . what have you been up to, Kitty?"

I kept my glass up and gave him a half-shrug. "This and that."

"Where'd you take off to when you left?"

"Tulsa," I lied.

"Working in the industry?"

"I got out."

"You leave with Branson? He took off around the same time, from what I hear."

"Nope." I took a drink, hoping my hand didn't shake. Branson. I wasn't surprised Stan had asked. "Once I found out he was cheating, I took off."

Stan snorted. "That's a lie."

Jed's hand curled into a fist, but Stan didn't seem to notice.

I gave Stan a look so cold I was sure his testicles shrank to the size of acorns. "Excuse me?"

"It's just that he cheated before that . . ." he stammered, caught off guard. "And you didn't do anything about it then."

"The last time was different. He was cheating with my best friend."

I took another drink and looked up on the stage. Nothing much had changed. Same sad décor. Same damn poles—I could tell by the chip at the top of the one on the left, although the indentation was bigger now. Even a few of the same damn customers. I felt dirty being here, not necessarily from what I'd done on that stage—the money I'd made here had helped me survive—but everything else. Being here was like toweling off from a shower with an oily rag.

Branson. Beasley. Stella.

They were in my past, yet I still hadn't lost the stink of them. Maybe I didn't deserve to.

I downed the glass and set it on the counter. "Get me another."

"Only the first one's free," Stan said.

"She's covered," Jed growled. "Now get her drink."

I finally glanced back at him. He seemed like a firework about to go off at any moment. Why was he pissed? Did he want to leave? It seemed unlikely, since he'd insisted Stan get me another drink.

Stan refilled my glass, and I took a generous sip. I felt both hollow inside and full of regret, kind of like when you have a stomach virus and you can't tell if you're hungry or need to vomit. It was a familiar feeling even if it had dulled over the last few years. I had yet to find a cure, but at least I had a crutch. I took another sip, needing to drown it all out.

What was I doing here? I needed to accept that I'd done terrible things. I should be running to the farthest corners of the earth and praying I was never found.

The things I'd done . . .

They were locked up tight in my vault of secrets, but the liquor burning through my blood made it feel like someone was loosening the handle.

Jed leaned over to my ear. "Neely Kate, is there anyone else you want to talk to here?"

I glanced back at him, surprised by the softness in his eyes.

"No." I needed to talk to Carla, but I didn't want to give her a heads-up either. I turned to Stan. "I want to surprise Carla, so don't tell her I came in, okay?"

"Sure, sure," he said, wiping the bar again. He was nervous. Why?

Jed looked torn, but he pulled out a ten-dollar bill and tossed it on the counter before he stood.

"Hey! Drinks are fifteen!" Stan protested.

"Please," Jed sneered. "It's watered down and a knockoff at that, poured into a top-shelf bottle. You're lucky I'm payin' you at all."

Stan glared but didn't say anything.

I downed the rest of my whiskey, feeling the burn all the way to my toes, then stood. I rarely drank anymore, and watered down or not, the alcohol was going straight to my head.

Jed tossed another bill on the counter, this time a twenty. "I take it this will ensure that our visit never happened?"

"Yeah," Stan said, sliding it off the counter and stuffing it eagerly into his pocket. "Never saw ya."

Jed leaned closer. "I'm counting on your discretion. If I find out—"

"You won't! I'll be quiet."

"Good." Jed put his hand at the small of my back and pushed me toward the door.

It felt like a choker was tightening around my neck.

As soon as we left the building, Jed rushed on ahead, moving several steps away from me. I felt my lifeline to my new life—my life with Rose—tighten and threaten to break. Jed was taking it with him.

How could I have been stupid enough to trust him?

"Go ahead," I said as I held my hands wide.

"Go ahead and what?" he asked with a scowl as he continued to barrel toward his car.

I stayed in place and called after him. "You know my truth now. One of my dirty little secrets. Just keep on walkin'."

He stopped and turned around, looking furious. "What do you want from me, Neely Kate? You want me to condemn you for working here? Seems like you've done that enough on your own."

"I disgust you, don't I?" I asked, taking a step closer.

His face hardened even more. "No."

"So you like that I used to be an exotic dancer?" I asked coyly, yet my voice had an insincere edge. "You want me to show you my moves?"

"Get in the car, Neely Kate."

Why, so he could ditch me later? It would be best to save myself a mountain of pain and get this out of the way now.

"Have you changed your mind about not sleeping with me?" I asked, moving closer with slow steps as I grabbed the skirt of my dress and hiked it up, exposing my upper thighs. I slinked toward him.

Jed's eyes dipped to my legs before lifting to my face, his expression unreadable again.

"Do you want me to give you a lap dance?" I put my hand on his chest and pushed him backward. His butt hit the trunk of his car.

I expected a reaction out of him, but he just watched me with guarded eyes, his hands on the trunk beneath him.

My hips started to sway to unheard music as I straddled his leg and began to grind. "I slept with men for money, Jed," I said in a hard voice. "You didn't know that when I asked you if you wanted sex in exchange for the gas money to drive me here. I'd understand if you changed your mind."

"Neely Kate." His voice sounded strangled.

I turned around and lifted my hair from the back of my neck. Reaching back in a practiced move, I spread his legs and began to rub my ass into his crotch. "Do you want to screw me right here in the parking lot?"

He stood, wrapping his arm around the front of my waist to keep me from losing my balance. "Neely Kate," he said in a sad voice, "I want you, but not like this." He spun me around and held me to his chest.

I tried to pull back, but he held on tight, refusing to let me go.

"It's okay," he said. "That's not you. It's in your past."

I started to cry. "No. It's not. It's right here."

"You don't have to live like that anymore."

"But I'll always be that girl. I'll always be that eighteen-year-old girl who sold her virginity for two hundred dollars. Slut. Whore. *Prostitute.*"

He held me tighter as I sobbed into his chest, seven years of pain and regret drenching his shirt. "It's my fault my babies died."

"No," he said, burying his face into my hair as he pulled me even closer. "It's not your fault."

"But it is. All those STDs destroyed my insides. And the baby before them . . ." I sobbed even harder. "It was my punishment, only they paid the price. They counted on me to keep them safe, but I killed them."

"No, Neely Kate. *No.*"

"I deserve every bit of pain this world gives me, but they were innocent. Why did they have to die?"

He cupped my face and pulled me back to search my eyes. "I don't know. But you would have made a wonderful mother."

I cried harder, loud, embarrassing wails. "How could I be a wonderful mother if I killed them?" I tried to pull away from him. "Let me go!"

He lowered an arm to my back, continuing to search my face with compassionate eyes. "I'm not letting you go, Neely Kate."

"Why?"

He didn't answer.

"See?" I demanded, through heavy sobs. "I'm worthless. I can't even take care of babies so small they were the size of lima beans." I tried to jerk away again, but it was a halfhearted attempt. If he let go of me, I'd be lost in my misery forever, yet I didn't trust him to stay. "Let me go."

"No," he said, the word thick with emotion.

"*Why?*"

"I don't know."

I tried to pull free, but his arms were tight bands around my back, holding me to his chest. I fell into him, crying so hard my face went numb. But he held on.

"I'm here, Neely Kate," he said, stroking my hair. "I'm here, and I'm not going anywhere. You can't be worthless, because you mean something to me."

Chapter Eleven

I didn't believe him. Not for a minute. He was only saying that to make me stop crying, but I was too distraught to argue.

I sank into him, sobbing so hard I could hardly catch my breath. My legs went limp, but Jed's arms were tight around me, holding me up.

"Let's go find a room, Neely Kate. Okay?"

I didn't answer. I didn't care. Part of me wanted to disappear right here . . . just evaporate into a wisp of a cloud and be gone forever.

He led me to the passenger side and gently helped me in, then shut the door.

He got behind the wheel and started driving. For all I knew, he was heading straight back to Arkansas, not that I blamed him. But I knew if he took me back there, I'd promptly turn around and leave. I couldn't go directly from the stench of *this* to the goodness of Rose and the hopefulness I felt with Joe, and that knowledge only made me cry harder.

But when Jed drove into town, he pulled into the parking lot of a Motel 6 instead of taking the highway south.

He got out without a word and went inside, but he was back in only a few minutes. I couldn't bring myself to look at him. What did he think of me? What had I done? I'd just disgusted the one person who could possibly help me out of my nightmare.

He drove to the back of the lot and grabbed my bag as he got out. Seconds later, he opened my car door and squatted next to me.

"We're goin' inside now."

I lifted my gaze to stare at him. Preparing myself to face his scorn.

The worry and concern I saw instead made me reel.

He gently grabbed my arm and helped me out. We started toward the stairs, but I was exhausted and dizzy from the whiskey. He swooped me up into his arms, carrying me as though I weighed next to nothing. Something inside of me told me to stop him, but I didn't want to fight. I'd been fighting all my life, and I was so *weary* of it.

Maybe it was time to just let things be.

Maybe it was time to give up.

After opening the door, he turned on the light. Then he set me down on the king-sized bed as gently as if I were made of porcelain. He tossed my bag onto the dresser on his way into the bathroom, and less than half a minute later he was back, sitting on the bed next to me.

He grabbed my chin and gently turned me to face him.

I stared at his chest, too humiliated to look him in the eyes. He lifted a wet washcloth and tenderly began to wipe my mascara-smeared face.

I lifted my hand to stop him, still focusing on his shirt. "Jed. Stop. You don't have to do that."

"I know," he said softly as he pulled my hand from his. "When was the last time someone besides Rose took care of you?"

The thought made me teary again. "Ronnie. After my miscarriage. He tried, but he didn't understand."

"Didn't understand what?" he asked as he continued wiping my face.

"He knew I was upset over losing the babies, but he didn't get why I felt so guilty."

"Wasn't he upset too?"

"In a way, I guess. I think he was partially relieved, especially when he found out they were twins. Part of me wonders if he really wanted them. I was so eager for it all, it was almost like he got caught up in the wave." I looked up at him. "Now I wonder if he wanted any of it for himself."

"Wanted what?" he asked quietly, but I could see a storm brewing in his eyes.

"The house. The baby. Our marriage. He wanted those things, but I think I pushed him into them a whole lot sooner than he had planned." I shrugged. "Maybe I was scared he'd see the real me and run." I took the rag from him and finished wiping.

Turned out I'd been right to worry. I'd spent plenty of sleepless nights thinking about it all. Realizing it couldn't be a coincidence that Ronnie had turned cold and distant right after the doctor told us I was unlikely to get pregnant again because I'd had too many STDs.

"He must have wanted all of that if he gave in."

I shook my head. "I can be . . . insistent."

"He was a grown-ass man, capable of saying no," he said in a rough tone.

"Maybe." But I couldn't help thinking that things might have been different if I hadn't pushed so hard. In that alternate world, I wouldn't be trying to get a divorce from a man who'd abandoned me. And I definitely wouldn't be blubbering to Jed now. I'd made an utter fool of myself tonight. I lowered the washcloth. "I'm sorry for earlier . . . I'm humiliated beyond belief. I shouldn't have . . ." I paused. "I couldn't stand to think you thought less of me—"

"Don't you ever be ashamed of doing what you needed to do to survive."

"Still . . ." My face felt hot. "I've made it weird between us. I plan to visit my old trailer park tomorrow. I'm sure I still have friends there. You don't need to come. I can even stay with them so you can head back and try to work things out with Skeeter."

"I'm not leaving you, Neely Kate," he said in a tone that let me know it wasn't up for debate.

"I know you made Rose a promise—"

"You think I'm staying for Rose?" he asked in disbelief. "Let's get one thing perfectly clear: I'm here for me."

I searched his face for answers. I still couldn't understand why he was willing to deal with my thousands of pounds of baggage. "Why?"

"Because you need a friend. I'm your friend."

I glanced down, still embarrassed. I wanted to believe him, but Jed didn't seem like the kind of guy who tolerated weakness, and I'd shown plenty of it tonight. "But you were so angry with me . . ."

He shook his head and said emphatically, "Not with you, Neely Kate. I was angry at the situation." He scooted over a few inches. "Look," he said in frustration. "I could see you were hurt . . . that someone or several some*ones* had hurt you bad. You've told me next to nothing, so I don't know who the people who hurt you are or what they did . . . and then I saw you drowning your sorrows in cheap whiskey, talking to that lowlife you used to work for . . . and it makes me *so angry* that I can't fix this for you." His voice rose and he stopped. "That's what I do, Neely Kate—I fix Skeeter's problems—and I'm damn good at it. I'd give anything to fix this for you, but I don't even know what *this* is."

I still wasn't sure why he wanted to help me, but I believed that he did.

Overwhelmed by him—that he had chosen to be here with me, that he genuinely wanted to help despite the many times I'd tried to push him away—I threw my arms around his neck and pulled him close. It felt so good to lean on him, but I couldn't put this on him. I needed to handle the situation myself. "I have to do this on my own."

His arms tensed. "Are you going to try to ditch me again?"

The fact that he wasn't running gave me the courage to be honest. "No. I like having you here." I shot him a grin to lighten the mood. "And it's not so bad having badass backup."

His seriousness faded and he looked amused. "You think I'm a badass?"

I snorted and rolled my eyes, unable to stop my smile from spreading. "Please."

"So you'll keep me around?"

I plucked at his still-damp T-shirt. "You make a pretty good pillow to cry into."

He grinned, looking more relaxed than he had since we'd left Slick Willy's parking lot. "At least I have a purpose."

There was no forgetting what he'd said to me earlier. *I'm irredeemable.* I lifted my hand to his face and searched his eyes, serious now. "You're a good man, Jed Carlisle."

He snorted and tugged my hand down. "No. I am *not* a good man. But we'll exorcise *your* demons, Neely Kate, and then we'll bury the bones and light it all on fire. I'll make sure you're free of whatever happened here. No more running."

I froze. His words hit a little too close to home.

"Are you hungry?" he asked. "Thirsty? You probably have a headache after crying so hard."

I shook my head.

"Do you want anything?"

I studied him, worried about how he'd react to my request. "Can I ask you a favor?"

"Of course."

His warm smile gave me the courage to ask. "I'm exhausted, but I've had a lot of nightmares lately . . . Will you hold me?"

He took so long to answer, I was sure he was going to ignore the question. Finally, he said, "I was going to sleep in the chair."

I gasped in horror. "In the chair? You paid for the doggone room. If you don't want to sleep with me, then *I'll* sleep in the chair."

The glint in his eyes warned me that he was digging in his heels. "Like hell you will."

I wasn't sure if he was trying to prove he was a gentleman or if he really didn't want to hold me. But part of me *really* needed him right now, which made the humiliation of begging slightly more bearable. "How about a compromise?" I asked. "You can sit at the head of the bed and hold me. Just for a few minutes. *Please.* If you'd like, you can move after I fall asleep."

His face softened. "Of course."

He kicked off his shoes and scooted up on the bed, rearranging the pillows to support his back and head, and stretching his legs straight in front of him. Then he reached out his arms in an invitation.

I slipped off my jacket and sandals before crawling up the bed and snuggling into his side. I'd intended to curl up beside him, leaving him plenty of room, but my body seemed to react of its own accord. I sank into him, our bodies practically fusing together—my leg curling over his upper thighs, my arm draping across his chest, my hand cupping the back of his neck. His arm curled possessively around me, his hand resting on my hip.

He felt *right*, more so than any man ever had. And that scared the spit out of me.

Jed reached over and turned off the light, but I held on to him, worried he'd change his mind. I realized this made me a *literal* clingy female—every sane man's nightmare—but it was too late to turn back now.

To my surprise, when he sat back against the pillows, he lifted his free hand to my hair and began to slowly stroke, a soothing motion that brought fresh tears to my eyes.

"I'm not leaving," he whispered.

No. Jed wasn't running. I wasn't sure that was such a good thing, but I was too tired to reason it out. I soon relaxed back into him and started to drift off.

Tonight, I'd give myself the illusion that I was safe and protected and loved.

The harsh reality of tomorrow would come soon enough.

Chapter Twelve

I woke up with my legs tangled with Jed's, splayed halfway across his chest. His body had slid down to a more reclined position, his head propped higher with pillows, but I was still wrapped around him like a monkey to a tree.

I glanced up at his face, surprised to see his eyes open.

"No nightmares?" he asked.

"No. It's the best night's sleep I've had in months."

He reached up and brushed a strand of hair from my face. "Probably because you were so exhausted."

No, more likely it was because of the man still holding me. I'd never felt safer than I did right now in his arms. In fact, I felt safer with Jed than I'd ever felt with anyone. Period.

Guilt quickly followed that thought. Rose had gone out of her way to make me feel safe and loved, especially after Ronnie left. Shoot, she'd let me move in with her. But deep down I had always known I wasn't good enough for her. While we'd both been abused as kids, she'd only occasionally dipped off the straight and narrow path. I'd veered off it entirely, getting permanently stained in the process.

But Jed . . . Jed was more like me. We'd both done things we were ashamed of. And while he might think less of me by the conclusion of our Ardmore trip, I hoped he'd at least understand me. Maybe it was selfish, but I was glad he was here with me.

I lifted up on my elbow to check the time on the digital clock on the nightstand. "8:50!" I said in dismay. "How could I have slept that long? How long have you been awake?"

"Not that long."

"Why didn't you wake me up or, at the very least, shove me to the other side of the bed so you could get up?"

He put his free hand under the back of his head, propping it up. "I told you," he said. "I haven't been awake that long. It's the first time in years that I haven't had to get up for some purpose. It felt good to sleep in, and you were sleeping so soundly I didn't want to wake you." His gaze drifted down, and I realized my dress had hiked up on my legs. My butt cheek was hanging out and revealing a hint of my nude-colored panties. They'd been intended for camouflage under my white and blue dress, not seduction.

The memory of my behavior in the parking lot last night rushed back with excruciating detail. Horrified, I started to snatch back my arm and my leg, but Jed wouldn't let me.

"Neely Kate."

I looked up into his face, my cheeks burning, then quickly looked away. "Last night . . . I have no excuse. I was . . . it's just . . ."

"Hey, no apologies."

"I . . ." I squeezed my eyes shut. "I humiliated myself. I disgusted you . . ."

His body stiffened. "How could you think I was disgusted?"

"You . . ." I couldn't go on; his rejection still suffocated me, not that I blamed him. I had no desire to relive last night's disgraceful performance.

He slowly rolled me over to my back, his leg spreading my legs apart. He propped up on one elbow, looking down into my face. For a man who'd lived hard, his eyes were incredibly soft when he looked at me. "You could never disgust me."

"But I was ridiculous."

"No. You were hurt and you came on to me for the wrong reasons. I want you to want me for the right ones."

"And what are the right ones?"

His gaze lowered to my mouth and he lifted his hand to my neck, his thumb lightly tracing my jaw. "You'll know when you're ready."

I held my breath as my body jumped to life. Jed hadn't even kissed me, yet he'd made me feel more alive, more desired, than I'd ever felt with any man.

His gaze lifted to my eyes. "Thank you for trusting me."

"What does that mean?" I forced out, struggling to focus as his hand slid to my collar bone, his thumb tracing a lazy path down my neck.

"Last night. You trusted me enough to take me into Slick Willy's."

"I didn't have a choice."

"Not true," he said softly, lowering his mouth to my ear. "You could have tried to make me stay in the car," he whispered. His breath, hot on my neck, sent a shiver down my spine.

"Would you have stayed?" I asked, sounding breathless.

He chuckled. "Not a chance in hell."

I nearly jumped out of my skin when I felt the lightest of kisses behind my ear.

I lifted my hands to his shoulders, wanting more, but he sat up slightly and put my hands back on the bed. Then he placed a soft kiss at the base of my jaw.

I closed my eyes, my body burning with lust and anticipation.

"You have got to be the sexiest woman I've ever known," he murmured against my neck as he licked and nibbled his way to my collar bone. "It's important you know that." He moved his hand to my waist and lightly skimmed upward, stopping underneath the rise of my breast. "I don't want you to think I rejected you last night."

My breath came in hard pants. I was dying to touch him, but I grabbed handfuls of the bedspread to stop myself.

His mouth traced the scooped neckline of my sundress, lingering over the curve of my breast before dipping down the shallow valley of my cleavage and continuing up my other breast.

White-hot heat pooled between my legs, and it took everything in me to keep my hands off him.

He leisurely kissed a path up my neck. "I told you that you were in control, and that's still true. But nothing has changed for me. I want you." His mouth hovered over mine, and his tongue traced my full bottom lip before darting in for a second and then tracing my upper lip.

His hand lifted to my face again, and he gently held me in place as his lips brushed mine, his tongue still performing its dance, darting into my mouth and taunting my tongue to join in.

I was completely turned on and ready for his seduction to move to the next level, but his mouth continued its lazy plunder of mine. He sucked my bottom lip into his mouth, raking it between his teeth, and then gave me the gentlest of kisses. Then, as if sensing what he was doing to me, he lifted his head.

"I want you, Neely Kate, but not now. Not yet. I don't want there to be any doubt in your head that I want you for *you*, not whatever sleazy image of yourself you have in your head." He sat up and gave me a soft smile. "Now I'm going to go get us some breakfast. Do you want to shower while I'm gone? I can take a shower when I get back. Then we'll come up with a plan for the day.

Gaping, I sat up in disbelief. He'd gotten me all worked up, but for all his big talk, he was going to walk out the door?

I suddenly realized that while I'd brought a bag with clothes and toiletries, he had nothing. "What are you going to do about a change of clothes?"

He stood. "I have a bag in the trunk. I never know when I'll be gone overnight."

"You're like a Boy Scout."

His smile got smaller, tighter, but it didn't fall away. "Not even close." He grabbed his phone off the nightstand and checked the screen.

I didn't even remember him taking it out of his pocket. I'd still been too drunk and out of it. Great. The man had lost his job, maybe permanently damaged his relationship with his best friend, to haul me to the middle of nowhere and watch me make a drunken fool of myself. And here I was, moping because he wanted to grab a change of clothes and get me something to eat.

"Hey," he said, stepping in front of me as he shoved his phone into his front jeans pocket. "No negative thoughts." He cupped the side of my face again and tilted my head up so I was looking into his face. "Remember what I said? *I* see a sexy, smart, loyal, and loving woman. I'm not sure what you see in that head of yours, but if you don't see those things, you need a new mirror."

I gave him a soft smile. "I'm not sure if any man has ever told me anything so sweet before."

His grin spread. "Then you obviously need to spend more time with me." He leaned down and gave me a gentle kiss. "I'll be back in less than half an hour. Put the chain on the door after I leave. Got it?"

"Yeah."

"That's my girl."

I watched him leave, then put the chain on the door. As I showered, I thought about the man I'd gotten to know over the last few months. If someone had told me three months ago that I'd spend the night in Jed Carlisle's arms, I would have called them a liar. Yet here I was . . .

But where exactly *was* I?

From what little I knew about Jed, he didn't have girlfriends. He dated, though perhaps that was a generous word. I'd asked around a little, overheard some, and it sounded like the most serious he got was still pretty casual—multiple-night stands rather than one-offs.

So where did that leave me?

Jed wasn't acting like he was going for some short-term lay, but at the same time, I couldn't see him in a real relationship. As for me . . . I was technically still married (a true technicality since Ronnie, wherever he was, had already moved on), and I wasn't sure what I wanted. And now didn't seem the time to dwell on it. I had bigger issues to deal with.

I was glad Jed was here with me, and I'd have to leave it at that for now. I couldn't forget why I'd come here in the first place.

I wore another dressy dress, but I only put on mascara and a little bit of blush. It was July in southern Oklahoma. I would have sweated off any makeup in less than five minutes.

True to his word, Jed knocked on the door thirty minutes later and called out my name. I slid off the chain and opened the door a crack. "What's that wonderful smell?"

His smiling face made my stomach flutter. "I found a place with real breakfast—none of that fast-food crap." He held up two bags in one hand and a drink carrier with two large steaming cups in the other.

I stepped back and let him in. He gave me an appraising glance, taking in my white dress with its off-the-shoulder sleeves, and the look of appreciation in his eyes told me he did want me. "It's already hot out there."

"Welcome to summer in Oklahoma."

As he set the food down on the dresser, his eyes landed on the notebook on the bed. He gave me an inquisitive look.

"I was making notes . . ." I said. "Coming up with a plan for today."

He gave me a nod. "So if you plan to go back to the strip club tonight, we'll be hanging around here for at least another day, right? I'm going to pay for tonight so we can leave our stuff while we're out."

I hesitated, but it was ridiculous to keep things from him. Besides, it was a legit question. "Yeah. But I'll pay for it, Jed."

He shook his head. "No. I'll deal with it before we leave. But let's eat and you can tell me your plan of attack." He pulled out several containers. "I got pecan pancakes—it's supposed to be their specialty—and then there's an omelet, a waffle with sausage links, and I also got a Southern breakfast with eggs, bacon, hash browns, and grits."

I laughed. "You must be starving."

He gave me a half-shrug. "I wasn't sure what you'd like."

He had bought four breakfast entrees so he'd be sure to get something I'd like. I had an overwhelming urge to kiss him, but instead I reached over and grabbed one of the coffee cups. "Black?"

"Cream and sugar added."

"Perfect." I popped up the little flap and took a sip.

He lifted a Styrofoam container. "Which one?"

"How about we set them all on the bed and share?"

"Sounds good." He set them out—a great big breakfast buffet for the two of us—and we sat across from each other on the bed, plastic cutlery in hand.

Jed glanced over at my still-open notebook. "So where to first?"

"The trailer park where I used to live with my mother."

He opened a container of syrup and set it to one side of the pancakes. "You hoping to find clues about where she went?"

"*That* trail went cold the day she left to dump me on my granny when I was twelve. She left and never came back." He didn't ask questions, just waited for me to continue. "When I graduated from high school, I took all $438 of my graduation money and bought a bus ticket to Ardmore, hoping to find my mother. The most logical place to look for her was where we used to live . . . only, she didn't live there anymore." I stabbed my fork into the scrambled eggs.

"Why didn't you go back to Fenton County?"

"For one, I was pickpocketed on the bus. By the time I landed here, I had $21.09. Not enough to buy a return bus ticket, not that I would have anyway. My granny had told me not to come. My momma didn't want me anymore, she said, so I shouldn't waste my time and money. I was stubborn enough that I wasn't about to go home and eat a heapin' slice of humble pie. Besides . . . when I got off the bus that day, I didn't know she wasn't here. For all I knew, she was sleepin' off the previous night's drunk in the La-Z-Boy. So I got a ride from some guy at the bus stop, and he dropped me off at the entrance of the trailer park. When I found someone else living in her trailer, with no idea who she even was, I sat down on the steps and had a good cry. That's when Zelda found me."

"Zelda?"

"She was our next-door neighbor when I was a kid, and she was still there when I came back. She took me in."

"So you lived with Zelda?"

"Yeah, for nearly a year . . . until I met Branson." But I didn't want to talk about Branson. I wasn't ready to go to that dark place yet. "Zelda's niece Stella came to live with us after I showed up. She was a couple of years older than me, and despite everything my momma had put me through, I wasn't as worldly as I thought."

Jed's gaze stayed on me—interested but not judgmental.

"I was lookin' for jobs at the grocery store and retail stores, but Stella wasn't havin' none of that. She wanted a more glamorous job, so she started workin' at Slick Willy's. Miss Zelda knew Stella had some kind of night job, but she didn't know what. Stella told her she was workin' in a bar, which was technically true, just not the full truth. So Stella claimed she was makin' all this money, while I was still broke and desperate. I'd find a job, but it would never last because I didn't have a car and my rides didn't always come through. Stella started trying to convince me to work with her. She promised to give me a ride every night. Finally, after two months and havin' even less money than I showed up with, if you can believe that's possible, I told her yes."

"So you became an exotic dancer." His voice had a strange tone of detachment.

"I know how it sounds."

Jed leaned closer. "Neely Kate. I've spent more time running the Bunny Ranch than Skeeter. I know the girls who work there. Most are down on their luck, and some of them are supporting kids because their loser partners left them with no financial support. That's why Skeeter and I insist on paying them a set wage and giving them benefits."

"How can you afford it?" I asked. "Stan hardly paid us anything. All our money was from tips . . . and extras." I tried not to shudder at the thought.

Jed's eyes darkened. "There are no extras at the Bunny Ranch except for lap dances. There's no sex in the club. Period. And we encourage the dancers not to arrange it after working hours. You're right, though, the business can't afford it. It loses money just about every month."

"And yet you keep it open?"

"What would happen to those women if we closed it? They'd end up working for some shady place like the exotic club that opened in Fenton County last fall. Or worse."

Skeeter Malcolm purposely hung on to a business that was losing him money so he could give desperate women jobs? Truth was, I'd never thought much of Skeeter. I'd always lumped him into the same category as Stan, who didn't give a fig about the women who worked in his club. Sometimes Skeeter had served as a means to an end, but Rose's friendship with him had never sat easily with me.

Maybe there was more to him than I had thought. Rose always told me there was goodness in him, and here was Jed saying the same thing.

Jed gave me a wry smile. "Before you think Skeeter is completely altruistic, he uses the deficit as a tax deduction. Still, it's a pain in the ass to run. The sheriff's always sticking his nose in the business. It would be easier to close it, but Skeeter insists on keeping it open."

The sheriff. Had Joe been there? What did he think of the women there? Did he find them disgusting? Would he think the same of me?

How about Rose?

I glanced up at Jed. "When Rose and I went to Gems last fall . . . I told her I learned how to pole dance in my cousin's garage. I don't want her to know the truth."

"I'm not gonna tell Rose anything about our trip. Whatever she learns will come from you. I'm a vault."

"I suppose you'd have to be, after working for Skeeter all these years. So many secrets . . ."

"Including the fact that the Bunny Ranch is losing money. We like to keep that info under wraps."

I gave him a soft smile, honored that he'd shared it with me. "I won't tell anyone."

"So you started working for Stan . . ." Jed encouraged.

My mind went back to that first night and how scared I had been. I couldn't go there, not right now. I felt too content sitting here with Jed. I wasn't willing to lose that feeling yet. Still, he deserved answers. Skeeter was forever making him do things, and Jed didn't always know the why of it. It was obvious Jed hated it. He deserved better than that from me.

"Neely Kate."

My eyes lifted to his again.

"You tell me *what* you want *when* you want. Okay? Only when you're ready."

"But you need to know to help me."

"You're an investigator and you haven't done half bad. I'm content to be your backup until you're ready to talk. All I ask is that you give me warning before we walk into something dangerous."

"You *really* think I'm an investigator?" I asked. I was still trying to convince Rose of it.

"You and Rose have solved a heap of mysteries, and then you found that necklace half the county was lookin' for. No one else figured out where it was."

I grinned. "Sorry about shoving you into that pile of pig crap."

He grinned back. "I have to admit, I didn't see it comin'."

"I can't believe you're smilin' about it now. You weren't so happy at the time."

He laughed. "I wasn't. But a couple of weeks removed, I can see the humor in it. I remember the look on your face right before you shoved me. You were furious."

"I'd just found out you were double-crossing me for Skeeter."

"I never even thought about the cell phone in my pocket. But when you realized . . . I knew there would be hell to pay."

I lifted my eyebrows. "And you think that's *funny?*"

His grin faded, but there was merriment in his eyes. "There is nothing funny about you when you're riled up and ready to take on the world."

I cocked my head. "And when have you seen me like that?"

"Countless times with Rose. With Merv . . ." His smile fell. "Merv blames Rose for the changes in Skeeter, and he's becoming more and more out of control. When he saw you walk into the pool hall alone, I think he figured he'd teach you a lesson about meddling in Skeeter's business." He set down his fork, then grabbed my hand. "I had no idea I'd find him manhandlin' *you.* If you hadn't broken his nose and his hand defending yourself, I would have beaten him to a bloody pulp myself."

I turned his hand over to display the bruises and scrapes on his knuckles. "And how did you get these?"

His grin returned. "Okay, so I may have made sure he got the message that if he ever touches you again, he's a dead man." His look turned sober. "But I'm telling you, Neely Kate—if you hadn't beat him up first, I probably would have beaten him to near death." He paused and released my hand. "There's a darkness inside me. You may have done some bad things, but you ran from them. I've been marinating in mine for years."

I shook my head. "Not anymore. Skeeter cut you loose. You can do anything now. What do *you* want?"

Lust filled his eyes, and I was sure he was going to kiss me, but he stood. "I better take my shower."

I crawled off the bed, blocking his path to the restroom. "Jed, wait."

He glanced down at me but didn't say a word.

"You said you thought you were irredeemable. Do you really believe that?"

"Neely Kate . . ."

He didn't need to tell me. I knew. I reached up on my tiptoes and gave him a soft kiss, worried about rejection but willing to take the risk. "You're not irredeemable, Jed. You're a good man, and you keep showin' me that man over and over again. You . . . you told me that you see something different in me than I see in myself. Do you know what I see when I look at you? I see someone strong and brave. A man who's willing to risk his job and his life to help the people he's loyal to. I see a man with a heart so full of goodness he doesn't see strippers and prostitutes as whores—he sees them as women doin' the best they can to get by. Let *me* be *your* mirror, Jed. See the man that I see."

His mouth covered mine with a raw hunger that caught me by surprise, but I quickly met him in kind. I wrapped my arms around his neck, and he lifted me up and then pressed my back to the wall as his mouth ravaged mine. I wrapped my arms around his hips, and my dress gathered up to my waist. The cool, air-conditioned air hit my scantily clad butt, but his large hands quickly warmed me as he held me to him.

His pelvis pushed into mine, his erection pressing in at exactly the right spot to make me moan. But my response must have set off some alarm. He lifted his head and horror filled his eyes. "I swore I wouldn't do this."

"You kissed me before," I reminded him.

"Not like this. Before it was to show you how beautiful you are inside and out. This . . ."

He tried to put me down, but I locked my feet together behind his back. "Jed, I changed my mind. I *want* you to touch me."

He shook his head and gave me a tug to dislodge me. "Not like this."

I let him slide me down, but I hung on to his neck, refusing to let go. "Not like what?"

"Not with anger and recklessness."

I gasped in surprise. "Are you angry with me?"

"Not you, Neely Kate. God, not you, but I'm angry with the world, and I refuse to punish you for it." Then he pulled my hands loose and escaped to the bathroom.

I watched the door shut, wondering what had happened. If Jed's kiss had been fueled by anger, what had fueled mine?

Chapter Thirteen

After his shower, Jed walked out wearing nothing but a towel, and I got an eyeful of what I'd missed out on.

Jed was solid muscle.

From his pecs to his eight-pack, from his arms to the knotted muscles on his shoulder blades as he bent over his bag and pulled out some clothes and a small toiletry bag. There was so much for my eyes to feast on, they didn't know where to look. His hand held the towel slung around his hips, and the rise of his butt peeked out under the towel's edge.

Sweet baby Jesus.

He turned around, and I froze when our gazes met—he'd caught me ogling him. What should I do? Pretend our earlier kiss hadn't happened? Throw myself at him and try to resume where we'd left off? The latter wasn't an option because a new tension had filled the room, and it wasn't sexual. Plus, I got the distinct impression that Jed would prefer to be a million miles away from me at the moment.

"Like I mentioned before," I said nervously, "I plan to go to the trailer park first. I don't expect anything dangerous there. If you want, you can stay here, and I can use your car—I promise to come back. I'm not going to drive off and leave you here." His gaze didn't waver, and I found myself adding, "Great, now you probably think I'm gonna run off."

He watched me for another second longer, and then the intensity of his gaze softened slightly. "I know you're not gonna run off. But we're sticking together."

"It's just that I get the impression you need to be alone. I want to respect that."

"We stick together." Then he disappeared into the bathroom and shut the door.

He emerged a few minutes later, wearing jeans and a white T-shirt that clung to his still-damp skin. Jed may have been able to shut down his libido, but mine had just ratcheted up a few more degrees.

He tossed his dirty clothes on top of his bag as he crossed the room to me. His hands landed on my shoulders, and I was sure he was going to kiss me again, instead he spun me around, putting my back to his chest. He lifted his hands into my hair, and I held my breath with anticipation.

One of his hands rested lightly on my shoulder, and he said softly, "I want to look at your stitches. I need to make sure you're okay. I just slammed your head against the wall a few minutes ago." The last sentence was full of bitterness, but I knew it was directed inward, not at me.

"You didn't hurt me, Jed."

"I could have."

I glanced over my shoulder at him. "I'm not some fragile flower that's gonna be crushed."

Both of his hands turned my head to face in front of me while his fingers gently separated my hair.

"It's up higher," I said.

His fingers moved up until he found it. "Are you putting anything on it?"

"I can't wash my hair for a week. Do you think I'm going to put ointment in there?"

"Sit on the bed."

Part of me wanted to argue with him, but he was working out some inner demon of his own, and I didn't want to stand in the way of that. He was being respectful of the way I was handling the skeletons in *my* closet. I could be respectful of how he handled his.

He went into the bathroom, only to return seconds later. "Let me know if this hurts."

"Okay." I felt a cool salve touch my scalp as Jed's finger lightly traced my stitches.

"Does that hurt?"

"No, Jed. I'm fine."

He went into the bathroom again, and I heard water running in the sink. "I need to put that on you twice a day."

"I'll be fine."

The water stopped and he appeared in the doorway, drying his hands with a towel. "I've had some experience with stitches." The corner of his mouth lifted slightly. "Trust me on this."

I nearly cried with relief that my Jed was peeking out of the surly man who had replaced him. "Thank you."

He tossed the towel into the bathroom. "Let's go."

Twenty minutes later, Jed pulled into the Winter Haven Mobile Home Park, and my anxiety shot through the roof. I grabbed the armrest attached to the car door and squeezed tight.

Jed pulled over to the side of the gravel lane. "Neely Kate. Talk to me."

"I'm okay," I said between pants. But I wasn't, of course. Everything was rushing back in horrific detail.

"You don't look okay."

"Just give me a moment. It's been a while."

He leaned over me and opened the glove compartment, then pulled out a small handgun.

"You won't need that," I said, trying to catch my breath. "It's not like that."

He popped out the clip, looked at it, then popped it back in. "Nevertheless, it's better to be prepared."

Maybe that's what I was doing now, preparing myself. My reaction had caught me by surprise. I'd loved Zelda like a mother. Rose's old boyfriend's mother, Maeve, reminded me a lot of her. Only, Maeve was the sweeter, more genteel version of Zelda, who could best be described as a character.

I expected Jed to tuck the gun somewhere on his body, so I was surprised when he handed it to me.

"Why are you giving me that?"

"Because I know you know how to use it. I need to know you're covered."

"Jed, I don't need it."

He grabbed my hand and placed it in my palm. "Neely Kate. I have no idea what to expect here, so please humor me."

I put the gun back in the still-open glove compartment. Before he could protest, I opened my purse and partially lifted out my own gun. "Remember this? I think Merv's still pretty well-acquainted with it."

He studied me. "Would you really have shot him?"

"I'd like to say no, but Kate already had me on edge. If he'd attacked me again, I'm not sure what I would have done, although I wouldn't have aimed for anything vital." I paused. "Not looking so innocent now, am I? Changed your mind about me yet?"

"Why wouldn't I respect your ability to take care of yourself?"

"If I can take care of myself, then why are you here?"

"Because even Skeeter and I need backup. I'm backup."

I closed my purse. "Thanks."

"Are you ready, or do you need more time?"

I took a deep breath, grateful Jed had once again pulled me out of my spiral of anxiety. "I'm good."

"Then tell me where to go."

We drove to the back of the park, then turned left on the last road in the place. "Go slow," I said.

He obeyed without question, slowing down to a ridiculous 5 MPH, yet that was almost too fast for me. I took a deep breath as I pointed across the street to the trailer Zelda had lived in, but my eyes were on the hellhole I'd lived in with my mother. When I thought of this place, a whole host of images and memories filled my head, none of them good. Cigarette smoke and a parade of men. My fear of unleashing my mother's temper, reinforced by her stinging words and the back of her hand. My desperation to escape. Then, after she dumped me off with my grandmother, my determination to find her again.

No wonder I was screwed up.

He pulled over to the side of the road and put the car in park. "How do you want to play this?"

Ignoring him, I opened the door and got out, the heat blasting me in the face. I took two steps toward my mother's old trailer before I stopped myself. Why was I drawn to the trailer I'd lived in with my mother? I'd come back to this trailer park seven years ago and lived next door to Momma's old place for a year. I'd never given it the time of day—not after learning my mother had long since moved on—so why was I so drawn to it now? Maybe it was because my mother had been a complete mystery at the time. I hadn't known if she was living or dead. Kate had proven she was not only alive, but living in West Virginia.

Or had she?

I'd taken her word for it, which was unlike me. I'd trusted a certified psychopath.

What if she'd never met my mother? What if she didn't know anything about my past at all?

But she knew about Beasley and the azaleas. Even if she was lying about Momma, and my gut told me she wasn't, she knew plenty.

I felt Jed's arm around my back, his hand resting on the rise of my hip. "You okay?"

"Yeah."

He gave me a dubious look but didn't say anything. "How do you want to explain my presence?"

"I hadn't thought about it, but I'm sure you have."

"I want to play it like I did last night—I'm your boyfriend. People will be less likely to mess with you if they think you have a no-nonsense guy interested in your well-being."

"Okay," I said, a little more pleased with the idea than I had any right to be. "But that's not really an issue here."

"I guess we'll find out. It's been five years. Do you know if she's still here?"

I pointed to the car in her driveway. "I'd recognize that gold Charger anywhere."

Taking another breath, I headed across the gravel drive, the wind blowing my skirt. I grabbed the edge to keep from flashing the whole neighborhood. I was equally excited and terrified. I was eager to see Zelda, but as soon as she opened her door, a can of worms I'd buried—literally—five years ago would be opened too. I wasn't sure I could handle facing what I'd done.

But then I felt Jed's hand on my back, and I drew in a deep breath and climbed the two short steps to the faded cream and brown trailer. The metal door felt hot under my fist when I knocked on it.

Several seconds later, the door opened, revealing a hunched-over elderly woman.

Zelda. I almost gasped. With her now-snow-white hair and deep wrinkles, she looked like she'd aged a decade. "Neely Kate? Oh, my stars and garters!" she exclaimed, then started to cry. "You came home."

"Hey, Miss Zelda."

She reached for me, pulling me over the threshold, and memories washed over me. I tried to focus on the good as the woman who'd been my surrogate mother pulled me into an embrace. "You came home," she repeated. "I thought you were dead."

I wasn't a tall woman and I was wearing flat sandals, but Zelda's arthritis must have gotten worse—she was shorter and more hunched over than I'd remembered. I led her to the worn blue-and-white plaid sofa I recognized from my time here.

I could see why she might have feared the worst. I felt guilty for hurting her, but I'd been young and stupid at the time, too concerned about self-preservation to spare a thought for anything or anyone else. Now I realized how selfish I'd been, especially leaving her with Stella.

I gave her a sad smile. "I'm alive."

"You never came home."

"I know. I'm sorry."

She clung to me for several long seconds, silently crying while Jed stood by the now-closed door. He scanned the small space, and I couldn't help but wonder what he was thinking. Zelda's trailer looked pretty much the same as it had years ago, only a lot more used. Same thrift store furniture. Same worn brown carpet, although there were more worn spots.

But there was also the same feeling of being enveloped in love.

Zelda seemed to be recovering, and when I noticed a gleam in her eyes, I knew I was in trouble. "Where have you been, girl? Did you fall off the face of the earth? Or maybe you was put in deep freeze like that Lieutenant America."

I laughed. "Captain America, Miss Zelda."

"Captain, Lieutenant, he can be the damned general for all I care; I'm sitting here wondering how you couldn't bother to pick up a phone for five years."

"I'm sorry, Miss Zelda. I have no excuse."

She pointed her gnarled finger in my face. "You were runnin'."

I didn't answer. I didn't feel like lying to her, and I sure wasn't about to tell her the truth.

Her gaze turned to Jed. "And who might you be?"

"Jed Carlisle, ma'am," he said in a deep voice, holding his hands together in front of him and his feet shoulder-width apart. "I'm Neely Kate's boyfriend."

It was a cover story, but hearing him say it still sent a thrill down my spine.

Zelda gave me an ornery look. "He's a big boy, Neely Kate. Is he big everywhere?"

"Zelda!" I exclaimed. I had no visual confirmation of his size, but what I'd felt earlier suggested that I wouldn't be disappointed if and when we ever slept together. I was usually the one dishing out innuendos, but I felt my face heating up, especially since Jed was watching me.

She looked pleased as punch. "Judging by the smug look on your young man's face, it must be true."

Jed's eyes lit up. He seemed amused by my embarrassment, and no wonder.

She waved toward the chair in the corner. "You don't have to stand back there, Jed. Come sit."

"Thank you, ma'am." The chair looked so dilapidated I wasn't sure it would hold Jed's frame, but he sat anyway, proving how brave he really was.

"You found yourself a nice young man, Neely Kate," Zelda said, reaching over to pat my hand while she eyed Jed. "Polite and respectful."

"Yes, ma'am," I said. "Jed's one of the best."

She turned back to me, narrowing her eyes. "I can see why hooking up with this young stud would make you want to hide away from the world and screw your brains out, but I suspect you haven't been screwing Jed for all five of the years you've been gone, so tell me where you went."

I started to chastise her, but Jed was having way too much fun listening to her. In the past, I'd found the best way to discourage her was to move the conversation along. "I went back to my granny in Arkansas."

"You just took off, without a word. When you disappeared, and Branson too . . . well, Stella was beside herself."

Stella had never felt one ounce of guilt or regret in her life. If she'd been beside herself, it was only because she no longer had me around to manipulate. Nevertheless, as bitter of a pill as it was to swallow, I needed to find her. "What's Stella up to these days? I hear she quit her night job."

Zelda scowled. "Night job. You two thought you were pulling one over on me, but I always knew you were working at that peep show." She cast a glance at Jed and waved her hand dismissively. "And if you didn't know, young man, then I'm sorry you heard this way. But if you two have any hope of makin' it, there can't be any secrets between you."

"I already knew." Jed's smile fell, but the warmth in his eyes seemed to say he trusted me to tell him what he needed to know until I felt comfortable telling him everything.

"Ah . . ." Zelda murmured, bobbing her head. "Then you two are on the right track."

She turned to me with sharp eyes. Maybe age had finally caught up with her, but it hadn't dulled her mind any. "Are you still livin' that life?" she asked in a voice full of worry.

"No," I said quickly, before she could say anything else.

She nodded. "Good. Now tell me why you finally decided to stop by after all these years."

It felt like my tonsils were tied together, something Jed must have sensed. "I want to know everything about Neely Kate's life," he said. "I asked her to bring me to meet you."

Zelda's eyes teared up. "Why?"

"Because Neely Kate was at a sad and desperate point in her life when she showed up here seven years ago, and you took her in out of the kindness of your heart. I wanted to personally thank you for being there for her."

My mouth dropped open in amazement. Jed had come up with his story on the fly, only the look on his face suggested it wasn't totally a cover story.

Zelda sniffed. "I was the lucky one. Our girl is something special."

Jed nodded and gave me a tentative smile. "That she is."

I threw up my hands, feeling uncomfortable. "Enough of this mushy nonsense. What have you been up to, Miss Zelda?"

"Same ol', same ol'. I started goin' to the Free Will Baptist Church instead of the Southern Baptist, and you would have thought I'd become a devil worshipper accordin' to my former Bible study group."

I laughed and listened to her stories about her new church and what the old neighbors had been up to these last few years. Fifteen minutes into her tales, I noticed she hadn't said more than a word about her niece.

"What's Stella been up to?"

She scowled. "She found her a new man." Her scowl deepened. "Only, this one's rougher than the last half dozen."

"Does she come visit often?" I asked.

"I'm lucky to see the girl every few months, and then she only comes around to beg me for money, but I know what it's for." She pointed her finger at me. "I don't support drug addicts."

My heart sank. Even though part of me was still furious with Stella, I was sad to hear she was using. "Is she still in Ardmore?"

"Oh, yeah. She can't leave now that she's got the baby."

I gasped. "Stella had a baby?"

"Yep, she's bound to be a little over a year old. I've only seen her twice. She said the father tried to sue her for full rights, but she cleaned up enough for the courts to believe she was a fit mother." She gave me a knowing look. "Child support. But then I heard the man she sued wasn't the baby's father after all, so I'm not sure what to believe anymore."

I wasn't surprised that Stella would put the needs of herself over her child, but it made me ill. Especially since I'd so desperately wanted the babies I'd lost.

"Can you tell me where she lives?" I asked, trying not to look like I was about to gag. "I'd love to pay her a visit."

"Oh, she'll be so surprised to see you," Zelda said with sad eyes.

She'd be surprised all right. It would be like the Ghost of Christmas Past had showed up to haunt her.

Chapter Fourteen

*J*ed took another glance around the room, then asked, "Miss Zelda, would it be all right if I got a glass of water?"

Zelda cringed. "Where are my manners? I should have offered you something straightaway since it's already beatin' hot. I was just so taken by surprise." She made a move to get up. "I'll get you something now."

Jed was already on his feet. "You sit and enjoy your visit with Neely Kate. I'll get it."

She smiled up at him as if he'd announced she was a bingo winner. "The glasses are in the cabinet to the left of the sink."

Jed moved the few feet into the kitchen and opened the cabinet.

What was he up to?

"Oh," Zelda said, slapping her leg. "I forgot to tell you—some people came looking for you."

My heart slammed into my ribcage. *People?* "Were they together or did they come separately?"

"Separately. The woman showed up months ago . . . right around Thanksgiving, but the man was here back in the spring."

My mouth went dry.

"The woman . . ." Jed said, setting his glass of water on the kitchen counter. "What did she look like?"

"It looked like her clothes came straight out of the Salvation Army, and when I asked her how she knew you, she said you'd worked together . . ." Zelda turned to face me. "But I didn't fall off the turnip truck. Something about her didn't seem right, so I asked her to remind me of your boss's name. She said she couldn't remember. As big of an asshole as he was, I figured she'd remember Shitty Stan if she'd ever set foot in that dump." Her mouth pursed. "She was a slick devil, trying to twist the conversation around to get things out of me. The only thing the she-devil got out of me was Stella's name, and that was only so I could set her up to see if she knew Stan."

I wasn't thrilled Zelda had given her Stella's name, but in the scheme of things, it wasn't the worst thing for her to have divulged.

"Did the woman tell you her name?" Jed asked.

Zelda shook her head. "No, and I asked her who she was, but she weaseled out of telling me, which was my first clue that she wasn't on the up and up. Plus, she seemed too classy to work at the place. Ratty clothes aside, she looked like the type to hold her pinky finger out when she sipped her coffee."

"What did her hair look like?" I asked.

"Short and black." Zelda lifted her hand to her shoulder. "To about here, and it had blue streaks."

Kate. My gaze lifted to Jed's, but he was expressionless.

"Did she say why she was lookin' for me?" I asked.

Zelda shook her head. "No, but I wondered if she might be a bill collector. Margo's grandson skipped out on one of those payday loans, and he listed her as an emergency contact. They called and showed up at her door hoping to catch him." She glanced at me again. "Are you in money trouble, Neely Kate?"

I was always in money trouble, but I was in much better shape than I had been the entire time I'd lived with her. "No, Miss Zelda. I'm fine."

She frowned, obviously not convinced.

"She's fine, Miss Zelda," Jed said. "I'm looking out for her."

She nodded and her body relaxed. "You're a good man, Jed."

She echoed my words from this morning, but he seemed to believe her, his back straightening some.

"You said there was a man," I said. "Who was it?"

"I think he was some kind of police officer, but he didn't show me his ID, so I'm not sure. He wasn't wearing a uniform, but he acted all official."

Police? My gaze jerked to Jed's in a panic.

He moved to the sofa and sat beside me, resting his hand on my knee. "Did he say anything to indicate where he was from?"

Frowning, she shook her head.

"That's okay," Jed said. "He was probably being careful. Why don't you start from the beginning and tell us everything you remember?"

"I was outside watering my petunias when he pulled up, getting out of his car and ambling toward me like he was large and in charge."

"What kind of car did he drive?"

She pointed toward the front door. "Kind of like the one you're driving."

"A dark sedan?"

"Yeah, like the ones on all those cop shows."

"What happened then?" he pressed. I was glad he'd stepped in—my mind felt like a hamster on an out-of-control wheel.

"He walked up and said he was lookin' for a missing person, then asked, 'You know Neely Kate Rivers?' and I asked, 'Who's askin'?'" She shook her head with a frown. "He didn't like *that* answer one bit. He moved up close enough that I could smell the whiskey on his breath when he said, 'Unless you want to get what's coming to her, you'll answer my damn questions.'"

I sucked in a breath.

"And what did you say?" Jed asked, not fazed at all.

"Well, I wasn't sure what he was talking about, but I was pretty darn sure I didn't want it, so I told him the truth—that I hadn't seen Neely Kate in five years. But it didn't matter if it was the truth or not because he wasn't buyin' it. He called me a liar. I let loose, telling him he needed to respect his elders and that you can catch more flies with sugar water, but he wasn't the least bit impressed. He told me I had to earn his respect."

"Zelda," I said. "I'm sorry."

She blew a raspberry. "I'm not about to let some punk kid push me around."

"Kid?" Jed asked. "How old do you think he was?"

She waved off his question. "Anyone under fifty is a kid to me. But he looked to be in his thirties."

"What was he wearing?"

"A suit, but it was a nice-lookin' one. Not one of those cheap knockoffs. And sunglasses. I couldn't see his eyes. Never trust a person who won't look you in the eyes."

"So did he ask anything else?"

"Yeah, he wanted to come inside my home and look around. I asked him to show me his badge first. He bugged off instead, saying he'd be back to deal with me, but I never saw him again."

Jed nodded. "Thanks."

"Are you in trouble with the law, Neely Kate?" Zelda asked with worried eyes.

"No," Jed answered, wrapping an arm around my back. "It's just some crazy man who's stalking her. If he comes back, don't answer the door, and if he tries to break in, call 911. He's not a police officer."

"I knew I was right," she said, snapping her fingers. My heart swelled with love for her.

"You have good instincts, Miss Zelda," Jed said.

"I didn't get this far in life playin' the fool."

Jed grinned, but my mind was whirling. Had that man been working for Kate? I didn't think so, somehow.

We left soon afterward, and I gave Zelda a long hug. When I released her, she reached up and patted my face. "Thank you for comin' to see me, but you need to leave this place and never come back."

My mouth dropped open. "What?"

"Nothing good ever came to you here. Don't go searchin' the past, Neely Kate. You need to find your future."

Tears stung my eyes.

"You're a good girl. You just needed someone who believed in that too. Someone besides me."

I hugged her again, realizing how much this woman had done for me and how little I'd given back. Wishing I'd done better by her. "I'm sorry."

"Hush now," she said with a watery smile. "I'm proud of you, girl. Now go live the happy life you deserve."

Jed put his hand on Zelda's shoulder and shook her hand. "It's been an honor to meet you, ma'am."

"You too, young man." Then she made a shooing motion. "Go on now. I always hated goodbyes."

Jed opened the door and put his arm around my back as we walked toward his car. He opened the passenger door to let me in before circling around to the other side.

I studied him as he turned on the ignition. Until Ronnie, no man had ever opened my car door, and even Ronnie had to be trained. When Rose had told me about the man who had kept watch over her during meetings with possibly subversive criminals, I never in a million years would have pictured the man with me now. Was this the real Jed Carlisle, or was it all an act? After seeing him with Zelda, I would bet money this was genuinely him.

He pulled into the gravel driveway in front of my mother's old trailer. "We should have asked Zelda about your mother."

"It would have been wasted breath. I asked plenty of questions when I came back. Zelda said something spooked Momma and she took off. After she dumped me at Granny's, she disappeared for good."

"Do you think J.R. found out about her . . . and you?"

I gasped. "I hadn't considered that."

"It might explain how Kate learned the truth. And if J.R. *did* find out about you, it wouldn't have been hard to track you down to the Rivers' farm. Why'd he leave you alone all those years? It stands to reason he'd keep an eye on you . . ." His voice trailed off and he looked taken off guard.

And I knew why—it didn't take a genius to figure out who would have been tasked with watching me.

Jed looked furious.

"We have no way of knowing if Skeeter was involved, Jed."

"Oh. I *know* he was. He did J.R. Simmons' dirty deeds and kept it all from me for *years.*" He backed out of the driveway and headed down the road toward the trailer park entrance.

"But there's a good chance J.R. never knew the truth until the end."

"Had your mother ever taken off like that before? And why did she leave you behind?"

"The second one's easy: I attracted too much attention from Momma's boyfriends." Somehow Kate had known about that too. Only, she hadn't gotten it entirely right—Momma may have let one of them sleep with me, but she'd absolved her guilt by telling him I had to technically be a virgin when he was done.

While I was taking my haunted hayride down memory lane, Jed had been piecing together my last words to him.

"Your mother got rid of you because she was jealous of the attention her boyfriends were giving you?" he asked in disbelief.

"I didn't say she was jealous," I backtracked.

"You didn't have to."

"She did me a favor in the end, but it goes to show that there could be any number of reasons why she took off. For all we know, someone turned her in for pimping her twelve-year-old daughter to her boyfriend for drugs."

Jed remained still so long that if he hadn't been driving, I would have wondered if he'd fallen asleep. But one look at him proved he was alert—and angry enough to wring someone's neck.

A good two or three minutes later, he said, "You may be right about why she ran, but the J.R. explanation would still make more sense. If she was worried about getting turned in for your *molestation*"—he spat out the word—"I would think she'd keep you around to make sure you stayed quiet. If she was running from J.R., she'd have run far and wide. Ditching you would have made it easier for her to hide. She'd know that the first place J.R. would look for you would be your granny's farm. Which means he probably knew you were there, and he had Skeeter watching you."

But it also meant she had literally thrown me to the wolves. She must have known J.R. would be tempted to *destroy* any potential claims to his money. That was the sole reason she'd run twenty-five years ago. To save her skin.

I let that settle in, waiting for the familiar pinprick in my heart, but maybe my heart had been hurt too many times. Maybe there wasn't enough of me left to feel.

That thought was quickly dashed when I considered that Skeeter Malcolm might have been stalking me. "But Skeeter hasn't worked for J.R. for the past five years," I objected, wanting him to tell me it wasn't possible after all.

"I guarantee you that he was watching you when you came to Fenton County the first time." Jed looked like he was about to rip someone's head off. "You were a kid."

"You don't know that he was watchin' me, Jed."

He kept his eyes on the road. "I do." He paused. "He may not have known why he was watching, but he did it anyway and reported it to Simmons. And when all of this shit came to pass this past winter, he never said one fucking word to anyone."

"Jed. It's okay."

"The hell it is." He swallowed, and I could see a war waging on his face. "I'm done."

I shook my head as I tried to grasp what he was saying. "You're gonna quit?"

"He already fired me, Neely Kate. I told you that."

"But you know he'll change his mind and call you back."

"Maybe I don't want to go back." He turned to look at me. "Maybe this is the last straw."

"Because of *me?*"

"Seems like a pretty damned good reason to me."

"But—"

"I'm not letting anyone hurt you, Neely Kate. Not while I'm around." His voice was hard when he added, "And that includes Skeeter Malcolm."

Chapter Fifteen

We decided to get lunch and come up with a plan for the rest of the day. Zelda didn't have a solid address for Stella, but she knew the name of the apartment complex. We picked a place with Wi-Fi and Jed brought in his computer bag. He set up his laptop on his side of the booth and began to search for Shenandoah Apartments, leaving me with plenty of time to think.

I wasn't sure how to handle what Jed was going through. He and Skeeter went back a long way, so I understood why he felt betrayed, but I had no idea how to comfort him.

"Jed, I think we should talk about it."

"Talk about what?" he asked as he continued his search.

"Skeeter."

His fingers stopped typing and he glanced up at me. "There's nothing to talk about."

"That's not true. He hurt you."

His gaze returned to the screen. "He didn't hurt me."

"But he did. He's like a brother to you, and you thought you shared almost everything. When you found out he'd spent all those years working for J.R. without ever telling you . . . that had to sting."

"I trusted him, Neely Kate." He didn't look at me.

I covered his forearm with my hand. "I know.'"

"I knew his story about running off to Memphis to make seed money for the pool hall was a lie, but I didn't press him. I figured he'd done something he was ashamed of." He shook his head. "He wasn't ashamed of it. He came back and worked for the man. He cleaned up your brother's messes."

"*Joe's?*"

He glanced up at me. "Joe kept him pretty busy at times."

Joe had rebelled against our father's expectations, enough so that he'd gotten himself into trouble with the law in his earlier days, despite the fact that he worked for the Arkansas State Police. I'd heard that J.R. had always sent in a cleanup crew to smooth things over. I had no idea that Skeeter was the one who'd pushed the broom.

"Skeeter was always running off to do some secret task. I started to get more and more suspicious about what he was doing, but he'd shut me down straightaway whenever I asked. Then the secretive trips stopped one day five years ago. No explanation. I guess that was when he quit doin' J.R.'s grunt work, but I never heard a word of any of it until last winter . . . when he was working with Rose." He shook his head. "Even when shit was goin' down last fall, he never breathed a word."

"Maybe he was ashamed after all," I suggested. "Skeeter's a powerful man in his own right. Being on J.R.'s leash had to chafe. Even years later. I would guess that could wound a man's pride."

Jed seemed to consider my words. "Maybe. But it doesn't fully explain why he'd keep something so important from me."

I glanced out the window. "Rose doesn't know about this part of my life, and I don't want her to *ever* know."

"But you're telling me."

I turned back to him. "And I'm dolin' it out piece by piece. Maybe that's how Skeeter did it . . . with Rose."

Jed didn't look any happier.

"Maybe we need different friends for different things," I said. "I don't know why I feel more comfortable sharing this part of my life with you . . . Maybe it's because you're more worldly when it comes to seedy doin's. Or maybe it's because Rose has always believed in the sugar-spun version of me, and I can't stand smashin' that image to bits. But I do know that I always feel like I'm pretending, like someone's gonna point at me and shout, 'She's not wearin' any clothes.'"

He frowned. "Because you were a dancer?"

I laughed. "*No.* Because of the story of the emperor's new clothes."

He gave me a blank look.

"You know . . . the story about the emperor who gets bamboozled by some tailors who claim they can make a suit only smart people can see. Only, there is no suit and they charge him a lot of money, and the king won't call 'em on it because he doesn't want to look stupid."

"Anyone who would fall for such bullshit is stupid."

I laughed. "It's no different than a princess sleepin' on a stack of mattresses on top of a pea to prove she's royalty. They're fairy tales."

His frown deepened. "There's no room for fairy tales in my life."

I held his gaze. "Maybe it's time you started makin' room for them."

His expression softened and the hint of a smile appeared just as the waitress showed up to take our order. When she left, Jed turned back to his computer.

I let the subject of Skeeter drop. Jed Carlisle didn't strike me as a man who went around talking about his feelings. I was lucky to get what I had out of him.

A few minutes later, with his eyes still on the screen, he said, "Based on satellite maps, the Shenandoah Apartment complex looks fairly small, which means it will be easier for us to figure out where she lives. She has a baby, which should make it even easier. What does Stella look like?"

"She looked like a model. Tall and thin, with long, shiny blond hair. She was a favorite at the club. Men would go in on her nights just to see her. She's gorgeous . . . or at least she used to be . . ."

He picked up on my train of thought. "Zelda suggested she's an addict. What would she be using?"

"Meth," I said. "She used it before. She liked it. A lot. But she fought it." I looked up at him. "So she might not be as pretty as she used to be."

He nodded.

The waitress showed up with our food, and I let out a little laugh when she set the large salad bowl in front of Jed.

"What?" he asked as she walked away.

I picked up a fry from the pile next to my BLT sandwich. "You don't look like you need to go on a diet."

He had a playful look that made him seem years younger and more carefree. "Have you been checking me out, Neely Kate?"

"It was hard not to notice there wasn't an ounce of fat on you this morning . . ." I let my voice trail off suggestively, but I was grinning like a fool. Jed made me feel like the seventeen-year-old version of myself, the one who had compartmentalized all the crap from her past and pretended it never existed. The one who had foolhardily believed in love and romance and happily-ever-afters.

But that seemed crazy, in and of itself. Jed was seeing the ugliest bits of me. So why did I feel so much lighter with him? Why did this feel okay?

Belatedly, I worried that reminding him of this morning would make him turn surly again—just like he had after our second kiss—but he grinned back at me. "Maybe I'm tryin' to be healthy." He pointed to my plate with his fork. "Maybe I don't want to clog my arteries."

I laughed and ate another fry.

We turned quiet for a minute as I took several bites of my sandwich and Jed ate his salad, which I had to confess looked delicious. I picked up my fork and stabbed it into his bowl, fishing out a piece of chicken along with some lettuce and a piece of apple.

"Umm . . . this is pretty good."

He laughed. "You want more?"

I took another bite, and he reached over and picked up half my sandwich.

It was such a simple thing, but the unstudied intimacy of it floored me.

Not the time or the place, Neely Kate. Here I was back in Ardmore, Oklahoma, reopening my own version of hell, but I was flirting with Jed over a stupid salad and a sandwich. Still, there was no denying he was keeping me suspended above all the bad memories rather than lost in the thick of them. I wanted him to stay—and our visit to Stella would help determine if he could handle the rest of it.

He noticed the change in my mood. "You thinkin' about Stella?"

I stabbed my fork into his salad bowl again and nodded. "Yeah."

"How close were you?"

"Close. Or so I thought. After Momma dumped me on my granny, I had a lot of friends in school, but it's easy to keep people at a distance when you're popular." I realized now that I'd held them back out of necessity. "I never had a close friend until Stella."

"And Stella helped you get the job at Slick Willy's?"

I nodded. "Zelda tried to stop me, even though she pretended to believe we were working at a bar. I'm not surprised she knew. She was lettin' us keep our dignity." I paused. "Or more accurately, me. Stella wasn't ashamed."

"If you were so reluctant to do it, how did you handle the job after you started?" he asked, lowering his voice. "Some of the girls at the Bunny Ranch take to it like ducks to water, like Stella probably did. But some of them only stay because they're desperate. You can always see it in their eyes. The Ranch is literally the last place on earth they would choose to work, but they need the money too much to leave." He paused, looking uncomfortable. "The customers notice, of course, and those girls make less tip money. When that happens, I always try to quietly find the girl another job. Working as a waitress or a maid doesn't pay as much as the successful performers in the club rake in, but those girls never get to be top earners anyway. Plus, they don't feel like they're selling their souls for a wad of one-dollar bills."

He stared at his salad, looking embarrassed, but I was staring at him. This was further proof of what a good man he was. Leaving Skeeter was the right move for Jed. Granted, Skeeter Malcolm was a better man than I'd expected. Jed and Rose had made me realize he had morals of a kind, a rarity for someone in his position. Still, I knew in my heart that Jed deserved better. Something told me he felt like he was selling his soul, just like those girls at the Bunny Ranch did. Only, I suspected Jed did it out of loyalty.

"It was hard for me at first," I said, picking up my half of the sandwich. "But I got used to it. I just had to become the person I created on stage, and when I left, I left her there." I shrugged. "It wasn't that hard. I was used to pretending to be someone I wasn't."

"Kitty?"

I gave him a wry smile. "Yeah, Stan gave me that name. He could see how shy I was when he interviewed me. He said I was as innocent as a newborn kitten."

"How long did you work there?"

I shuddered. "Nineteen months."

"And you worked there until you left town? Stan said you took off after something big happened. You said it was after Branson cheated on you with your best friend. Stella."

I knew it would be easier to come clean, but I still wasn't ready to face what happened the day before I left, let alone tell Jed.

"How long had Branson been your boyfriend?"

I released a bitter laugh. "That depends on how you look at it. Did I stop calling him my boyfriend the day I left, or somewhere around the middle when he started doing things to me that no real boyfriend would ever do?"

"The cheating?"

"Yeah. But that was only one small part. The others were worse."

He let that sink in, and I could see he was full of questions, so I was surprised by the one he chose, the most innocuous of all. "And Stella was one of the women he cheated with?"

I sat back in my seat, my greasy french fries not settling well. "Yeah."

"When was the last time you saw Stella?"

"The day before I left."

"The day something big happened."

"She doesn't know everything." My hands began to shake, so I put them under the table. "She only knows parts."

"Does anyone besides you know everything?" Jed asked.

A tsunami of guilt crashed into me. "Beasley." Tears filled my eyes as I said his name.

Jed studied me for several seconds. What was he thinking? He knew Beasley had gone to prison. Did he realize it should have been me?

He closed his laptop and started to slide out of his seat. I knew in my gut this was it—this was when he left me. But he surprised me once again by moving to my side of the booth and sliding in next to me. Without a word, he wrapped an arm around my back and pulled me to his side, my head resting on his shoulder. Out of instinct, I wrapped an arm over his stomach and held him close.

We sat like that for a couple of minutes. The waitress came back to check on us, but Jed told her we were good and sent her away.

"How much danger are you in?" Jed finally asked. "People are looking for you. I suspect the woman was Kate, but I doubt that guy was a cop. The question is, who was he?"

"I have no idea."

"Was there anything to his missing persons line of questioning?"

I hesitated. "Maybe."

"Was the missing person he was asking about you?"

"No."

He was quiet for several seconds. "Can it be traced to you?"

I hesitated again. "Maybe."

I thought he'd press me for more information, but he went down a different path. "Kate was here asking questions before she showed up in Henryetta at the end of December. Which only supports the idea that J.R. found you thirteen years ago and that your mother ran because of it. Is it possible she might have kicked a few sleeping dogs in regard to what happened when you left five years ago?"

"Yes." There was one common denominator in all of this, and I was going to have to face him again, sooner rather than later. "After we talk to Stella, we need to find Beasley."

"I know he was in prison. What was he convicted of?"

My anxiety skyrocketed, and Jed held me tighter.

"You don't have to tell me yet."

"But I do."

"Do I need to know before we talk to Stella?"

"She'll probably mention it."

"Are you opposed to me finding out from her instead of you?"

I needed to face this head-on, but learning about Beasley's conviction would probably only confuse him. Besides, call me a masochist, but better for him to learn that and plenty more from Stella. The ugly truths he'd already learned were only the tip of the iceberg.

I sighed. "I don't know."

"You seemed surprised when Kate told you that Beasley was out of prison. How long was his sentence?"

"Fifteen years."

"So he could have gotten out on good behavior," Jed said. "Or he could have gotten out due to outside influence."

I gasped and sat up. How had I failed to consider that? "Kate?"

"Maybe. Was he incarcerated in Oklahoma?"

"Yeah."

"Kate would have had more influence in Arkansas, but a lot of her strings must have snapped after her father's downfall."

My father's downfall.

"Still," he said, "I wouldn't put it past her." He paused and then his voice softened. "I know you're reluctant to give me details, but I'd like to look into his release and see if anything looks suspicious. To do that, I need to know his full name and what he was convicted of." Another moment of silence hung between us before he continued. "Neely Kate, I need to ask you something else. I noticed your reaction when Kate mentioned his release. Should we be worried for your safety in regard to Beasley? Will he come after you?"

Once, I would have said no. We'd maintained regular contact for years, and even two years ago, he'd eagerly accepted my calls. Something had changed, though—and abruptly—about a year ago. He wouldn't talk to me on the phone anymore, wouldn't answer my notes. "I'm not sure."

His body tensed. "Do you think he's here in Ardmore now?"

"I don't know. He had some family here, so maybe. All I know is that I need to talk to him." I paused. "He's the only one who knows about the azaleas."

"Okay," he said matter-of-factly. "So he goes on the list of people to talk to." He considered something, then asked, "Were Stella and Beasley close?"

"No. They couldn't stand each other, but they were kind of stuck together."

"Why?"

"Because Stella was my best friend and Beasley was Branson's brother."

"And where's Branson?"

"I don't know."

And I hoped I never found out.

Chapter Sixteen

A half hour later, we were parked at the Shenandoah Apartments complex. The place had seen better days. The paint was peeling off the siding, and the playground equipment was missing the swing. The apartments all had outside entrances, and the doors all had peeling paint. Stella would hate living in a dump like this.

"So what's the plan?" I asked.

"People fall for free crap all the time. All we have to do is start knocking on doors and telling people that Stella's won a contest for free diapers for a year. Most people will fall all over themselves to let us know where she is. But it will work better if you do it. They'll trust you more than they do me."

It was pretty brilliant. "I take it you've used something like this before?"

"Multiple times. It's effective."

I filed that idea away for future reference. It might come in handy if I could convince Rose to open our own investigation business. Jed might have all kinds of helpful ideas for us.

I was thinking about a future with Rose. I took that as a good sign. I cast a glance over at the man next to me, realizing he'd given me a hope that I could actually fix this.

"Okay. Any suggestions for where to start?"

"The first apartment, and hope you find someone who knows sooner rather than later. The problem with these kinds of places is the neighbors often don't know much about one another. They tend to keep to themselves."

"Then let's get started. Why do you look so nervous?"

He suddenly looked like a surprisingly buff actor in a commercial for constipation medication.

"It will work better if you're alone, but after hearing that someone was looking for you, I'm hesitant to let you go without me."

I opened the car door. "I'll be fine."

"I'll be watching you. So don't try to run off."

My mouth parted to ask him what in tarnation he was talking about, but then I realized he had every right to be concerned. Rose and I had, on more than one occasion, purposely lost him while he was tailing us. I offered him a sweet smile. "I won't."

He looked even more suspicious. "Whatever you do, don't go in anyone's apartment."

"I'm not stupid, Jed."

"I know you're not, but I also know you have a big heart. Your kindness might overshadow your sense of self-preservation."

I gave him a questioning look.

"Elderly people tend to live in lower-income places. They're lonely, and they'll see your friendly face . . ."

"And you think I'll go in to keep them company."

"Yeah. But don't. Stick to the task."

I leaned over and kissed him on the cheek.

"What was that for?"

"For being you. Thank you." I bolted from the car before he could say anything.

My cell phone rang seconds after I bolted, and I wasn't surprised to see Jed's name on the screen.

"I can do this, Jed."

"If I didn't believe that, I wouldn't have sent you to do it. But I want you to leave our call going so I can hear what's going on."

"Okay."

I stuck my phone in my pocket and then walked up to the first apartment and knocked on the door. No one was home there or at the next two places. But the fourth door revealed an elderly man and his small dog. He didn't know anything about Stella, but every time I tried to move on to the next apartment, he kept talking. His scruffy dog reminded me a bit of Muffy, and I realized I probably would have stayed longer if Jed hadn't given me his warning.

I had multiple strikeouts after that—the occupants weren't home or didn't answer (a real possibility) or they'd never heard of Stella. I only had a few doors left to knock on, at least on this side of the second floor, but I knocked on the next one with as much confidence as I'd knocked on the first one.

A young woman with a baby on her hip answered. A toddler was hiding behind her legs, stealing looks at me.

"Hi," I said with a big smile. "I'm Tiffany from Baby Dearest, and I'm looking for Stella St. Clair."

"What for?" she asked.

I'd expected her to say no and slam the door in my face, so it took me a second to catch up. "Uh . . . I'm here to deliver the good news—she's won a year's worth of diapers."

"Stella's a private person," she said, jostling the baby on her hip. "Why don't you leave it with me, and I'll give it to her."

"That's so sweet of you," I said in a saccharine voice. "But I really need to deliver the prize to Stella personally."

She scowled, probably thinking she could sure use a year's worth of diapers, but then leaned out and pointed to the door at the end. "She lives down there, but she's not the most pleasant of people, so be prepared."

"Okay," I said. "Thanks." But she'd already slammed the door in my face.

I pulled the phone out of my pocket. "Did you hear that?"

"I'm already on my way up," he said, and I noticed him walking toward the staircase. "Don't go down there without me."

My stomach was in knots by the time Jed reached me. The unreadable expression on his face sent a jolt of fear skating down my spine. "What are you planning on doing?" I asked.

"I'm not planning on anything, Neely Kate. This is your visit. I'm here to make sure you're safe."

"You jumped in with Zelda."

He looked taken aback. "You're right. I'm sorry. I overstepped my bounds."

"No," I said, my hands starting to shake. "That's not what I was trying to say. I was all wound up in knots, and you asked questions it wouldn't have occurred to me to ask—at least not in the moment. When Rose and I question people, we usually tag-team it. That's what it's like with you and me too. We're a team."

His smile was reassuring, telling me he believed in me. I smiled back, suddenly less nervous.

"Okay," he said. "We do this as a team."

I led the way to Stella's apartment and took a deep breath before I knocked on the door. No one answered, so several seconds later, I knocked again—a little harder this time.

The door opened seconds later, and a haggard woman answered. "I've got a baby sleeping—oh, my God," she gushed. "Neely Kate?"

"Hey, Stella," I said softly, every ounce of hostility washing out of me. She looked like a shell of the woman I once knew.

"What are you doin' here?" Then she glanced over at Jed and took a step backward. "I didn't mean to sell all your stuff, but you just took off—"

I glanced back at Jed and realized she saw a beefy-looking guy who looked like an enforcer. She thought I'd brought him as backup. "That's not why I'm here, Stella. I wanted to see you, that's all."

She nodded toward Jed. "Then who's the guy?"

He stepped forward and reached out a hand. "I'm Jed. Her boyfriend. We're here in Ardmore for a visit, and when she said she was coming to see you, I insisted on comin' along."

Her eyes narrowed. "Why?"

He dropped his hand. "You used to mean a lot to Neely Kate."

"Until the end."

"You still meant a lot to her."

She eyed me as though trying to determine if it was a trick, but I must have passed her test because she stepped back and let us in. "My baby's sleepin', so keep it down."

"Okay," I said as I entered the dark room.

The drapes were pulled closed, but a bit of light shone through a crack. My eyes adjusted enough to take in the details of the small living room with a sofa and a recliner. There was a playpen in the corner, and baby toys were strewn all over the floor. Dirty dishes covered the kitchen counter and baby bottles filled the sink. The entire place reeked of sweat and cigarette smoke, and I fought the urge to gag.

I stepped through the minefield of crap on the floor toward the sofa, and Jed sat next to me.

"I see you traded up from Branson," she said, flopping into the chair. She opened her arms and spread them on the chair arms as she ogled Jed. "Still opposed to sharing, Neely Kate?"

My mouth dropped open, but Jed remained quiet and still.

"Relax," Stella said, "I was joking."

The set of Jed's jaw suggested he didn't appreciate the joke.

"You have a baby?" I asked, looking for an icebreaker, which was hard given how awful her life seemed to be. She hardly looked like herself. She'd always been thin, but now she looked like a bundle of bones. Her once-beautiful hair was thin, stringy, and lifeless. Her flawless complexion was blotchy, and then there were the missing teeth . . . A before and after shot of Stella would probably scare a bunch of bored teenagers off drugs.

"Joke's on me, huh?" she asked. "I was always the one warning you not to get pregnant. And then you went and got knocked up. But at least you were smart about it."

My stomach clenched at the reminder.

"Now you know why I was so eager to drive you to Oklahoma City for your abortion," she said in a brittle voice. "I didn't want anything to tie you to Branson."

"I was leavin' him anyway."

"Sure you were . . ." She reached over to an end table and picked up a pack of cigarettes and a lighter. "Well, neither one of us has 'im now."

"Do you know where he went?" I asked.

She lit her cigarette, took a long drag, and blew out a bit puff of smoke. She lifted her eyebrows. "Do *you*? Rumor had it you ran off together after Beasley was arrested."

"I never saw him again after our argument." That was a flat-out lie, but unless she'd heard differently from Branson, Beasley, or Carla, she might believe it.

She released a derisive laugh. "Argument. Ha." She took another long drag of her cigarette. "Is that what you want to call it?"

I didn't feel like dragging *that* confrontation out for examination. "Stan says you're not working at the club anymore."

Her eyebrow quirked up. "You went to the club, huh? Stan fired me after I got pregnant. Nobody wants to stick dollar bills into a G-string under a baby bump. *Not. Sexy.*" She took another drag. "But he was itchin' to get rid of me even before that. He said my 'recreational drug use'"—she used air quotes to get her point across—"was interfering with my work."

"So what are you doin' now?" I asked.

"Livin' the sweet life on the government dole," she said with a caustic grin. "The kid's good for *something*."

I felt a tiny stab in my heart, one that buried in deeper every moment I spent in this hellhole.

"Why did you keep her?" I asked. "You were the one who pushed me hard to abort mine."

"For the exact opposite reason," she said, flicking her long trail of ashes into a nearly full ashtray. "I was trying to *keep* my man. That's the whole reason I got knocked up, only the joke's on me." She let loose a laugh that sounded like a bark. "He hooked up with someone younger and prettier, and my new man's meaner than him."

I didn't respond.

"How about you, *Kitty*?" she asked. "What are you up to with your hunky man?"

"You know I hate that name," I said.

She took another drag of her cigarette and let out the smoke with a humorless laugh. "I know."

"I'm living in Arkansas," I said, trying to feel sorry for her to replace my disgust. Trying to remember that she'd once seemed like a friend. "After I left Branson, I went back home to my granny."

"And you didn't tell Zelda." She tsked. "The woman was heartbroken. Never mind that *I* was still here."

"I wasn't her favorite, Stella," I said, sounding exhausted even to my own ears. We'd had this argument more times than I could count. "*You're* her niece."

She took another drag, then stood. "Whatever. Want a drink?"

I shook my head, and she turned to Jed. "What about you, hot stuff?"

"No, thank you." His voice sounded cold and impassive.

She stubbed out the last of her cigarette and then headed into the kitchen. I watched as she made her drink—filling the glass half full of coke, topping it off with a more than generous pour of Jack Daniel's, and finishing it with a few ice cubes.

As she headed back into the living room, she lifted the glass with a partially toothless smile. "It's five o'clock somewhere."

Neither of us said anything.

She sat back down. "Why are you really here, Neely Kate?"

"Jed told you."

"Jed's a damn fool if he believes you, but then again, you always did have a way of wrapping men around your little finger."

"You used to think that about Branson, didn't you?" I asked before I could stop myself. "I hated him in the end. He treated me worse than shit."

"Which is why I found it so hard to believe you actually left him," she said. "You never found the gumption before."

"I did the last time," I said. "That was the last straw."

She didn't look convinced. "You did a lot of other kinky shit for the guy."

"I wasn't about to let a man beat the crap out of me while he screwed me, Stella. Why would I put myself through that to save Branson's sorry ass?"

Her eyes narrowed. "But it probably cost Branson his life, don't you think? That's why you're asking about him. You feel guilty because you didn't go through with it, and Branson got snuffed out."

I swallowed the bile rising in my throat. If she only knew the truth . . .

She grabbed another cigarette and stuck it between her lips, mumbling, "I bet he's buried out by an oil well somewhere."

"If he is, then it's his own damn fault."

She lifted her shoulders into a shrug as she flicked her lighter and lit her cigarette. "Maybe it is, but can *you* live with it?"

I didn't answer. I'd lived with it all just fine until Kate's letters started sending me down nightmare lane. Until I realized the walls of the new life I'd built for myself were made of paper.

"Have you seen Beasley since he got out?" I asked, my voice shaking a little.

A knowing smile lifted her lips. "Have *you*?"

"No."

She laughed. "That boy loved you . . ."

I didn't answer.

"I know you had something to do with it. He was so tight-lipped. The only time he got like that was when it came to you."

"Maybe he didn't want to incriminate himself."

She took a drag. "Not likely."

"Do you know if he came home when he got out?"

"Rumor has it he went to his aunt's house, but I can't be sure. Last week I heard he had a job at a hardware store." She grinned. "I always heard he was good with his hands. Was he?"

My face burned. "It wasn't like that, Stella."

She laughed. "That's what you always said. Beasley begged Branson to let him screw you. Did you know that?"

I didn't respond, but I hoped to God it wasn't true. Beasley hadn't been like his brother, which had made it even harder for me to accept what he'd done.

"So why are you here?" Stella repeated. "I find it hard to believe you were just takin' a stroll down memory lane."

"I wanted to check on you is all."

"More like gloat," she sneered, then took another long drag. "You and your perfect life and perfect man. I bet you're just livin' the life high on the hog."

"I have a job, Stella. I work at a landscaping office."

She waggled her eyebrows. "Sounds *fancy*."

Damned if I do and damned if I don't. It had always been like that with Stella, so why was I still trying?

A baby began to cry in the back, and Stella released a groan. "That damned kid."

I cast a glance at Jed, but his face was completely expressionless.

Stella leisurely sipped her drink as the baby began to wail louder.

"Don't you need to get her?" I asked, starting to get anxious.

She waved her hand. "She's fine. She can cry for another twenty minutes or so; then I'll get her up."

I felt like I was going to be sick. "Can I see her?" I asked. "Before I go?"

Stella rolled her eyes. "You're gonna screw up her schedule, but what the hell. I've gotten good at tuning her out."

How long did she let her baby girl cry? I stood and started toward the back, then stopped, sidelined by a sudden thought. "What's her name?"

"Crystal."

I wasn't surprised. Stella had always been attached to Crystal. It had been her stage name.

The back of the apartment was equally as dark as the front, but I didn't have any trouble figuring out which of the three doors led to the baby's room. Her sad cries led me right to her.

The tiny bedroom had a dresser, a rocking chair, and an old crib. All three pieces looked like they'd been around for half a century. The crib didn't have the bumper pads and bed skirt I'd already gotten while I was pregnant. It only had a crib sheet and a kicking, crying baby.

I moved to the side rail and peered down at her, my heart breaking into pieces. I was pretty sure Zelda had gotten her age wrong because she looked like she was eight or nine months old. She was naked except for her very full disposable diaper. Dried baby food covered parts of her face, and dirt was caked in her crevices. An empty bottle lay next to her, and I watched as she grabbed ahold of it and began to suck in vain, bursting into more cries when it proved empty.

I was devastated.

"Hey, Crystal," I said in a soothing tone. "I'm Neely Kate, and I'm gonna take care of this diaper, okay?"

Her eyes widened with fear when she didn't recognize me, and she continued to cry in earnest while I looked around the room, frantically searching for diapers and wipes. I found a nearly empty package of diapers on the floor at the foot of the crib, but there were no wipes, and the smell coming from her told me that the fact she needed a bath wasn't the only reason she stank.

"Stella?" I called out. "Do you have any wipes?"

She released a bitter laugh. "Wipes? That's a good one. Who has money for wipes?"

"Then how do you change a poopy diaper?"

"Just rub it off with the old diaper. If it's a bad one, I'll spray her off with the sprayer in the sink."

I gasped in horror, but I said nothing. Talking back would be a quick way to get us thrown out, and something told me Stella wouldn't be too quick about changing Crystal's diaper or feeding her. I went into the bathroom and turned on the hot water while I opened drawer after drawer, looking for a cloth. Each one was filled with makeup, used tissues, and handfuls of unlabeled pills—aspirin, Tums, and others I didn't recognize. Finally, I found a cloth, which I dampened in the now-warm water, and a nearly empty tube of diaper ointment.

When I got back to the baby's room, Crystal was still crying and getting frustrated that nothing was coming out of the bottle. "I'll get you a new bottle in a minute, sweet girl," I cooed softly. "Let me change your diaper first."

The poop was dried and caked to her bottom. I put the warm rag over it to get it loose, then gently wiped the red, angry skin. She cried harder as I put ointment on her, and I was about to fasten her new diaper when I felt Jed standing behind me.

"I made her a bottle," he said quietly. He stared at her bottom as I closed up the diaper and fastened the tabs, and while he didn't say anything, I felt him tense.

I picked her up and held her close, and she grabbed a handful of my hair and clung to me for dear life.

Jed handed me the bottle before picking up the dirty washcloth that was sitting on top of the dirty diaper on the dresser. "You start feeding her and I'll get another washrag."

I nodded, nearly in tears as I carefully sat on the rocking chair and put the bottle to the baby's mouth.

She began to suck in earnest, as though worried I was going to take it from her. I held her close while she ate, and she wrapped her tiny hand around my ring finger.

Jed returned and crouched in front of me, watching her with that same empty expression. What was he thinking? Was he upset I was doing this?

Holding this baby made me think of my own childhood, born to a woman who'd had me for selfish reasons . . . just like Stella. But Crystal also made me think about the babies I'd lost—two due to my miscarriage and one of my own doing. How could Stella get this precious gift and treat her so badly? How could I walk away and leave this baby with her heartless mother? What would Stella do if I insisted on taking her daughter with me?

Jed stared up at me, and I realized his mask of indifference had finally dropped. The pure rage I saw on his face scared the bejiggers out of me.

"We can't take her with us."

My mouth dropped open. "How . . ."

"Because I know you, Neely Kate. I know it's killing you to see her like this."

"You're angry that I want to take her with me? I'll find another way home."

"I'm not angry with *you*. I could literally kill that woman for treating her baby like this, but we both know I can't do that. And if that coldhearted bitch talked you into an abortion so your loser boyfriend would be available for her to steal, do you really think she's going to let you walk out of here with her baby?"

"But she doesn't want her, Jed!" I whisper-shouted.

"That may be true, but she's getting welfare money for her. She's not going to let this baby go, and she's especially not going to let *you* have her. She's so jealous of you she can't see straight."

I knew he was right, but it killed me to think of leaving Crystal with the woman in the other room. "Do you expect me to just walk away and leave this poor baby to that monster?"

"No. As soon as we walk out that door, I'm going to report her to the authorities."

"But Stella will know we did it."

"So? It doesn't sound like she's got anything to hold over you."

"But my past . . . with Branson . . ."

"Who's she going to tell? It's not like you're running for president."

"But . . ."

"Neely Kate, we've all done things we're ashamed of, even Rose. But if Stella doesn't have anything to hold over your head that could land you in jail, then there's nothing stopping us from reporting her." He was still speaking in an undertone, but his voice was full of conviction. "I know you don't want to leave the baby like this," he said, reaching over and putting a hand on my knee, "and neither do I, but we really don't have a choice. If you take this baby with you, Stella can have you arrested for kidnapping, and I wouldn't put it past her."

"Let me finish cleaning her up." I reached for the new washrag in his hand.

"No," he said, refusing to relinquish the rag. "We need to leave her dirty. The authorities have to see how badly she's treating her."

Tears filled my eyes. "I can't walk away from her like this."

"I don't like it any more than you do, but we don't have a choice. This is our best course of action to save her."

He was right, of course, which wouldn't make it any easier to leave.

When she finished her bottle, I put her on my shoulder and burped her, tears streaming down my face. How could God take away my babies and leave this poor baby with Stella?

Jed pulled me out of the chair and wrapped me up in his arms, holding me for a few moments, the baby sandwiched loosely between us. She looked up at Jed with curious eyes and reached for his face. He took her from me and held her close, giving me a worried look. "I need you to be strong and trust me on this. Can you do that?"

He gently bounced her as though it was instinctual. She was reaching for his face again, and he rubbed her back with his free hand. Watching him hold Crystal was all the confirmation I needed that he wouldn't let her stay in this situation for long.

He reached out and brushed the tears from my face. "You can't let Stella see you upset."

"I know." But it was easier said than done.

"Why don't you get yourself together in the bathroom? I'll take care of the baby until you come out."

"Okay."

The sooner I did this, the better, so I gave the baby a soft kiss on the cheek and left the room. Once I was in the bathroom, I shut the door.

The walls were paper thin and I could hear Jed's voice, only it was a low murmur and I couldn't make out the words. He was talking to Crystal.

Fresh tears sprang into my eyes. I'd let myself start imagining something with Jed, wondering what a life with him would look like. After Branson, I couldn't build a life with a man on the wrong side of the law. Of course, that hadn't worked out so well for me. I'd thought Ronnie was safe, but he'd been as tangled up in organized crime as a fly in a web. At least I *knew* Jed had worked for Skeeter, and if he didn't intend to go back, he could do anything. Get a job on the right side of the law. Shoot, he was good at this investigating thing, better than me. Maybe he'd be open to starting an investigating business with me and Rose (once I talked her into it, of course).

But there was no future for us. I saw Jed as a father—he'd already told me how he planned to raise his future children, and there was no denying how sweet he was with Crystal. Maybe it was a mistake to look so far down the road, but I saw the roadblock from a mile away. I couldn't give him babies.

The thought brought fresh tears to my eyes, which was defeating the whole purpose of being in here. I flushed the toilet and then turned on the faucet as I leaned my head back and took several deep breaths. Jed was right. If we didn't leave here as though nothing was wrong, Stella might figure out what we were planning and run with the baby. They needed to catch her off guard.

I turned off the water and took another deep breath. I could do this.

Chapter Seventeen

W hen I walked out of the bathroom, Jed and the baby weren't in her room, but I heard Stella's voice in the living room.

"You look mighty fine bouncin' that baby on your leg," she said in a seductive voice. "If you ever want a real woman, leave Neely Kate and let me take care of you."

"I'm pretty happy with what I have," Jed said in a tone that made his stance clear.

"You and half the men we ever met," she spat out.

I stopped in the hallway.

"Is that why you hate her so much?" Jed asked flatly.

"It's hard to compete with someone like her. The men at the club loved her because she had that whole innocent vibe. Branson figured that out pretty quick and decided to use it to his own advantage. Did she tell you about that part of her life?" she asked with a leer in her tone.

"No."

She laughed. "I won't lie; he was taken with her too, but it wasn't long before his friends and clients also noticed her. He knew a gold mine when he saw it."

I nearly burst into the room to stop her, but something held me back. Her version wasn't far from the truth, and this way I wouldn't have to tell him myself. It was the chickenshit way out, and I knew it, but I closed my eyes, leaned back against the wall, and let her go on.

"And what did Branson do?"

She laughed again, this time with more genuine merriment. "What did she even tell you about all of us?"

"Enough to know you were like a cancer to her."

She chuckled. "And I thought you said you were here because I meant something to her."

"That's what makes what you did even shittier. She trusted you, and you hurt and used her."

"Bullshit," Stella said, getting angry. "She was the one all the guys wanted. I was tired of competing with her. I was prettier than her! I only got her a job because I felt sorry for her. And then that backstabber betrayed me."

"Betrayed you? Because men could see the witch you really were beneath your shiny exterior? Men are easily fooled at first, but it doesn't take long for the smart ones to see through the glitter. You saw the goodness in her and tried to kill it. But guess what? Neely Kate's one of the sweetest, kindest people I know—you didn't defeat her. She has a good life with friends who love her and support her. And you're the worthless, dried-up bitch with no one but this poor baby, who deserves a much better mother than you."

"Get out."

"Gladly. Just remember karma's a bitch, Stella, so maybe take a good hard look at how you got here."

"Neely Kate!" she screamed, and the baby started crying.

I braced myself and walked into the living room.

Stella was livid—more so than I'd ever seen her. "Get the fuck out!" she screamed, pointing to the door. "Get out of my house!"

Jed tried to put the crying baby in the crib in the living room, but she wrapped her small hands around his arm, clinging for dear life. His jaw clenched as he pried her off. He stood there for a moment as if to gather himself, then turned to stare down at Stella. "There's a special place in hell for people who mistreat defenseless children, and I suspect you've already got your place reserved."

"*Get. Out!*" she screeched. "And don't you come back, Neely Kate!"

Jed moved to the door and opened it, waiting for me to exit. I didn't say a word to Stella as I headed outside, trying to shake loose from the desperation and hopelessness that had soaked into my soul. Jed followed, closing the door behind him. I expected him to slam it shut, but he seemed more controlled now that we'd left Stella's hellish den. He was reaching for his phone and tapping on the screen before we even reached the staircase to the parking lot.

I didn't say a word as he placed his call, an anonymous tip about a mother neglecting her baby, giving Stella's name and address. Then he got into the car and grabbed the steering wheel.

I got in next to him, slightly unnerved by the rage he was suppressing. I waited for him to back out of the space after he started the car, but he didn't move, just watched the door with narrowed eyes.

After a minute or two, some of the tension eased out of him and he turned toward me. "I'm sorry. I blew it in there."

I shook my head. "No. You didn't."

"I did. Now I'm worried she'll run before the authorities show up."

"No," I said. "She won't. She wouldn't dream of me doin' it. She thinks I'm too weak. And you . . . she would expect you to defend Crystal with your fists, not by calling Family Services."

"That's sick and twisted."

"And yet that's her life."

He kept his eyes on the door. "It used to be yours."

"Until I left. But I lived through a lot of shit before I left, Jed."

He didn't answer, and I started to get nervous.

"How long do you plan to stay here?" I asked.

"Long enough to make sure she doesn't bolt."

"I never asked her about Kate," I said. "I don't know if Kate found her."

"We found Stella in less than half an hour. If Zelda talked about her, then it's a safe bet that Kate found her too."

He was probably right.

His body was so tense it was practically twitching, but he relaxed slightly as he turned to face me. "What did he make you do, Neely Kate?"

I swallowed, my fear rising.

He shook his head, turning back to stare out the windshield. "No. You don't have to answer that."

"Do you want to know?" I asked.

"I thought I did. Now I'm not so sure."

"Because I disgust you?"

He gripped the steering wheel and squeezed. "More like I'll want to beat the ever-lovin' shit out of someone, and it sounds like Branson's already dead, which means Stella might be next on the list. What about Beasley? Where does he fall in this mess?"

What Jed had said earlier was true. I had family and friends. I had a good life. I was scared that if the truth about my past started oozing out, it would poison everything I had now. Could I risk it? But Jed had been dealing with this piece by excruciating piece, and he'd finally put voice to the question he must have been asking himself all along. It wouldn't be fair of me not to answer.

"When I first started working at the club . . ." My voice came out so soft I wasn't sure he could hear me, but he went stock still, so I guessed that he could. "I was scared spitless, but I'm a quick learner and, like I said, Kitty was someone else, definitely not me. I'd been working there a few months when Zelda got sick. She had a cough that wouldn't get better, and they kept giving her medicine that cost more and more money. They gave her a prescription that would cost her three hundred dollars. After all the other medicines she'd bought, she was flat broke. She couldn't afford it. I tried to get Stella to help me cover it, but she said she didn't have the money, even though she raked in fifty dollars in tips on a good night. So . . . I took Stan up on an offer."

"Sex?" he asked in a dead voice.

"Yeah. Everyone knew I was a virgin. It was kind of Stan's thing with me. It was a big draw." I paused to let the wave of self-disgust wash over me. "So there were quite a few regulars who offered to pay to be my first."

"You sold your virginity to pay for Zelda's medication." It was a statement, not a question.

"Yeah." I took a breath and clasped my shaking hands together. "Two hundred dollars."

"And what was Stan's cut?"

"He got two hundred too." I turned to look out the side window, too embarrassed to look at him. "Stan wanted me to sleep with other customers. It was illegal, of course, but somehow he got away with it. A lot of guys requested me, but after that one time, I swore I would never do it again." A lump filled my throat as I remembered that night . . . the fear, the shame, the pain. "So I kept saying no, which only made them more intrigued."

I snuck a glance to Jed, but he was still clutching the steering wheel.

"Do you want to hear the rest?"

"I want you to tell me what you feel comfortable telling me," he said, but his voice was tight and far from comforting.

Would he really look at me the same way after I told him everything? Did it matter? I was guilty of everything I'd done. If he was revolted by me after this, I deserved it.

"I met Branson after I'd been working at the club for a little over a year," I said. "Stella had hooked up with his friend. He had these boy-next-door looks, and he didn't mind that I worked at Slick Willy's. Sometimes he'd even come to the club and watch me dance. I thought he was different because he was paying me so much attention, and we weren't even sleeping together yet. Just hanging out, and sometimes he'd kiss me." Tears stung my eyes, but I blinked them back. "I thought he was different, so I finally slept with him, and while it wasn't awful like it had been with the guy who won Stan's auction, it wasn't anything like Zelda's romance novels either," I said. "He wanted me to be Kitty when we had sex, not Neely Kate."

"And you stayed with him?"

"Yeah," I said. "Stella told me I was makin' too much of nothin' and that was the way men were. Besides, he was nice to me at first, and he had money even though he only had a job at the loading dock. But sometimes he would disappear for an hour or so and come back with a wad of cash. One night, I was with him when he made a *run.*"

I'd never told anyone this story, and a quick glance to Jed made me question whether I should continue.

"Drugs?" Jed asked.

"Yeah. Meth. Crack. And some pills I didn't learn about until much later."

He remained silent.

"I stayed in the car while he made his trade, but the guy noticed me and told Branson he'd pay to screw me. When I told the guy I wasn't for sale, he laughed and told me *everything* was for sale. Branson didn't contradict him." I stopped. I'd already come this far. I needed to finish the story. "A couple of nights later, I had a night off, and Branson was being unusually nice. He told me he wanted to take me out. He told me to dress up from head to toe, including sexy lingerie and my stiletto heels. I didn't think much of it since it wasn't unusual for him to ask me to dress like that, and besides, he was takin' me out, something he didn't usually do."

"You don't have to tell me the rest, Neely Kate." His voice was thick.

"I do. I need you to know."

"Okay."

"So we went out to a club and we were dancing. Strangely enough, I'd been thinkin' about breakin' it off with him and movin' back in with Zelda, but I decided to give it one more chance. And I was happy," I said in a pathetic voice, clogged with tears. "All I ever wanted was for someone to love me, and Branson was finally makin' some kind of effort, you know?"

"Yeah," he said softly.

"But then the guy from the drug deal showed up. I got uncomfortable and told Branson I wanted to go. He said fine, but we needed to have one drink with this guy or Branson would offend him, something that would be bad for business *and* his personal well-being." I closed my eyes. "So, like an idiot, I agreed. My last memory of that night was drinking with them while the guy undressed me with his eyes. The next thing I knew, I was waking up in bed the next morning. Naked, sore, and with a terrible hangover."

"Branson roofied you."

I swallowed and looked down at my lap. "Yeah."

"Did you realize what happened?"

"No. Branson told me that I'd gotten drunk and we'd gone home early. I'd asked him for rough sex, which was why I was so sore. That sounded so unlike me—all of it—but I never dreamed that Branson would let some guy screw me for money. Not even when he had a new used iPhone later that day."

"It happened again?" Jed asked.

"Yeah, two weeks later, only Branson didn't even try to fool me by takin' me out. He invited some friends over for a party. I hadn't had a drink since my blackout, but Branson convinced me to try some moonshine punch. Sure enough, the next day was the same."

"You didn't figure it out?"

"I know I sound like an idiot, but I mentioned it to Stella and she told me not to worry about it. That she'd seen me drinking cup after cup of punch. She said I'd practically dragged Branson into our room to screw him while the party was still goin' on." I shook my head. "But that wasn't me. It wasn't adding up. So I asked Beasley what was goin' on—and he buttoned up tighter than a clam. He was usually talkin' ninety miles a minute, so I knew something was up, yet I still couldn't let my mind go there. I thought maybe Beasley was embarrassed by my behavior.

"Branson started having more parties after that, and always on my nights off. Sometimes nothin' would happen, but other nights I would black out again and there would be bruises on my arms or legs I couldn't explain. And not only that, Branson had more money than usual and Beasley would hardly look at me, which made it awkward since we were all living together. Everything changed the night I refused to drink anything except from my water bottle. Branson got pissed and accused me of being a nagging bitch—which made no sense since I'd sat in a corner and kept to myself. When I pointed that out, he told me that I was bringing down the party, and I needed to get with the program and quick."

"He had someone who didn't like waiting," Jed said as though he was talking about the weather.

"Yeah, and Branson got *so pissed* when I still refused. He backhanded me and told the guy that he could have me fully conscious since he liked it rough. So the guy dragged me to my bed and screwed me. He didn't care that I was screaming and clawing the whole time—" My voice broke. "He loved every minute of it. All while Branson was filming it from the corner."

Jed remained completely still.

"When he was done, he got up and tossed Branson several hundred-dollar bills. He said he'd pay extra if he could have me like that again." I paused. "After he left, I told Branson I was going straight to the police, but he laughed and said he had plenty of videos of that guy and others screwing me without any resistance. Besides, he said, who were the police gonna believe? A stripper who had sold herself for sex before or a man who was the foreman on a construction job? And I realized he was right."

"Neely Kate." His voice sounded strangled.

"I left. I packed up my stuff and headed to Zelda's, but he followed me and beat the shit out of me in Zelda's front yard. He told me he owned me. From that moment forward, he said, I couldn't so much as take a shit without his permission."

"Zelda let him get away with that?" Jed asked, incredulous.

I released a tearful laugh. "She'd gone to visit her sister, Stella's mom."

"And Stella . . . ?"

"She told me I was lucky to have a man to take care of me." I swallowed my tears. "Branson left my car at Zelda's and told me that he would be driving me to and from work from then on, and when I was home without him, he'd lock me in our room, dead-bolting it shut."

"And his brother still lived there?"

"Yeah."

"And he still sold your *services*, I presume?"

"He didn't drug me after that, but I wasn't so sure being conscious was any better. Some men just wanted to screw. Others wanted me to role play. Some wanted to rape me, and every single time someone screwed me, Branson was there filming it all. All the while, Branson kept getting richer and I felt more and more like dyin'." My mouth lifted into a soft smile. "And then I met Carla."

"At the club?"

"Yeah. She saw something was off . . . She told me I had dead eyes, and then she met Branson and guessed he was the cause. When she saw how controlling he was, she offered to help me leave him."

I snuck a glance at Jed, who seemed like a solid statue.

"She knew Branson liked to watch me dance, and Stan gave him the schedule so he would know when to expect me on stage. That gave me a window of about five to ten minutes from when I left my hostessing duties to get changed in the back to when I went up on stage. Carla came up with a plan that she would give me the keys to her car as soon as I went into the back. That would hopefully buy me a good ten minutes to get away before Branson figured it out. She said she'd loan me a hundred dollars for gas money, and the plan was for me to take off for my granny's house in Arkansas. She'd stay behind and cover for me. We agreed that I'd figure out how to get the car back to her later."

"It didn't work?"

"I found out I was pregnant a week before we planned for me to leave." I shook my head. "Or rather Stella figured out I was pregnant. I was viciously ill, just like with my last pregnancy. Branson was pissed because I was too sick to entertain, and I couldn't dance on the pole without losing my lunch. So Stella got a pregnancy test because I couldn't shop on my own. Sure enough, there were two pink lines.

"The last thing I needed was a baby tying me to Branson—or one of those horrible men—but I wasn't so sure Carla's plan would work. I suspected Branson would track me down to Henryetta, and if he found out I had a baby, there'd be no escaping him. So when Stella suggested the abortion, I decided it was my only chance to save my baby from the hell I'd lived through, as sick as that sounds. One day, when Branson was going fishing with his friends, she got me out and drove me to a doctor in Oklahoma City. There's a waiting period, and Stella knew this was a one-shot deal, so she found someone to do it off the books."

"How'd you pay for it?" Jed asked.

A single tear slid down my cheek. "Stella paid for it."

"What'd she get out of it?"

"Her shot at Branson? She was sure he treated me like he did because I was weak. She believed she would be different. I just wanted out. But a few days later, I was still bleeding from my procedure and Branson told me he had some big deal in the works and that he needed me to do something special. He said if I went along, he'd give me part of the money. I knew right away that this had to be big. He'd never offered me anything before other than the promise not to beat me. It was a ridiculous offer. I never went anywhere to use money, and he kept every penny I made at the club, but I asked him what he wanted me to do."

"Neely Kate. You don't have to tell me." Jed's voice shook. "I already heard enough from Stella."

"No. You need to know it all. We're close to the end now."

He gave a small nod.

"He said he had a rich customer from Dallas who'd heard about me. Branson said he wanted to buy me for one night, but I had to sign a waiver promising not to press charges. Well, that perked my fear right up. No one else had ever been worried about such a thing. Branson saw my hesitation. He played down the agreement, saying it was no big deal. The guy had a reputation to maintain, and if word got out that he was into something kinky, it could ruin him. I said I'd think about it, then

177

told Carla I needed to leave sooner. The guy was coming the next night. He was going to watch me dance; then I was supposed to leave with him. Branson would come pick me up after six hours. That was when the guy would pay him. But I had to sign the agreement. If I didn't, the guy would leave and neither of us would get anything."

"So what happened?"

"I didn't give Branson an answer, but he took my silence as agreement to go through with the deal. In the meantime, Carla had scraped together gas money for me. We had a plan worked out, only Stella was working that night and knew something was up.

"When it came time for me to escape, I got in Carla's car, but Branson was waiting for me. He told me that I was still going with the guy, but I wasn't gettin' a dime. When I told him I refused to do it, he threatened to hurt Zelda."

"You agreed."

I couldn't tell what he thought of that. "I had to. I could handle his fists, but she was frail . . . I couldn't risk it."

A car pulled up next to Jed's side, and a woman got out. She looked to be in her forties, and the expression on her face suggested she didn't take shit from anyone.

"Family Services?" I asked.

"I suspect so." He put the car in reverse but didn't back out.

Sure enough, the woman marched up to Stella's door and knocked. As soon as Stella answered, Jed backed out.

I hadn't finished my story, but now that Jed knew someone was going to make sure the baby was okay, his whole demeanor had changed.

"Where are you going?" I asked, worried about where I stood with him.

"We're going to find Beasley." The look in his eyes suggested Beasley should be very afraid.

Chapter Eighteen

"Jed, hold up," I said, reaching for his arm. "You don't even know where to find him, and you don't know why I'm lookin' for him."

"Neely Kate, I know I said I was lettin' you handle this, but I'm taking over with Beasley."

"Jed."

"No," he snapped. "That man has a lot to answer for . . . and I'll be the one makin' him atone for what he did."

"He's already atoned for it, Jed. He went to prison for something I did."

"What was the charge?"

"*Jed.*"

"*What was the fucking charge?* Because unless it's for murdering his brother, he's not even begun to pay."

"Jed! *Stop!*"

He pulled over into a gas station parking lot and got out of the car, leaving the engine running, and began to pace the length of the car.

I got out and walked over to him, half-scared to confront him, but I had to fix this.

"Jed."

He continued to pace, his fists clenching and unclenching.

"Jed. I'm sorry."

He shook his head, looking incredulous. "Why the hell are *you* sorry?"

"You told me not to tell you, and I did anyway. I'm sorry."

"No! Don't you ever be sorry for telling me the truth. How many people have you told that story to?"

"No one. Just you."

He stopped pacing and lunged for me, pulling me against his chest. "God. Neely Kate." He sounded so anguished. Because of me. I couldn't take it.

I jerked away. "Stop. *Just stop.* I don't want your pity, and I don't want your condemnation. I only told you so you'd know what I've been running from, and I haven't even finished."

He shook his head. "No condemnation, Neely Kate. Not one little bit."

"I could have run and I didn't," I said.

"When?" he asked in disbelief. "When could you have run?"

"When Stella took me to Oklahoma City."

"Did she ever let you out of her sight?"

"Only once I was prepped and ready for the procedure."

"And then she came right back, didn't she?"

I didn't answer. We both knew that she had.

"You were beaten down, Neely Kate. You were . . . *fuck!*" he shouted, then spun away and began to pace again. After a couple of lengths, he leaned his hands on the top of the car, then cursed and shook his hands when he realized how hot it was.

He spun and turned to face me, rage twisting his familiar features into something unrecognizable. "You realize he knew, don't you?"

My blood ran straight to my toes. "Knew what?"

"He knew you were pregnant. He paid for the abortion."

"What? No . . ."

"*Yes*. He knew. Trust me. If he was using you like that, he knew your cycle. He had to schedule his . . ." His voice trailed off, and if possible, he looked even angrier than before.

"But why would Stella . . . ?"

"What would you have done if he took you to get an abortion? Probably fought him on it, right? But damn, he knew you'd trust your friend to have your best interest in mind. How else would she be able to get you out of that room?"

I stumbled backward, my butt hitting the back of the car. "I'm so stupid." It all came rushing back, viewed through a different lens, and now I could see that he was right.

Branson had known all along.

Horror washed through me. "Oh, my God. I killed my baby. And that's exactly what he wanted. *I'm so stupid.*"

"No!" he shouted, drawing the attention of the few people brave enough to face the heat to pump their gas. "Don't you dare accept any guilt in this." Then his expression morphed into horror. "You blame yourself. You think you deserved it."

I took several steps to the side, clearing the back of the car.

"Oh, my God. He made you think you deserved it."

I started to cry.

He was close to me in an instant, pulling me into his embrace. "I'm sorry," he said into my hair. "I'm making it worse. I'm sorry."

I shook my head. "I can't see Beasley right now. I can't handle it."

"I know. It's okay. Let's go back to our room."

I nodded and he helped me into the car again. As soon as we were settled, he took off, ignoring the curious stares.

He drove straight to the motel while I sat in silence. I didn't dare cry or I'd cry away every last part of me until there was nothing left but an empty shell. When he parked in the lot, he came around to help me out, but I was already halfway to the stairs. He wrapped his arm around my back, but I shook it off, feeling dirty and claustrophobic. I was waging an inner battle over what I wanted. Part of me was desperate for him to hold me and tell me everything would be okay, but another more vocal part of me was on edge and ready to fight. That part couldn't stand anyone's touch, not even Jed's.

"I'm sorry," I said after I recoiled. "I just feel . . . so . . ."

"Don't apologize." But he stayed close until we reached the room, as though he worried he'd need to be there to pick up the pieces if I fell apart.

It was a legitimate concern.

As soon as we entered the air-conditioned room, I climbed onto the bed and curled into a ball. I couldn't handle the world anymore. I couldn't handle my shame and embarrassment. I couldn't handle the pain I'd been through and the pain that had lingered with me for so long. All I wanted was to sleep for a million years and wake up feeling nothing.

I woke with a start, bolting off the bed, fresh from a nightmare I was already forgetting, except I could see the man's looming face, turning first red and then pale.

It was still daytime, which made me feel a little better. Jed was slouched in the chair next to the bed. He sat up when he saw me stir.

"Jed?"

"I'm here," he said, leaning forward. "What do you need?"

"Will you hold me?"

He was beside me in an instant, helping me lie on my side. Then he curled up behind me without hesitation, wrapping his arm over my stomach. "Is this okay?" he asked. "Is this too tight?"

"No." A moment later, I whispered, "I need you. And I hate that I do."

"Did you ever think that I need you too?"

I turned to glance back at him.

"It's true," he said, leaning over and kissing my bare shoulder. "Skeeter . . . I've been loyal to him for so long I've forgotten there are other choices. Other lives. I'm confused and pissed, but you help me put it all in perspective. No one else has ever made me feel like this . . ." He closed his eyes and groaned. "I suck at this, Neely Kate."

I rolled over so that my stomach pressed against his. "No. Jed. You don't." I lifted my hand to his temple, stroking it with my fingertip. "But I'm messed up. I'm broken. You deserve someone who isn't so complicated."

He gave me a sardonic smile. "And my career choice isn't complicated?"

"It's more than that, and you know it. I haven't even finished my story." I searched his eyes. "I killed someone, Jed."

His hand brushed a strand of hair from my face. "I know." I started to sit up, but he pulled me back down. "Shh . . . Lie still. It's okay."

"It's okay that I killed someone?"

"We've talked about this. I've killed someone too. *Multiple* someones. You should kick me out of this room right now and take my car to go back home."

"I'm not goin' to do that, Jed."

"Why?"

"Because I know your heart. You must have had a reason."

"Some of those deaths were self-defense, but in some cases I played judge and jury. I offered to kill someone for Rose, and she begged me not to. I gave Rose what she wanted, but the bitch turned around and tried to kill Rose right after I left. Looking back on the whole thing, I wish I'd gone ahead and killed her. What do you think of me now?"

I only saw a man who was protecting my friend. "I'm not kickin' you out, Jed."

He placed a gentle kiss on my forehead, then leaned back to look at me. "So why in the hell would I leave you? You killed in self-defense," he said. "I haven't figured out who you killed yet—although I have my suspicions—but I'm not running, Neely Kate. I'm still here. I'll help you with whatever you need to do."

I closed my eyes and buried my head underneath his chin. "Thank you."

"What do you say we take the night off and start back on this tomorrow?"

"No. I want to finish it and go home. What time is it?"

"Six."

"So we have a few hours before we can go see Carla," I said, then sat up. "We need to find Beasley."

Jed's jaw clenched.

"Jed, I *need* to find out if he talked to Kate. He's the only one who knows about the azaleas, and my life could be on the line. Especially if a guy came looking for me a few months ago."

He sat up and picked up my hand, linking our fingers. "Then we talk to Beasley. And I promise not to beat the ever-lovin' shit out of him until after you get everything you need to know out of him."

"Jed."

"No, Neely Kate. Don't you dare make me promise to play nice to a man who sat back and watched that asshole abuse you." His face reddened. "*Don't you fucking dare.*"

I closed my eyes and leaned my forehead into his shoulder. "It's complicated."

"The hell it is."

I sat back and studied his face. "He went to jail for me, Jed. That isn't something that can be taken lightly. He forfeited years of his life to protect me. You're not beatin' him up."

His face softened. Slightly. "Fine. I won't beat the shit out of him unless he does something that warrants it. That's the best I can do."

I narrowed my eyes, but he stared at me unapologetically. "Okay."

"Then let's go find Beasley."

Chapter Nineteen

I t was all well and good to know that Beasley might have worked in a hardware store, but there were nine possible locations. It was disconcerting, especially since it was already after six thirty.

Jed frowned. "You said Beasley has an aunt. Do you know where she lives?"

I searched my memory. "I was only there a couple of times. I don't know an address, and I'm not sure I could find it."

"How about her name?"

"Beverly Desoto."

Jed searched his phone, then gave me a grim smile. "Jackpot." His smile fell. "Maybe I should do this without you."

"He'll never talk to you, or at least I hope *to God* he wouldn't talk to you." When Jed looked taken aback, I said, "I'm counting on the fact he's never told anyone. If he blabs it to you without me around, then who else has he told?"

"Yeah, you're right. I'm only trying to protect you, Neely Kate."

"And while I appreciate it, I still need to face it. Maybe it's the only way I'll ever truly be free."

He took me by surprise and kissed me, his lips soft on mine. I wrapped my arms around his neck and held tight. Jed was my lifeline in this turbulent sea of my past.

"When we finish here," he said, pulling back to stare into my eyes, "let's not go back to Henryetta, at least not at first. Let's you and me go somewhere, just the two of us, and *just be*. No danger. No painful past. Only you and me."

"For how long?" I asked, feeling anxious. "I know you might never want to go back, but I've got Rose and Joe . . ."

"A week? Two? As long as we want until we decide to go back, but Neely Kate—" He turned serious. "Joe will never approve of you being with me."

"You don't know that."

"*I do.* We're legally at odds."

"But you won't be working for Skeeter anymore."

"But I have. For years. Something's bound to turn up and bite me in the ass. Carter Hale will help me get out of it, but Joe will *not* approve."

I frowned. Jed was right, but I wouldn't let them be at odds with each other. "We'll deal with that when it comes." I kissed him again, because I could, and it felt so right.

Was this what love felt like? Being around the one person you wanted to be with more than anyone else in the world, who made you feel like you were lying in the warm sun on a soft bed, surrounded by warmth, love, and protection until you were bursting with it. Because that's what I was feeling right now with Jed, and while it scared the dickens out of me, part of me basked in it.

But while all of that was happening on the surface, underneath it all, I was like a molten vat of boiling lava about to erupt. I wanted Jed like I'd never wanted another man. As scared as I was to bare everything to him—body and soul—part of me knew he'd not only accept my scars, but appreciate me more because of them.

I finally pulled back, more than a little pleased to see Jed had been as affected as I was. "We need to find Beasley."

"And then we'll escape somewhere. Where's the one place you've always wanted to go?"

I cringed. "You're going to think it's silly."

"I doubt it."

"I know you mentioned Florida, but I've always wanted to go to the mountains in Colorado and see the chipmunks. Did you know they come right up to you and eat out of your hand?" Jed was grinning like a fool, so I gave him a mock scowl. "I told you it was silly."

"It's not silly."

"Then why are you smilin' like that?"

"Because you've lived through some horrible things, yet you're still so . . ."

"Stupid."

"No. So full of life and joy, and you still see the good in people—"

"Not all people."

He tilted his head in acknowledgment. "Okay, not all people, but most people. There's something about you that makes me think maybe I'm not so bad. That maybe I can have love and a family too."

My smile immediately fell.

"What?" he asked with a worried look. "What did I say?"

"I can't have babies, Jed."

He blinked. "What?"

"I can't have any more babies. I'm too scarred inside from all those infections . . . I was lucky to have gotten pregnant with my babies last winter, but one of them got stuck in my fallopian tube and . . . I can't have babies, Jed. And you deserve babies."

He shook his head. "There are other ways to have a family besides having babies. Look at you and Rose. You're like sisters, and you only met a year ago."

"I know, but . . ."

"I'd love to have kids someday, Neely Kate, but knowin' you can't have them doesn't change my mind about being with you. If we reach the point where we want kids, then we'll deal with it, okay?"

"But—"

He shook his head. "No buts. Now let's go."

We were halfway to the car when he asked, "What part of Colorado?"

"I don't know, the part that has chipmunks."

He laughed, that belly laugh that filled me with happiness. "You don't know?"

"No, but surely it can't be too hard to find out."

He opened my car door, grinning from ear to ear. "I need you in my life, Neely Kate. I meant what I said, no one makes me feel like you do."

"But a lot of it's bad," I said.

"The bad makes you appreciate the good so much more, don't you think?"

"Yeah," I said. "I do."

While we drove to Beasley's aunt's house, Jed had me look up chipmunks in Colorado on my phone. We settled on a town called Estes Park, and by the time he pulled up in front of the small bungalow house I recognized, we'd even picked a place to stay. We only needed to make the reservations. Only then did I realize what he'd done for me—he'd purposefully kept me distracted so I wouldn't worry about Beasley.

I took a deep breath. "Give me a minute."

Jed left the engine running. "Whenever you're ready, Neely Kate. We'll sit here all night if you need to."

I forced a smile. "That won't look suspicious."

"Then I'll keep circling the block. You're setting the pace."

I turned to look at the house. It had never been in good shape, and that hadn't changed. "I think maybe I need to do this alone."

"Not a fucking chance in hell," he grunted.

I couldn't help my small chuckle. "I guess you made that clear."

"You're damn right."

"Then play it like you did with Stella. Let me do the talking. I'm worried you're going to scare him off."

"How do you know he's here?"

I pointed to the driveway that ran down the side of the house. "That's his truck back there."

Jed didn't answer. I wondered if I should tell Jed the rest. He was bound to be confused when he heard about Beasley's conviction, but I was already opening the car door and getting out. He'd have to figure it out like he'd figured out everything else.

He met me on the sidewalk and gave me a reassuring look, not exactly a smile, but there was something in his eyes that told me I could do this.

I knocked on the door, and an older woman opened it. "Can I help you?"

"Hi," I said, sweet as you please. "I'm looking for Beasley."

Her eyes narrowed. "Who's asking?"

"An old friend." When she didn't budge, I added, "Neely Kate."

She stared at me for a moment, looking like she was going to tell me to go away, but I heard a man's voice behind her say, "Let her in."

I glanced back at Jed, giving him a warning look before I stepped inside.

Beasley was sitting on the sofa with a beer can in his hand, watching a game show on the TV. He looked a lot like he did the last time I saw him, only he was wearing jeans and a Harley-Davidson T-shirt instead of prison orange. His dishwater-blond hair had grown out enough to graze his ears, and he was trying to grow a mustache over his lip. He stood when we entered the room—rising to his full 5'8" stature—and he looked nervous when he noticed Jed.

"Neely Kate," he said, his gazed shifting back and forth between us. "I'm surprised to see you."

"I was back in town and thought maybe we could chat."

His aunt stood in the doorway of the living room and kitchen, watching me with interest. "You used to be Branson's girlfriend."

Hearing people call me that was like fingernails on a chalkboard, but this wasn't the time or place to make a fuss. "That's right."

"I ain't seen hide nor hair of that boy since Beasley crashed Branson's car in his drunken stupor. You heard from him?"

"No, ma'am."

She shook her head and tsked. "Must have gotten up to no good."

I figured it would be best if I didn't say anything.

Beasley gestured toward the back of the house with his thumb. "Why don't we go into the backyard and talk?"

"Good idea," I said, following him past his aunt. We walked through a kitchen straight out of the 1950s and into a backyard that looked like a garden park. Beasley was already halfway across the yard to a small fire pit area.

Jed was practically on my heels as I followed. I sat in a chair directly across from Beasley, and Jed sat beside me.

Beasley nervously eyed Jed, but I was staring right back. Now that I had a better look at him, I realized Beasley *did* look different. Harder. More confident. After all the berating he'd tolerated from his brother, that was a good thing, so why did it make me nervous?

"Who's your friend, Neely Kate?"

"This is my boyfriend, Jed."

"Boyfriend. You always did go for the mean ones."

I supposed I could see why he'd think that about Jed, who was looking downright intimidating. I wondered if there was any truth to what Beasley said about the men in my past, but Ronnie wasn't mean. In fact, he reminded me a lot of Beasley . . . a little quiet, shy, and hated violence. Or so he'd said. Maybe that had something to do with why I'd picked Ronnie. Maybe I'd been trying to choose Beasley the second time around.

He turned to look at Jed. "Are you here to beat me up?"

None of Beasley's usual fear was present, and that set me on edge. Maybe I wasn't as safe with him as I had once thought.

"That's Neely Kate's call," Jed said in a no-nonsense tone.

"No," I said. "No one's beating anyone up."

Beasley didn't seem convinced, and the expression on Jed's face didn't look any friendlier. Maybe bringing Jed was a mistake. Only, something still felt . . . *off* about Beasley.

"You got out," I said, stating the obvious.

"Yep," he said, finishing off his beer. He crushed the can with his hand and tossed it to the ground. *That* wasn't a Beasley move. He'd definitely changed, but what had I expected? He'd been in prison nearly five years. Because of me.

"How long have you been out?"

"A few months." He leaned back in his chair, trying to look nonchalant, but the beads of perspiration lining his top lip and his forehead gave him away. Granted, it was hot, but that didn't explain why his hands were shaking on the metal arms of his chair.

"You stopped taking my calls," I said. "Why?"

"What good did they do?" he asked. "It wasn't like you were gonna pick me when I got out."

"We could still be friends. What you did for me . . . That made us friends."

"He said you'd try to play it like that."

My blood ran cold. "Who said that?"

He ignored me and stood. "I need another beer." Then he headed toward the house.

"Neely Kate," Jed grunted in a low tone. "Are you in danger?"

Confused, I watched Beasley disappear inside the back door. This was not the scared, bullied man who had watched his brother abuse me for months before finally stepping up to help me escape. This man was still scared, but he'd turned defiant and belligerent. I was pretty dang sure if faced with the same choice, he would have made

194

a different one now. And I was pretty sure he had a major case of buyer's remorse.

"I don't know," I answered honestly.

"I think we should go. Now."

But Beasley was already out the back door with two cans of beer in his hands. As he approached, he tossed one to Jed, who reached out and caught it without any effort. A look of mock appreciation filled Beasley's eyes as he sat down and popped the top of his drink. He looked at me with a sneer. "I would have gotten you one, Neely Kate, but I remembered how much you hate to drink."

I gasped at his obvious reference to Branson's parties.

"When did Branson start visiting you in prison?" I asked. It was a leap, but not a hard one to make. Beasley had always been desperate for his brother's approval, and he seemed like a mini-Branson in the making. It stood to reason that Branson had started poisoning his brother against me.

"A couple of years ago. You hadn't been calling as often, and I was lonely for visitors. I was pretty surprised to see him sitting at that table, but he said he hadn't forgotten about me. He just had to stay low so you couldn't have him arrested."

"I wasn't planning on having him arrested. All I cared about was breaking free, Beasley. You knew that."

"He said you'd say that."

My mouth went dry. "When did he say that?"

"Last time I saw him. Last November. He said someone was poking around into the past, and he was pretty sure you'd hired some woman to start covering your tracks. He told me that we Desoto boys had to stick together or else I'd end up doing more years. Only for murder this time."

I shook my head, fear coursing through my blood. "No, Beasley. I want the past buried. I want no part of it. That wasn't me."

"She claimed to be related to you. She visited me in prison, asking all kinds of questions about when you'd lived in Ardmore as a kid, but she was also interested in the more current stuff. Including how I ended up in prison."

"Did you tell her?" I asked, feeling lightheaded.

He watched me for several seconds; then a cruel look spread across his face. "I always wondered why Branson liked it so much."

Oh, God. "What?"

"Controlling you. Making you do things you claimed you hated."

"*Claimed?*"

He took a sip of his beer and turned a watchful eye on Jed. Satisfied Jed wasn't about to jump him, he gave me a leer. "Branson said you liked it that way. That you liked to be dominated. He told me that you'd tricked me into helping you."

I slowly shook my head, words escaping me.

Jed's hands gripped the sides of his chair.

I needed to get myself together, get my answers and then leave. "Did you tell Branson what we did?"

"You mean what *you* did?" he asked bitterly. "What you dragged me into."

"I never asked for your help," I said, my voice sounding far away. "I never asked you to take the blame."

"You didn't have to. Branson said you were like a siren, making men do what they didn't want to do. He says he didn't want to keep you like that, but you were sick and perverted and made him do it."

I shook my head. "You saw me, Beasley. How many times did you see me crying? You kept telling me you were sorry for not helping me escape."

"He said it was an act."

"Then I must be a really great actress," I said in disgust. Beasley had always been weak and easily manipulated by his brother, but this took the cake.

"Stella agreed with him."

I froze. "When did you speak to Stella?"

I'd gone to see Beasley once after he'd been convicted; then I'd called and written him multiple times until a little over a year ago, and he'd never once mentioned Stella. But maybe that explained why he'd suddenly changed.

"She came to see me. She told me that Branson wanted to come home, but he was scared I'd turn against him. She told me that I'd gotten everything all wrong, that you'd manipulated me."

"And you *believed* her?" He had always hated Stella. She'd treated him like shit, and because of his low self-confidence, he'd just taken it. It had provoked her to treat him even worse.

"He came to see me after that and told me that Stella was havin' his baby and they wanted to be together, but you were stoppin' them."

Crystal was Branson's daughter? I swallowed the bile rising in my throat. "I was livin' my life in Arkansas, trying to forget about the both of them."

"Like you were forgetting about me." His mouth twisted into an ugly sneer. "You never uttered one word about your *fiancé*."

"No . . ." Maybe. I'd met Ronnie by then, and transferred all those feelings of gratitude and obligation to him. Only, I hadn't realized it.

"Branson said I had to make sure he was protected."

And that meant giving him evidence to keep me in line. The edges of my vision began to black out, but I refused to lose consciousness. I was facing this head-on. I already knew the answer, but I had to ask anyway. I needed confirmation. "What did you do, Beasley?"

He gave me a defiant look. "I told him about the azaleas."

Chapter Twenty

"Neely Kate, are you finished?" Jed asked in a voice so cold it scared me.

Was I done? I was so shocked I wasn't even sure what to ask. "Yeah."

Jed was out of his seat in a flash. He grabbed a fistful of Beasley's shirt with his left hand and jerked him out of his chair and to his feet. "You thought you were safe, huh? That Neely Kate had me on a leash? Or are you just plain *stupid?*" He gave Beasley a shake. "I'm going with stupid, because that's the only explanation I can come up with to justify all the shit I heard pour out of your mouth."

Beasley grabbed Jed's hand and tried to break his hold. "Leave me alone."

"You stupid asshole, I haven't even *begun.*"

Pure terror washed over Beasley's face.

"Where's your piece of shit brother?"

"I don't know."

Jed punched him in the face. Beasley's knees buckled, but Jed's hold on his shirt kept him upright. "Let's try that again. Where's your brother?"

"I don't know!"

Jed gave him another punch, and Beasley sagged even more. Jed released his hold, and Beasley dropped to the ground in a heap.

"Let me make this perfectly clear, Beasley," Jed said in a cool, matter-of-fact voice. "I *will* find out where your brother is, so this can go as easy or as hard as you like. It's entirely up to you."

"He'll kill me if I tell you."

"I'll kill you if you don't, so I guess it's a matter of which one of us you would prefer to end your life."

Beasley started to cry.

"That's right," Jed growled. "Cry, but we both know it's an act. You really like it. You were just beggin' for this. You're using me to get what you want. Is this the point where I let someone screw you?"

I could only watch in horror. I knew I should stop Jed. I needed to stop him, but watching him turn the tables on Beasley was empowering, even if it was wrong.

Beasley continued to sob. "Don't hurt me."

"How many times did you hear Neely Kate cry, *begging* for help, but you ignored her?"

"I'm sorry," he said, glancing up at me. "I'm sorry."

"Too fucking little, too late," Jed grunted right before he kicked Beasley in the stomach.

Beasley grunted and curled into a ball.

I felt like I was going to be sick.

"Where's your brother?" When there was no response, Jed kicked him again.

Beasley cried out in pain, then said, "Kansas City! He's in Kansas City."

Jed took a step back. "What's he doin' there?"

"He has a job. He's an electrician now."

"Then why is Stella still livin' here with the baby he was so desperate to be with?" Jed asked.

Beasley sat up and hunched over, protecting his stomach. "I don't know. He said the timing wasn't right."

"And you believed him? You have *got* to be the most gullible piece of shit ever born."

Beasley glanced up at me, and I saw the defeat on his face, the same look he always used to get when Branson lit into him.

"Jed. Let's go."

He turned to look at me, and there was something feral in his eyes. "Go wait for me in the car."

"No. We're walkin' away from here together."

"Go wait for me in the car."

I marched closer and pointed my finger at him. "Let's get one thing perfectly straight: No one tells me what to do. Not anymore. We are walking away right now."

He was so pissed a vein on his forehead began to throb.

Beasley tried to reach over and lunge for me, but I kicked my heel into his face with enough force to send him flying onto his back. He stared up at me with a look of surprise—which quickly transformed into anger—but I put my foot on his throat with enough weight on it to cut off part of his airway.

"You even think of knocking me over, and I'll crush your windpipe before I hit the ground," I said in a calculated voice.

He lowered his hands.

"You know I've killed someone else in a very similar way," I said, watching the anger and terror on his face. "Don't think I won't do it again."

He blinked.

"Jed was wrong. You're not stupid. You know I wanted no part of any of it. What you are is *deluded*. Not that you believe I begged to live like that, but that you believe your sorry excuse for a brother cares one iota about you. But that's on *you*, Beasley. *You* can believe whatever you want. But now you've put my life and safety in danger, and I don't like it one bit." I pressed a little harder. "When I lift my foot, I'm going to need more information about how to find Branson. And if you don't give it to me, I'll find creative ways to get it out of you."

I stepped back as Beasley rolled to the side and began to cough.

"*Now*, Beasley," I said, knowing full well that he couldn't answer, but I was high on the rush of power from dealing with someone who had hurt me, even if he'd helped me in the end.

"Overland Park," he said in a hoarse voice. "But I don't have an address, and I don't know who he works for."

I glanced up at Jed. "Is that enough?"

He stared at me in pride and disbelief. "It will do."

I nodded. "Then we're almost done." I walked over and kicked Beasley between his parted legs. "*That's* for looking up my dress a few moments ago. Pervert." Then I turned and stomped toward the driveway.

Jed followed me. We were silent until we got into the car and he pulled away.

"God," I said. "That felt good." Then I turned to face him. "Don't you ever suggest I can't handle something again."

A sly grin twisted his mouth. "Wouldn't dream of it."

"I'm done being that cowardly girl."

"You were never cowardly, Neely Kate."

"I was. I could have—"

"You can second-guess every decision and every action you made from here to kingdom come, and it won't change a blessed thing. You are a strong, capable woman, Neely Kate Rivers, and God help any man or woman who tells you different. But I'm here as your backup, just in case you need someone cheering you on."

I smiled at him.

"Now where to?"

I glanced at the clock on the dashboard. "I'm starving. Let's eat."

His eyes lit up. "You worked up an appetite."

I shrugged, my mind whirling. "We still have a few hours before we can go to the club to see Carla, so now's as good a time as any. But I need to buy a shovel before we meet Carla."

"Time to face the azaleas?" he asked.

"Yeah, but not until after we talk to her. We'll need to wait until really late so no one sees us."

He nodded.

We stopped at a diner and ate, our conversation steering clear of what was going on in Ardmore.

"Can you get away from the landscaping office for a week?" Jed asked. "Can Rose spare you?"

I pushed out a breath. "She'll say that she can, but I'm not sure. Her sister's coming home next week, and I know she'll be dealin' with that along with everything else."

"Maybe she can get that new vet to help her."

My eyes widened.

"Skeeter knows she's been on two dates with him over the last two weeks."

"He's spyin' on her?"

"Makin' sure she's safe."

"And spyin' on her."

He was silent for a moment. "Skeeter's complicated. He has strong feelings for her, but he doesn't know how to handle them."

"Kind of like he doesn't know how to handle you."

He hesitated. "Yeah. I guess so."

"He's wastin' his time with Rose," I said. "I think she likes the dangerous side of him, but she'd never have a boyfriend who's on the other side of the law."

"And what about you?"

I gave him a saucy grin. "Skeeter never did anything for me."

He grinned back, but something was missing in his eyes. "Good to hear I'm not playin' second fiddle with *you.*"

"Is that how you feel?" I asked.

He didn't answer; instead, he asked, "What about being with a man on the other side of the law?"

"I'm not gonna lie. I would prefer to be with a man who's not, but I guess it depends on what he's up to." I looked into his eyes. "What do you think you want to do when you go back?"

"I'm not sure I can go back."

"What? Why?"

"Skeeter will ask me to come back, and if I tell him no, he'll see my rejection as a challenge. But more importantly, my leaving will make him look weak, and he can't afford to look weak now."

I started to panic. "You're not goin' home?"

He reached over and cupped my face. "I don't know what I'm doin' yet. I know you need to stay in Henryetta. I won't make you choose, Neely Kate. I would never make you choose."

Tears blurred my eyes. "I don't want to lose you."

"You won't," he said, but he didn't look convinced. "I'm not leaving you. Maybe we can figure it out while we're feeding chipmunks in Colorado, although our relationship might be short-lived if one of us gets bitten and dies from rabies."

I laughed away the tears. "We're not gonna get rabies."

"How do you know?" he asked. "Do they set up little cages so they can catch them and give them rabies shots?"

"I don't know, but my cousins would know how to catch them."

He had a mischievous look about him. "And eat them." When he saw my shocked expression, he added, "Your cousins have a reputation."

"You're terrible!"

He shrugged. "But it's true."

He wasn't wrong.

We stayed at the restaurant for over an hour, and I reveled in this time with Jed, filling up on his goodness, because I knew I'd need everything within me to get through the rest of the night.

Chapter Twenty One

We pulled into Slick Willy's parking lot at ten. There were several more cars tonight, but nowhere near as many as there'd be on the weekend. I couldn't help thinking it would be better to wait until tomorrow night, when we could get lost in the Friday night crowd, but who was I kidding? Jed drew attention from the guys due to his size and attention from the women for both his size *and* good looks. Besides, the years hadn't changed me nearly as much as they'd changed Stella. I looked pretty much the same, only I had a little more weight on me and probably looked less dead in the eyes. We'd draw attention no matter when we showed up. Besides, the sooner I did this, the sooner I could leave my past where it belonged and, hopefully, move on with my life.

Jed seemed nervous, and I couldn't say I blamed him after my behavior the night before.

"Jed . . . about my freak-out last night." Lordy, that seemed at least a week ago. "I know I already said it, but I'm sorry."

He snagged my hand. "Don't apologize. You're working through a mountain of shit. My job is to be here every step of the way and support you."

I turned to stare into his face. Several days ago, I would have taken his statement to mean he was following Skeeter's orders. Now I knew he was doing it because he cared about me, although I still didn't understand why. But he'd been helping me for months, and I was finally starting to understand how deep this went for him.

He started to let go and open his car door, but I tugged him back.

"Wait." I scrambled to figure out how to bring this up. "When I asked Skeeter to help me look for Ronnie a few months ago, you told me you were there for me. You said you wanted to help me for me, not because of Rose. Was that when you first started having feelings for me?"

He gave me a hesitant look. "No."

"When?"

He grimaced, clearly uncomfortable. I knew I should let it drop, but now that I'd had the nerve to bring it up, I wanted an answer.

"Honestly," he said, "it snuck up on me, but it probably started last winter, when Rose arranged to meet Mick Gentry without Skeeter. You insisted on coming as backup. I figured you'd be a waste of time—and worse, a liability—but you more than proved yourself."

"Really? I had no idea," I said in surprise. "You only seemed annoyed."

"I was annoyed, but more at myself than you. You didn't know, and I wanted to keep it that way. You were still married. But when you showed up to Skeeter's office a few months ago, asking him to help you search for the fool, I couldn't stand seeing you so upset. So I overstepped my bounds." A sly grin spread across his face. "But I'm not sorry I did. I was sure that was why you called me a couple of nights later."

I hung my head in embarrassment. Rose had gone to Houston to donate her bone marrow for her sister's transplant. I was pissed at the world and lonely without her, so I'd gone to a bar outside of town with the sole purpose of hooking up with a man. Finding someone was easy, but I changed my mind pretty much as soon as we got to his apartment. Things went south right quick, and I locked myself in the bathroom and called Jed.

"There's one thing I don't understand," he said. "The guy from the bar . . . why didn't you just beat the crap out of him?" He held up his hands in surrender. "Don't get me wrong, I thoroughly enjoyed beating the shit out of him myself, but you've proven multiple times that you can take down a man . . ." His voice trailed off.

"So why didn't I?" I finished.

"No judgment, Neely Kate. I need to make that perfectly clear."

I nodded. It was a fair question. "When I came back home to my granny five years ago, I was a hot mess. I huddled in my room for days, crying off and on and refusing to leave the house. But then a week later, my cousin Witt busted in and told me Rivers kids didn't mope and he and my cousin Alan Jackson were going to teach me how to shoot a gun. They gave me my grandfather's six-shooter, and it turned out I was pretty good at it." I looked up at Jed and saw his grin.

"I'll say." He'd seen me shoot targets a couple of weeks ago after Skeeter told him to take Rose for target practice.

"Now, I hadn't said a word about what had happened to me, but somehow Witt seemed to know what I needed. He never asked questions, and I never offered answers, but after I learned to shoot better than him and Alan Jackson, he suggested I learn some self-defense moves next."

"So Merv has Witt to thank for his busted nose."

I lifted my shoulder into a shrug and grinned. "Rivers kids are scrappy. After I ended up breaking a few of their bones, they ended the self-defense lessons."

"So what happened with that guy from the bar this spring?"

"I thought I'd built this perfect life with Ronnie, the one I'd always wanted—a husband, a house, babies . . . only, being married to Ronnie wasn't what I wanted after all and I was just plain stuck. He was a good man—or at least I used to think so—and I'd pretty much roped him into the whole thing, so it wasn't like I could say, 'Oops, I changed my mind.' Besides, by then I knew I was pregnant. And then I lost the babies. And Ronnie took off, not that I necessarily wanted him to stay, but it was just another rejection. My body rejected my babies, and then Ronnie ran off after he found out my body had been full of STDs . . . even though the doctor assured him that they'd all been cured. *After* they'd destroyed me. But the clincher was Joe. When I found out he was my half brother and then he left town first chance he got without one word . . . it was all too much. I felt like that girl again, that stupid girl who'd fallen for Branson's lies, hook, line, and sinker." I hung my head in shame. "I felt so rejected, so worthless, I just needed a man to think I was pretty."

"I wish I'd realized that," Jed said quietly. "I would have made more of an effort."

I shook my head. "No. The thought of you being interested in me scared the bejiggers out of me. I wasn't ready. But I wasn't ready to hook up with some random stranger either. Once he got me back to his apartment, everything with Branson came rushing back, and I suddenly lost every bit of self-confidence I'd gained over the past five years. I became that scared, stupid girl again, not the strong, kick-ass woman I'd worked hard to become."

I looked into his eyes. "I was scared and humiliated, so I called the person I thought would help me without judgment. You'd made your offer a couple of days before, and I knew you'd gotten Rose out of some tough situations. Calling you was the right thing to do, but I was still embarrassed." I paused. "And then you insisted on sleeping on my sofa to make sure I was okay." I squeezed his hand. "You have no idea how much that meant to me. When I woke up, I was so angry. I was angry *at myself* for getting into that situation and not fighting back. I was pissed at that guy for thinking he had a right to sex just because he'd bought me a few drinks. And I was mad at you for being so perfect because I knew you deserved someone less broken and used-up than me."

"Neely Kate."

"So I lashed out at you. Again and again. Even as I was doin' it, I knew it wasn't the right thing. It made me feel worse. Not only had I reverted back to that stupid girl, but I'd been ugly to the one man who was willin' to help me for no ulterior motive." I looked up at him. "I'm sorry for that too."

He shook his head, giving me a sad smile. "Have you ever thought that the reason we might work together is because we're both screwed up?"

I laughed. "You like me because I'm a mess?"

He grinned. "I wouldn't put it that way . . . but we just seem to fit, don't you think?"

"Yeah," I said softly. "We do."

He turned to study the outside of the strip club for nearly half a minute before he asked, "Do you think Branson was the man who showed up at Zelda's looking for you?"

"No. Zelda has seen Branson plenty of times. She would remember him."

"So we know some mysterious man is looking for you, and we know that Stella and Branson have been working together to turn Beasley against you. The question is why. Do you know?"

"I don't know for certain, but I will after I talk to Carla."

"But it's a fair assumption that you could be in danger. Agreed?"

I hesitated.

"Let me rephrase that," he said in a no-nonsense tone. "I know you're in danger. I'm making sure you're on the same page."

"I guess."

"And while we both know you can handle yourself and take on any asshole who comes at you, we also both know I've had far more experience dealing with situations like this. Also agreed?"

"I guess," I reluctantly conceded.

His mouth tipped into a hint of a grin, a fleeting expression that quickly faded. "Then I'm asking you to let me take the lead on this tonight. You can be in charge of talking to Carla or whoever you want, but let me be in charge of making sure you're safe." He squeezed my hand. "Please."

He was right. He was more experienced with this kind of thing, but he'd proven he knew when to hang back. Before stepping in with Beasley, he'd let me question him—even though he must have been itching something fierce to take control. "Okay."

Relief filled his eyes. "Thank you."

I took a deep breath. "Let's get this over with."

We got out and walked across the parking lot, Jed's possessive arm around my lower back. He paid the cover charge this time and headed straight toward an empty table in the back corner. Again, I caught some attention, but Jed held on tight, making sure every pair of eyes that landed on me knew they'd face his wrath if they dared to hit on me.

He held out a chair for me, and while he was being his gentlemanly self, I also knew he was placing me exactly where he wanted me—in the deepest shadows while he was more in the light.

There was a dancer on the stage and two girls working the crowd, but I didn't recognize any of them.

Jed rested his forearm on the sticky table and turned his attention to the stage, but I knew he wasn't watching the dancer swing around the pole. He had chosen this table purposefully—it gave him a perfect vantage point to assess the room around us. He could see a threat as soon as it walked in the door. He could see anyone who approached us. He could see who was on stage, who was behind the bar, and every hostess working the room.

I took note of this for my own future reference. My own surveillance skills needed some brushing up.

A few minutes later, one of the *hostesses* walked over to our table, wearing nothing but pasties and a G-string along with four-inch stilettos. She stopped in front of our table and popped her hip out to the side. "Hi, I'm Destiny, and I'm your hostess for the evening. What can I do for you two? Drinks? A private room?" She gave Jed a sultry look. "I can do girl on girl if that's your thing."

My face burned, but the shadows hid my embarrassment. I couldn't help but remember what it felt like to work here, to say tawdry things to complete strangers. Was Jed imagining me in this hostess's place?

He slid his hand off the table and picked mine up and held it on top of the table. "I'll take a beer. Whatever's on special." He turned to me. "Honey?"

I nearly startled at his term of endearment, but then I realized my name was much too uncommon to go unnoticed. "A bottle of water."

Destiny grabbed a strand of her hair and began to play with it. "What else, sugar? You can get a beer down the street."

"Do you know if Carla's here?" he asked.

She frowned. "She'll be here in another half hour. But I'll be more than happy to take care of you."

"That's enough for now," Jed said.

She walked off, looking disappointed, and I understood how she felt. I'd dealt with plenty of older, unattractive guys while working here, so I knew how much she must appreciate having a good-looking man in her section. But she must still be fairly new because the good-looking ones were often the worst.

I tried to pull my hand free, but Jed held on.

"We could leave and come back, but I think it would look suspicious. It would probably be better to sit here and wait. Are you okay with that?"

I knew he didn't like being in this dump any more than I did. "Whatever you think is best."

A huge grin spread across his face. "I'm goin' to remember this moment because I have a feeling it will be one of the only times I'll hear those words coming from your lips."

I laughed because he was right, and we both knew it.

Destiny brought our drinks, and Jed handed her a hundred-dollar bill and told her to start a tab. When she left, he picked up my water and examined it before unscrewing the cap and handing it to me.

So he knew why I'd ordered bottled water, not that I was surprised.

We sat there for a half hour. Jed ordered another beer, but he nursed the second, taking everything in.

Finally, I leaned over and whispered in his ear, "What are you looking for?"

"Patterns."

"What kind of patterns?"

"How the waitresses work the room. Who's asking for drinks, how many and what kind. Who's asking for lap dances. Who's leaving the room—where are they going; how long are they gone; who are they with? Which of the girls get the most attention, and how do the other girls deal with it."

I leaned back and stared at him in surprise. "Why? We're just here to talk to Carla."

"What if you talk to Carla and things go sideways? I'll know the expected behaviors of the people in the room. Besides, I don't know exactly what I'm dealing with here, so I want to know as much as I can."

That was my fault. I should have told him the rest. "The threat's not in this room, Jed."

"I'll be the judge of that."

I hesitated, then asked, "Will you teach me?"

He gave me a questioning look. "Teach you what?"

"How you take note of things like that. I'm trying to convince Rose that we're good at snoopin' things out, and we should become investigators."

"Like you did with the necklace."

"And lookin' for my missing cousin."

"And the money stolen from Rose in that bank robbery last fall," he said, turning more sober.

That was how Rose had first gotten tangled up with Skeeter. "Yeah."

He studied my face. "You really want to be a PI? For a job?"

"Yeah."

"NK, I'll help you with anything you need."

"*Really?*"

"Why wouldn't I? I've seen you and Rose investigate things in the past, and then you today . . . you've done really well in spite of all the emotional crap you've been through. I think you'd be great at it."

I nearly burst with happiness, barely believing what I'd just heard. I always had to convince Rose to investigate cases. Jed was the first person to believe I could actually do it for real.

Another half hour passed, and Jed asked Destiny about Carla again. She told him that she was running late but she was coming.

When she left, he turned to me, his face expressionless. I'd come to realize this was his game face. He expected trouble. "I don't see any sign of Stan. Do you know anyone else who's working tonight? Anyone who might recognize you?"

"No."

"And was this common for Carla? Did she often run late?"

"I only worked with her for a few weeks, Jed. She was new, so she was on her best behavior."

"How important is it for you to talk to her?"

"I think she might know what happened with Branson after . . . I left."

"Why?"

"Because he had started showin' an interest in her, and she was holding him at bay, especially since she knew I was in such dire straits with him. Not to mention she was letting me use her car and he found out." But mostly I needed to know what she knew about my meeting that night. As far as I knew, only Branson and Beasley knew the identity of the man who'd wanted to buy me. Stella had known a few details—I'd told her about the waiver and my suspicions about kinky torture—but no specifics. Branson could have told her later, of course, but I suspected he'd kept quiet. It was common knowledge she couldn't keep a secret . . . although she'd done a good job of keeping the fact that Branson was alive and well from me—and not dead and buried by an oil well.

Branson had brought me to the house that awful night, and Beasley was the one who'd set up the logistics. They were the only two who could link me to that man by name and location, and I needed to make sure it had stayed that way.

The dancer left the stage—one of the women who'd been hostessing when we first walked in—and the bartender announced Carla.

She slunk out, looking just like I remembered her, which made me unbelievably sad. I'd escaped this life, but she was still stuck in the thick of it. I was relieved she still had the same quiet dignity to her. Looking back now, I understood why Stella had practically hated her on sight.

Carla was wearing a few scarves and began her slow striptease. She was gorgeous and knew how to work the crowd. The belly dancing was a new act for her—well, new since I'd last seen her—but she could move her hips in ways I'd never even dreamed of. She had the full attention of the room, every eye on her, with the exception of Jed, who was watching me with concern.

"You okay?" he asked.

I nodded.

Carla danced for the next ten minutes, making more money than the other dancers before her. Destiny came around again at the end of the show. "Are you sure you don't want me, sugar? Carla charges a lot more. Or . . ." I could tell she was thinking fast. "You can have both of us together. How's that? We can find something else for your girlfriend to do while Carla and I take care of you in the back."

He pointed a finger toward the stage. "I want to see her. Just her. Out here."

Destiny made an exaggerated pouty face.

Jed slid her a twenty-dollar bill. "For your trouble. Tell her I'll make it worth her while."

That appeased her. She took the money and suggestively tucked it down the front of her low-cut G-string before moving on to the next table.

I leaned closer to Jed. "You want to question her here?"

He leaned closer so that his mouth was next to my ear. "Do they have private rooms?"

"Yeah."

He turned back to watch the people around us. "When she comes by, we'll see if she's agreeable to going to a private room to chat. You're sure no one's recognized you?"

"I don't see anyone else I know, customers included."

About five minutes later, Carla emerged from the door to the backstage, her gaze immediately landing on our corner table.

Jed's expression and posture didn't change, but he cast a glance at her as she approached. Then his eyes panned across the rest of the room—it was subtle, but I'd watched him do it all night.

She glanced over her shoulder before turning toward Jed. "I hear you were askin' for me. What can I do for you?" Her gaze traveled over his body, and I was surprised at the spark of jealousy burning through my veins. The feeling had caught me off guard, but I could still tell she was acting strangely.

Her gaze drifted to me. She looked afraid but not surprised. "Kitty."

"Hey, Carla."

"You need to leave."

Jed tensed. "Why?"

She moved closer to the table, leaning forward so that her boobs were right in front of me. While it might look like a seduction technique to anyone watching us, it was obvious she was trying to cover for what she was about to say. "He's lookin' for you, Kitty."

"Who?" I asked, afraid to hear the answer. Knowing it anyway.

"Branson."

Chapter Twenty Two

My blood ran cold.

Jed was on full alert. "When?"

Carla's eyes were filled with panic, but she moved closer, thrust out her hip, and said, "Give me twenty dollars."

I expected Jed to argue, but he reached into his pocket and slid a bill across the table. Carla began to gyrate her hips.

Jed sat back in his chair, watching her face. "You weren't late getting here, were you, Carla?"

"No," she said as she moved between his legs. "Destiny was told to try to keep you here. Stan kept me in his office until Branson showed up."

"They're both here?" Jed asked.

Her face moved to the side of his head, but her answer was loud enough for both of us to hear. "Yes."

Branson was here now. We were in the same building.

I was speechless, but Jed didn't react in any obvious way. He just sat still in his chair as she air-humped his leg. "Where are they now?"

"In the back." Her voice broke. "Branson wants me to keep you busy in a private room so he can come out and talk to Kitty."

All of my insecurities rushed back—my terror and my helplessness—but then fury rose up and burned those other emotions to ashes. I was done letting Branson scare me. I needed to stand up to him, and what better time than with Jed with me?

"I have a plan," she said, putting her hands on his shoulders and bending over to give him an up close and personal view of her barely covered breasts. "I'll go back there to set up the private room, and you take Kitty and get the hell out of here."

"How do we know you're not double-crossing Neel—Kitty now?" Considering a beautiful woman was flashing her nearly naked boobs in his face, Jed was doing a remarkable job of staying on task.

"Because I tried to help her escape before, and I'm doin' it again. Listen to me." She leaned across the table and grabbed my face with one hand, playing it off as another flirty gesture. "You need to leave. *Now.* If Jed isn't back there soon after this song ends, Branson will come out here lookin' for you, Kitty. He looks desperate, which means he's dangerous." She dropped her hold on me and began to swivel her hips for Jed again.

The music stopped, and a thrill of fear shot through me. Our limited time had been cut even shorter.

"Will he hurt you if we leave?" I asked, already feeling guilty about how Branson would react. I knew about his vicious temper firsthand.

"Branson Desoto can't hurt me," she said. "I have a few tricks up my sleeve." She popped up to standing, taking the money with a seductive sweep of her hand. "Run, Kitty. Run far away from here and never look back." Then she turned to Jed. "If you care anything about her, then get her out of here. Go. I'll keep them busy in the back."

"Come with us," I pleaded. I didn't look at Jed before making my request, but something told me that he wouldn't have a problem with it.

She shook her head. "Thanks, Kitty, but my life is here. Plus, I have me a good man now. He'll kick Branson's ass as soon as he finds out Branson messed with me. And that's something I'm dying to see."

She turned on her heels and started to leave, but I grabbed her arm, then handed her a piece of paper I'd put in my pocket in case I saw her. "Carla. If you change your mind, we're staying in the Motel 6. Call my number on the back."

She nodded, then jerked free and walked away.

"You shouldn't have given her that," Jed said as he grabbed my wrist and tugged me out of my seat.

"I had to. I owe her."

He started to drag me toward the front door.

"What are you doin'?" I asked, trying to break free. "This is our chance. We need to confront him."

"No. If Carla's right and this is a setup, then we need to get as far away from here as possible." Without so much as a backward glance, he pulled me into the entrance foyer and pushed me against the wall next to the bouncer. He squatted down and pulled a gun out of a holster strapped to his calf under his jeans. The bouncer's eyes widened, and he slunk back in fear.

Slick Willy's wasn't exactly the kind of place most people were willing to take a bullet for.

"We don't want trouble," Jed said as he stood, although his body language was broadcasting the exact opposite. "We just want to leave."

The bouncer raised his hands in surrender. "I've got no beef with you."

Jed nodded distractedly as he glanced out the door. Then he pulled me out with him and guided me toward the car.

"Jed."

"Don't fight me on this, Neely Kate."

Part of me wanted to try to get him to confront Branson, but I'd promised him I'd go along with his decisions at the club.

He put me into the passenger side and then circled around to the driver's seat. Seconds later, he was pulling out of the parking lot, darting glances at the rearview mirror to make sure we weren't being tailed.

"How did Branson know we'd be here?" I asked.

"Stan. He must have told Stan to call him if you ever showed up. Money talks. Plus, Stella and Beasley could have alerted him that you were asking questions." He checked his rearview mirror again. "You have something Branson wants. What is it?"

"I don't know."

"*Neely Kate.* This isn't the time to keep secrets from me. What does Branson want?"

The blood rushed from my head. "I don't know. Maybe he wants the video."

"What video?"

"The video of me committing murder."

Jed's face went blank. "Why would Branson want that?"

"I don't know. Payback?"

He dug his vibrating phone out of his pocket and then stuck it back in. "Who did you kill, Neely Kate?"

My mouth went dry.

"Was it the man who wanted you to sign the paper?"

I hesitated, but I couldn't keep it from him. He needed to know. "Yes."

"But you killed him in self-defense." When I didn't say anything, he cast me a questioning look. "It had to be self-defense."

I'd relived that night over and over in my head, trying to justify what I'd done, but no amount of self-reflection could change the facts. I hadn't *needed* to murder the man. There had been other options available to me. "I don't think it was."

"I need to know what happened. Who did you kill? What was his name?"

"I don't know," I said, starting to shake. "He never told me his name and neither did Branson. They said he was from Dallas."

"What's on the video, Neely Kate? Everything?"

"You mean what he did to me? Yeah."

"Where's the video now?"

"Buried under the azaleas. With his body. I didn't intend to bury it, but I wasn't thinkin' straight after . . . everything. I didn't realize the video was still in the camera until after we finished."

"Beasley helped you bury the body," he said.

My mouth dropped open. "How did you know?"

"You said he was in jail because of you. I knew he had to have helped you somehow, and I sure as hell haven't heard what he did to help you in any other way." He paused. "How do you know he hasn't told his brother where you buried him?"

"Because he doesn't remember."

"How is that possible?"

"He was drunk as a skunk."

"If only Beasley and Branson know the guy's name," he said, reasoning through it out loud, "and no one but you knows how to find the body, then Beasley couldn't have been arrested for anything to do with the murder." He shook his head. "Beasley went to prison for driving under the influence," he muttered to himself, then sucked in a deep breath. "Neely Kate, I need to know what's going on."

He was right. It was time to confess. "Beasley knew about the other guys, but he could tell something was off about this one. He couldn't handle the guilt because he was sure the guy was going to hurt me bad or kill me. An hour after the appointment was supposed to start, he showed up in Branson's car. I had just . . . the man was already dead. I wanted to call the police, but Beasley convinced me to help him load the body in the back of Branson's car. He was pretty wasted, so I got behind the wheel, and he climbed into the passenger seat and passed out. I didn't know what to do. I thought about calling the police anyway, but not only had I killed the man, but I'd moved the body too. I was scared, so I found a couple of shovels in the garage of the house and took off driving."

"Where was the guy's car?"

"I don't know. The only car there was Branson's."

"What about when Branson took you there? Was there another car?"

"No, and the guy was already there."

Jed turned to me. "How'd he get there?"

"I don't know," I said, getting agitated.

"It's okay, we'll figure that out later." His voice was calm and soothing. "Where'd you go after you got the shovels?"

"The house was in the country, and I headed away from town. I pulled off onto a deserted-looking country road and woke up Beasley. We went several feet into the trees, behind a clump of wild azaleas, and dug a hole."

"Can *you* find where you buried him?"

I swallowed, nauseated from the memories. "Yeah."

He was silent for a moment. "How far away from the house did you bury him?"

"I don't know. Maybe a couple of miles."

"And how obvious are the azalea bushes? They're not blooming now. It would be harder to find them."

"I know where they are."

"But could Beasley find them? He was in prison before, but what if Branson's making him look now? Could they stumble upon it? Was there any other landmark Beasley would recognize?"

"There was a light pole about ten feet away. Somebody had nailed in a bunch of silver nails to make it look like a cross."

"Can you see it from the main road?"

"No."

"But if they started driving around, they could find it?"

"Yeah. If that cross is still there. And if Beasley remembers it. He mentioned it while we were digging, telling me that God was watching and judging him for letting his brother get away with everything he did."

Jed was silent for a moment. "Let's assume he remembers the cross, which means, given time, he'll find it and dig up the body. What's he going to find?"

"The body and a video camera."

"Clothes? Was the man dressed?"

I cringed. "No."

"Did you bury everything he had with him?"

"I think so. We got all of his clothes and the camera, his shoes, and his bag and buried it all together."

"Were his clothes in the bag?"

"His clothes and shoes were separate. Beasley stuffed everything else—including the camera—into the bag."

"Was there a tripod for the camera?"

I nodded. "It was Branson's, but the camera belonged to the guy."

Jed was quiet for a moment. "Branson doesn't want the video, Neely Kate. He'll want it too if it's still there, but that's not why he wants to dig up the body. He's after whatever's in that bag."

"Yeah . . . maybe."

"No maybe about it." He was quiet again. "I'm tempted to leave it and let sleepin' dogs lie, but I think Branson will dig it up." He glanced at me again. "What will he find that ties you to his death? The video? What about the murder weapon? What was it? A gun? Did you leave blood evidence in the house?"

"There wasn't any blood." Then I added, "Not his."

"How much of yours?" When I didn't answer, he asked, "Enough to look like a crime scene?"

I still didn't answer.

"I'll take that as a yes." He was quiet for a good ten seconds before he said, "Then you killed him in self-defense."

"No," I said, surprised by how detached I felt. "I could have tried to run . . . but I didn't. I stayed and killed him."

"What do you mean you could have run? When Beasley showed up?"

I stared out the window at the passing landscape. Strangely enough, Jed was driving in the right direction. "When you get to that road up at the intersection, turn right."

"Neely Kate, what am I going to find on that tape?"

I gasped. "You can't watch the tape! Swear to me you won't watch it!"

His face hardened. "I can't promise you that."

I shrank back in horror. "*Why?*"

"Because that's the only way I'll know how to protect you. I need to know what really happened."

"No!"

"Then tell me." He slowed down and turned.

We were getting closer to where we'd buried the guy, but I was panicked by the thought of Jed seeing what I'd done.

He grabbed my hand, and his voice was softer when he said, "It's okay, NK. I'm gonna fix this. It's what I do, remember? I'm really good at it, so you have to trust me, okay?"

"You can't watch that video, Jed," I said, feeling defeated. Jed was helping me, but at what cost? No matter what he thought now, if he saw that video from beginning to end, he'd never see me the same way again.

He was quiet for so long I was sure he wasn't going to answer, but he finally said, "Okay, I won't look at it, but you have to tell me what happened."

I swallowed, feeling like I was going to throw up. "After Branson left me, my fears were confirmed. It was bad, really bad, and that's all I want to say about that."

And reason number one for why Jed couldn't see that video.

He didn't answer, so I continued, "I was kind of out of it, and—"

"Due to drugs or injury?" He was using his work face, the detached-from-the-situation one, and somehow that made it easier to tell him.

"He'd hit me too hard at some point, but I was lying there thinking I didn't want to die like this and be forgotten. I didn't want to disappear without anyone noticing, so I knew I had to fight back. He was bigger than me, but all of a sudden, I was filled with so much anger. At him, and at Branson, and at my momma and all the men in her life, and all I could think to do was lash out at the worst of them all. He had his back turned to me. I'm sure he didn't see me as a threat. He'd just proven he could do whatever he wanted to me and there was nothing I could do about it. My hands were tied to a rope that had a few feet of slack, so I jumped on his back and looped the rope around his neck and pulled tight."

"You strangled him."

"It wasn't easy. He was a big powerful guy, and he kept trying to throw me off, but I held on because I knew if I let go, I'd be as good as dead."

"What happened then?"

"He stood at one point and tried to slam me into a wall to get me off. I hit my head—hard enough that I let go—but the ropes were tied to my wrists, so I was dangling from his neck. The next thing I knew, he fell with me underneath him. I was still attached to him with that rope. I probably lay there like that for a good five or ten minutes, maybe longer since I kept drifting in and out of consciousness, but then I knew I had to get up or I'd die there too. I finally figured out how to push him up and get unattached. As soon as I did, I found something to cut through the rope. I was looking for a phone to call the police when Beasley showed up."

"Does Beasley know how you killed him?"

"He didn't ask, and I never offered any explanation, but there was a rope burn around his neck. I figured the whole situation explained itself. But I know it wasn't completely self-defense. I could have whacked him over the head and knocked him out. Besides, he obviously had money. I know how it works. I'd be facing jail time no matter who was at fault."

"Where was your blood?"

"On the sheets."

"And where are those?"

"Buried with him."

"Did it get on the mattress?"

"No," I said, feeling sick again. "Branson had one of those waterproof pads on there to protect it."

He took a moment before he said, "We have to get that video and those sheets and anything else with your blood on it. What about the form you signed? Is that with him too?"

"Yeah. But what if Branson's following us now?" I looked behind us but didn't see any cars. "What if he shows up?"

"He's not. I've been watching. And if he shows up, then he'll get more than he bargained for. Now tell me where to go next."

He pulled out his vibrating phone again, and this time he frowned as he tucked it back into his pocket. Part of me wanted to ask what it was all about, but I couldn't handle courting more trouble.

It took us fifteen minutes to get to the side road I remembered from that dark, dismal night. Then I had him drive slowly until I recognized the light pole. Jed pulled onto a small drive about fifty feet down the road, so as to look less suspicious, no doubt, and then he popped the trunk. He quickly swapped his shoes for work boots, put on a pair of work gloves, and grabbed one of the shovels and a bag out of the trunk.

When he started to close it, I said, "I'm helping dig, Jed."

He gave me a stern look, his hand on the still-open lid. "Like hell you are."

"This is *my* problem."

"Your problem is my problem now too, Neely Kate. The sooner you accept that, the better."

I barely took a moment to absorb what he'd said.

"Jed," I said quietly. "I need to do this." I didn't know why, and I sure didn't know how to explain it, but my gut told me that I needed to be a participant in this, not just stand back and let it happen.

He watched me for a moment before grabbing the other shovel and handing it to me. "You can help until we find the body. Then I'm taking over."

No problem there. I wasn't sure I could handle digging around the body. "Okay."

We walked down the side of the road until I saw the bushes, which were harder to recognize since it was dark and they weren't flowering. Jed didn't have a problem walking through the undergrowth with his jeans and boots, but I was still wearing my dress and sandals. When those azaleas had tumbled onto my desk, it had occurred to me that I might have to dig up the body. But it had seemed like a worst-case scenario. I'd hoped to show up in Ardmore and find out everything was okay. So even if Jed had agreed to drive back to the motel to change, I had brought nothing to change into.

The moon was mostly full and overhead, which helped light the road, but Jed turned on a flashlight and shone it around the ground behind the bushes, which were cast in deep shadows. "What do you think?"

I studied the ground and shuddered. "There," I said, pointing. "I think he's right there, but everything looks different, so I can't be sure."

He turned off his flashlight and tossed his bag to the ground. "That's okay. Did you bury him to one side or in the middle?"

"The middle."

"How big was the hole?"

"About three or four feet. We didn't lay him flat."

"Stand by my bag, and I'll tell you when you can help. Our goal is to leave the site as undisturbed as possible."

I watched as he shoveled a huge clump of weeds up and set it to the side, working until he'd cleared about a six-by-three-foot space. Then he started tossing piles of dirt and clay under the azalea bushes.

"Okay," he said, "you can help, but put the dirt into a pile under the bushes if you can. We want to make it as hard as possible to find this site."

"Okay."

Jed was much faster and more efficient. He moved several huge shovelfuls of dirt to my measly amount, but he never suggested I was in the way or that I should let him do it.

"You're pretty good at this diggin' thing," I said, trying to lighten the mood. "I'm kind of scared to ask how you got so good at it, but if you're ever lookin' for a job, Bruce Wayne's always looking for help with the landscaping business."

He looked up at me with a grin. "I'll be sure to put in my résumé."

About ten minutes in, Jed was now standing in a two-foot-by-four-foot trench.

I stood on the side so I wouldn't get in his way. Watching him work, I couldn't help but think that he was almost *too* good at this. His naked chest had looked like some kind of sculpture this morning, and that upper body strength probably helped, but even so . . .

He looked up at me. "My grandparents' farm."

"What?"

"I know where your mind's going, but I got plenty of experience diggin' posts and ditches at my grandparents' farm."

I couldn't help but grin at that.

About five minutes later, he stopped and looked up. "I think I found something."

I'd done a good job of telling myself we were just digging a hole up to this point, but now I was about to come face-to-face with the man I had murdered. Any way I looked at it, this was bound to be bad.

I stood to the side, telling myself I couldn't vomit, even though a stench had begun to fill the air.

Jed pointed to his bag. "There are a couple of masks in there. It won't help entirely, but it'll help some, not to mention it'll help protect us from the bacteria and shit we're diggin' up."

I turned on the flashlight and searched through his bag until I found a bunch of painter's masks. I handed one to Jed and put the other on myself.

"I need the flashlight now," he said. "You can hold it or I can prop it up, but I need to be more careful about where I'm digging." I appreciated that he wasn't babying me. He was treating this as a job that needed to be done—no more, no less—because he knew that was what I needed from him.

"I'll hold it." It was the least I could do. I'd insisted on helping, but now every part of me was shouting *run*.

But I was tired of running from this. I wanted it settled and left in the past for good.

I held up the flashlight and watched as Jed became more careful with his digging. Pretty soon, I saw what looked like the dirty bed sheet.

"Did you wrap him up in the sheet?"

"Yeah."

He nodded and kept digging until he had more of the sheet uncovered. "Where did you bury the bag?"

"At his feet."

"Which direction?"

"That way." I pointed to my right.

We heard a car engine in the distance, and Jed grabbed the flashlight and turned it off. "Get down."

We waited for thirty seconds before the sound faded into the distance.

"Sound travels out here," I said.

He nodded, then switched the flashlight back on and handed it to me. "It works in our favor and makes it harder for anyone to sneak up on us."

He resumed digging, to my right this time, and a few minutes later he discovered the edge of the bag. He was less gentle with it, prying it loose in less than a minute.

I started to hyperventilate.

His gaze turned toward me. "Neely Kate. Why don't you go wait in the car?"

I shook my head.

"You helped me find him," he said. "There's absolutely no reason for you to relive this. Let me handle it."

"I can't."

He studied me for a second. "Okay. Why don't you stand by my bag and watch the road for me?"

It was a bogus job, and we both knew it. But I wouldn't be helping either of us if I passed out beside the body.

I turned my back to him, and several seconds later he said, "I was right about Branson wanting the bag. There's probably ten thousand dollars in here. I wonder if he was making a drug deal too."

I swallowed the bile rising in my throat. "Because *I* couldn't be worth ten grand."

"Neely Kate."

I shook my head. "Just get this over with."

He tossed the bag behind me, then kept digging.

"Was the camera in there?" I asked, my voice shaking.

"Yes."

"His clothes should have been underneath it."

"I think I've just found them." After a few more shovelfuls of dirt, he stopped and squatted, then tossed a couple of pieces of fabric onto the ground behind me.

I glanced over my shoulder as he took off his gloves and reached his hand into a mass of fabric, removing a leather wallet. He flipped it open.

"Pearce Manchester. Sound familiar?" he asked.

I shuddered. Now I had a name to accompany the face in my nightmares. "No."

"I've heard of him. He was a Dallas businessman who went missing about five years ago. No one knew what happened to him, but his oil-rich family put up a reward. Branson may be after that too."

"Wouldn't he implicate himself?"

"Not necessarily. He probably figured he could make some bogus claim that he stumbled upon the body."

"And me?"

"Have you ever been arrested?"

"Once. For shoplifting. Not long after I got here. I pled guilty and got off with community service."

"Then they have your prints, but probably not your DNA. Still, I'm not leaving any evidence behind to tie you to the crime. He must have scratched you while you were strangling him, which means your DNA is under his fingernails and possibly on what's left of the lower part of him." He paused. "We have two options. We burn his body and destroy any DNA evidence, or we move his body so Branson never finds it."

"Where would you move it to?"

"I don't know yet."

"Which option do you prefer?"

He hesitated. "I want to move it. But I'm not sure how you'll handle that."

"I want this done. I never want it to haunt me again."

"Then we'll move it, but I'll need your help getting him out."

I swallowed, feeling ill. "Okay."

He climbed out of the hole and grabbed a tarp out of his bag. After laying it out on the ground beside the hole, he started to climb back in. He stopped to look back at me, though, and pulled down his mask. "How are you doing?"

"You're the one doin' all the work," I countered.

Sympathy filled his eyes. "Neely Kate."

I felt myself start to crumble, but I pulled it all back in and took a deep breath. "Just tell me what to do to make this go faster."

"Okay."

He soon had the body free, and he slid the tarp down into the hole and rolled the body on top of it before wrapping it up.

"This is when I need your help," he said.

I sucked in a breath, still smelling the lingering rancid stench through my mask. "Okay."

I climbed down into the hole, and we rolled the body up the incline and out onto the ground.

"I'm going to get the car and load the body and the bag into the trunk. If someone shows up and finds the hole, it's not ideal, but we'll make good and sure there's nothing tying it to you."

"I trust you, Jed."

"Are you okay waiting here?"

The answer was a solid *no*. But it was stupid for both of us to go get the car. "Yeah."

Jed took off and I waited for several seconds before curiosity got the best of me. I looked in Pearce Manchester's bag and found the video camera. I popped open the view finder and turned on the power switch, surprised when it actually worked. I rewound the tape and turned it on, steeling myself for what I'd find.

There I was on the bed. He was standing there above me, watching my bleeding body with a little self-satisfied smile on his face. Then he turned around and sat on the bed. I knew what was coming . . .

I fast-forwarded to the moment when I got up and lunged at him. The next part was how I remembered it except for the expression on my bloodied face. I looked like a murderer. If anyone saw this tape—especially if they didn't see the first part—they would never believe it was self-defense.

I heard Jed's car start, then park in the ditch in front of the bushes. I closed the screen and popped the tape out. There was no way I was letting Jed or anyone else near this thing. I replaced it with a loose tape from the bag.

He walked back around the bushes as I pocketed the tape. He had a small container of lighter fluid and squirted a generous amount into the hole before striking a match and lighting the hole on fire.

I considered tossing the tape in, but I knew Jed wouldn't be happy about it. Besides, I didn't think the fire would be big enough to destroy it. And I wanted that sucker good and destroyed.

"I can carry the body to the car," Jed said. "Do you want to start shoveling the dirt back in?"

"Yeah. Then what?"

"Then we rebury him."

Chapter Twenty Three

After we left the site as undisturbed as possible, Jed drove us back to the motel and pulled into the parking lot. He got out his phone and checked it again, then put it back in his pocket.

"Who keeps calling you?" I asked.

"Skeeter."

My eyes widened. "Don't you need to answer it? If he's calling after midnight, it's probably important."

"He's probably drunk off his ass and calling to chew me out. I'm not dealing with it now."

"But—"

"I need to take care of this mess first. I want you to wait here in our room while I take care of the body." I opened my mouth to protest, but he shook his head with a firm look. "I let you be part of digging up the body because you needed to do it, but I need you to trust me to take care of this. I can do it a lot faster and more efficiently if I'm not worrying about you, although I hope to God Carla didn't tell Branson where we're staying." He held up his hand to stop my forthcoming protest. "But while I wish you hadn't told her, I understand why you did."

"She won't tell him, Jed. And even if she does, he'll never know what room we're in."

"We found Stella," he said in a sardonic tone. "And we didn't know which apartment *she* was in."

I clenched my fists. "If Branson Desoto shows up at my door, you'll have to bury two bodies."

He gave me a smug look—not happy exactly, but bordering on pleased.

Crap. I could have used Branson as an excuse to go with Jed. While I didn't really *want* to go with him, it didn't feel right to let him take care of the body for me. I had no idea why he was putting himself at such risk, but the least I could do was let him set the rules.

"I trust you, Jed. You wouldn't be here with me if I didn't trust you."

He looked relieved. "If Branson shows up at your door, call 911, but shoot to kill if he finds his way into the room. Got it?"

"But . . . *the police?*"

"He can't hurt you now, Neely Kate. There's no body, and he would never want to tie himself to the crime anyway. At least not so directly. But if you're going to shoot him, make sure you call the police first; it helps prove self-defense. And if it comes to pulling the trigger, shoot to kill."

"Jed . . ."

He leaned over and gave me a quick kiss. "Why don't you get some sleep while you wait for me? But be sure to put the chain on the door and keep the gun by the bed. When I come back, we'll get a few hours of sleep before leaving. We can head to Colorado first thing in the morning. Sound good?"

"Yeah." Could my nightmare *really* almost be over?

"Good. The sooner we get out of Ardmore, the better." He glanced up at our room. "Call me at any sign of trouble."

"Okay." But I didn't get out of the car. "Are you burying the bag too?"

"No. I still need to go through it, but I won't be leaving it with the body."

I got out of the car, and he waited until I got inside the room. I fastened the dead bolt and then stood at the window and watched him drive away, wondering where he planned to go. Was it better not to know?

I dropped the curtain and took a long shower, washing my hair even though I wasn't supposed to get my stitches wet. I felt like I was covered in dirt and guilt, and I needed to get every part of me clean. When I got out, I dressed in a T-shirt and a pair of loose shorts and got into bed. According to the clock on the nightstand, it was after two in the morning, but I was sure I'd never get to sleep. I kept reliving that night five years ago over and over in my head, seeing Pearce Manchester's face as he turned around to look at me in disbelief as I strangled him.

For some reason, knowing his name made his murder more real, yet I asked myself if he'd bothered to learn *my* name. He'd called me plenty of other names, and Neely Kate hadn't been one of them. He had deserved every bit of what he'd gotten.

So why did I still feel so dirty?

I must have finally drifted off, because the next sound I heard was a rap at the door and my phone ringing next to my head. I bolted upright, sure Branson had found me. Before I could grab my gun, I registered that Jed's name was on the screen of my phone. The call ended as I got up, but there was no need to answer anyway. A few steps brought me to the door, and I could see Jed's face through the peephole.

When I opened the door, he looked exhausted and reeked of a bonfire.

"Why do you smell smoky?" I asked as I let him in.

"I decided it wasn't enough to bury him somewhere different. I burned the body, along with his clothes and the sheets. No DNA evidence to trace you to him should he ever get discovered." He looked into my eyes. "You're safe, Neely Kate. Branson definitely can't hurt you anymore."

"He still might try."

"But he has no evidence. You're free."

So why didn't I feel free? I wrapped my arms around his waist and hugged him. "Thank you."

He kissed the top of my head. "I'm going to shower, then climb in bed. How are you doing?"

"Fine." Or as fine as I *could* be given everything, and I had no doubt that was because of the man turning on the water in the bathroom. I had no idea how I would have done this without him.

I went back to bed, dozing again, but I roused when Jed climbed in beside me. He wrapped his arms around me and pulled my back to his chest. I could tell he was only wearing his briefs, but part of me was too tired to care.

"Thank you," I murmured. "For everything."

He didn't answer, just held me close.

I drifted off to sleep again, but I woke several hours later. Pale sunlight peeked through the slightly parted curtains. My phone was vibrating with a call, and I checked the screen, surprised by an Arkansas number I didn't recognize. Who was calling me at six in the morning?

I slid out of bed and went into the bathroom and answered with a whispered, "Hello?"

"Neely Kate."

I froze when I recognized Skeeter's voice. "Oh, my God," I said, breathless. "Is Rose okay?"

"How the hell would I know?" he grumped. "And why the hell would I care?"

I considered telling him what an idiot he was, but that seemed like a bad idea. "What do you want, Skeeter?" But I was pretty sure I had an idea.

"Put Jed on the phone. *Now.*"

I poked my head out of the bathroom and checked on the man still sleeping in our hotel bed. He looked as peaceful as could be after our night of hell. There was no way I was going to wake him to deal with Skeeter's crankiness. I snatched the room key from the bathroom counter, stalked out of the room onto the walkway outside, and stared down the ice machine at the end of the sidewalk as if it had become Skeeter Malcolm.

"Neely Kate!" Skeeter barked.

"I'm not your employee!" I said in a harsh tone. "I don't take orders from you."

"Just put Jed on the damn phone."

"I don't want to get in the middle of this, but maybe you should stop treating him like crap."

"*What?*"

"He's been loyal to you for a long time, Skeeter. Maybe you need to start treating him more like a partner and not an employee."

"What the hell are you talking about?" he demanded.

"Maybe you need to ask yourself that question."

"I don't have time for nonsense. I need Jed to get his ass home now. We've got trouble."

"When *don't* you have trouble?" I asked, turning to face the parking lot. I gasped when I saw the man standing at the bottom of the stairs. "Oh, my God." I started to drown in my fear.

"Neely Kate?" Skeeter's tone changed from demanding to concerned. But I was too busy staring at another nightmare from my past.

"Where's my hello, Neely Kate?" Branson asked, his arms held wide. An arrogant look covered his face as he started climbing up the steps. He thought I still belonged to him—it was written all over his face.

I backed my butt up to the motel room door and dropped my phone onto the walkway. "How did you find me?"

He ignored my question. "Working your way up in the world on your back, I see."

"Get the hell away from me, Branson."

"Now is that any way to greet your old boyfriend?"

I needed to get inside, but I didn't dare turn my back to him, not even for the quick second it would take to insert the plastic card into the slot. "I'm warning you to leave me alone."

"Or what?" he asked with a bitter laugh. "Will you kill me too?"

He was on the top step now, and all I could think was that I was *never* going to let that man touch me again.

"Maybe I will, Branson."

Laughing like I'd just said the funniest thing ever, he snaked out a hand to grab me.

Instinct took over. I punched him in the throat with the heel of my hand just like Witt had taught me, quickly followed with a heel kick to his groin. Shock filled his eyes as he fell backward in what seemed like slow motion, tumbling down the stairs to the first landing.

I descended several steps after him. "Get up."

He lay on his side, gasping for breath, but hate filled his eyes.

"How does that feel?" I shouted. "Do you like having your keister kicked by a girl?" I sneered.

"You're crazy," he said in a raspy voice as he lifted his hand to his throat.

"I was sure *crazy* to ever think you were worth my time, but I'm sane now, so let me make this perfectly clear, *you son of a bitch*," I said in a harsh tone as I stared down at him. "You have no power over me anymore."

He reached for my leg, but I stomped on his hand and followed up with a hard heel kick to his nose, flinging his head into the metal railing. Blood began to pour out of his nostrils.

"Who came around asking about me?" I asked.

He covered his nose with his hand and pure fear filled his eyes.

"You heard the lady's question," Jed said in a deadly voice behind me. "Answer her."

Jed? He stood next to me in his jeans and no shirt.

"A woman," Branson said in a hate-filled tone. "She came before Christmas. She said you'd screwed her over and she was looking for something to hold over your head. So I told her to ask you about the azaleas."

"And what did you tell her about the azaleas?" Jed asked.

"Nothing."

"Try again," Jed grumbled.

"I swear!"

Jed took a step in front of me. "Too bad I don't believe you. Maybe I should shoot out your kneecaps to show you how serious I am."

"Fine! I'll tell you!" Branson said in a panic. "I told her you buried something that was mine, but I didn't tell her what." Hatred filled his eyes. "I want my money, Neely Kate!"

"*Your* money?" I asked in disgust. "Are you *kidding* me?"

"I gave him what he wanted—drugs and you—but he refused to pay me until he was done. Now I want my money."

Jed tensed beside me. "Get up, you worthless piece of shit. You want what's coming to you?"

Branson didn't have the good sense to realize Jed probably wasn't referring to the ten thousand dollars. As soon as he got to his feet, Jed punched him in the face, then whipped out his gun and held the tip under Branson's chin. "Let's make something clear: Your claim on Neely Kate is over. From this moment forward, don't try to talk to her. Don't contact her. Don't try to find her. Don't even *think* about her. If I ever see your face again, I'll shoot you first, then ask your cold dead body whatever questions I have. Got it?"

Branson looked furious, but he spat out, "Fine."

Jed grabbed a handful of his shirt and hauled him to his feet. "You're lucky I don't kill you now. But your luck is about to run out. *So. Go.*"

Jed shoved him so hard Branson stumbled down the stairs. We stood there watching as he got into his car and pulled out of the parking lot.

As soon as he was gone, Jed turned to me. "Time to leave."

Sure enough, a few people had gathered to watch. Jed had put his gun away, but the last thing we needed was to talk to the police. Thankfully, the small crowd of five or six all seemed to lose interest as soon as we turned back toward our room, but one middle-aged woman lifted her fist and said, "Good job! Show 'em we don't take shit from men, honey!"

Jed ignored her as he squatted to pick up my phone, then followed me into the room.

"How did you know Branson was here?" I asked as soon as he shut the door. I could tell he was pissed.

"I *heard* you. What in the hell were you thinking going outside?"

"Skeeter called me."

"*What?*"

"I didn't want to disturb you, so I went outside." I caught his eye. "He says he needs to talk to you. There's trouble back home."

His jaw clenched tight. "There's always trouble back home."

"That's what I said." I started to walk around him, but he wrapped me up in his arms and pulled me close. I tried to ignore the fact that my cheek was pressed against his bare solid chest.

"You scared the shit out of me, Neely Kate."

"I had it handled, Jed."

His arms tightened. "I know you did, and I had no right to take over, but I wanted to kill that guy something fierce, and I hoped punching him would help."

"Did it?"

"Not nearly enough. We need to leave now."

I grabbed my few toiletries out of the bathroom and stuffed them into my duffel bag. Jed was already packed and sitting on the bed, staring at his phone.

I sat next to him. "Call him."

He looked at me with conflict in his eyes. "If I call him, it will be the same old shit, Neely Kate. And no Colorado."

"He claims it's important, so maybe you should hear him out."

He looked dubious, but he placed the call and stepped outside.

While he was gone, I looked at my own phone and realized I'd missed a text from Carla telling me she thought Branson had overheard her telling her boyfriend about Motel 6 and to be careful.

Too late for that warning.

But it made me think of Rose. I knew I needed to call and tell her everything was okay and that I would be home soon, but I couldn't do it. She'd be full of questions, which I understood. I would be too if the situation were reversed, but I had no idea how to answer her. So I took the chicken way out and texted instead.

I'm safe. We'll talk later.

She responded within seconds, even though it wasn't even six thirty yet.

I love you. See you soon.

A minute later, Jed came back in, looking like he wanted to punch someone again.

"What happened?" I asked as I climbed off the bed.

"I have to go back."

I moved in front of him and put my hands on his chest. "Do you *want* to go back?"

He stared at me with a blank expression. "It doesn't matter what I want."

"Yes, it *does*, Jed. If you don't want to work for Skeeter, you can do something else. We'll figure it out, then go back and deal with it together. Next week."

He shook his head with a sad look in his eyes. "No, Neely Kate. We have to head back now."

"Why?"

"That wasn't a call from my old boss. It was a call from my friend. Scooter's missing."

"*What?*" Skeeter's younger brother wasn't the brightest of men, but he had a sweet disposition and was loved by a lot of people. From what I'd heard, Skeeter tried to keep his brother out of the crime world. "What happened?"

He ran a hand over his head. "I don't know, but I need to get back and help look for him."

I put my hand on his arm. "You don't *have* to help, Jed."

"I do. Scooter is like family."

While I understood why he'd made that decision, it still ticked me off. For the first time in my life, I felt like fate had finally taken my side, just to snatch away my happiness again. "So you're just gonna go back to workin' for Skeeter just like that?" I snapped my fingers.

"No. It's not like that, Neely Kate. I'm not going back to be Skeeter's right-hand man. I'm going back to help find Scooter."

I put my hands on my hips and glared up at him. "You really believe that?"

He didn't answer.

We grabbed our bags and headed down to Jed's car, tossing our bags into the back seat. After Jed checked out, we stopped at a gas station to fill up the car and get some donuts and coffee. We were several miles down the highway before I said, "I'm sorry."

He turned to me in surprise. "What in the hell do *you* have to be sorry for?"

"I was upset about your decision to go back . . . I was being selfish, and I'm sorry."

"Neely Kate," he groaned.

"No. Of course you're going to help find Scooter. If you didn't, you wouldn't be the man I . . ." I what? Loved? Was falling for? "The man I care about."

He was silent.

"You think you're irredeemable, Jed Carlisle, and I know you've done some bad things. You know I have too. But maybe we buy back pieces of our souls with the good things we do. Calling the authorities about baby Crystal and stayin' until they got there. Goin' back to Henryetta to look for Scooter. Shoot, *helpin' me*. Don't you think those good deeds you've done help counteract the bad?"

He shot me a glance. "I didn't help you out of the kindness of my heart, Neely Kate. I did it for purely selfish reasons."

"What are you talkin' about?" I wasn't sure my heart could bear someone else betraying me. Especially if that someone was Jed.

He shook his head in frustration. "I mean, I couldn't let you go to Ardmore without me because I would have been sick with worry. If you'd cut me loose, I would have tracked you and followed you every step of the way. I wasn't about to let you do this alone."

A lump filled my throat, and I choked out a short laugh. "That's not selfish, Jed. That's called caring about someone."

He reached out and grabbed my hand. "I'm not sure you know how much you mean to me, Neely Kate."

I squeezed his hand back. "You mean a lot to me too." I considered everything he'd done for me over the last couple of days. Actions spoke louder than words, especially for someone like Jed. "Hey, where's the bag you dug up?"

"In the trunk."

"What do you plan to do with it?"

"Look it over for anything useful. I need to find out how close they got to tying you to his death. Maybe it'll help us figure out whether the guy who showed up at Zelda's was working for Kate or investigating Manchester's disappearance."

"Do you think I should be worried?" I asked.

"No. It's a dead end, and even if someone does trace it to you, there's absolutely no evidence."

"I sure as Hades hope no one gets that far."

"If Branson or Beasley talk, I suspect they know what will be waiting for them."

I wasn't so sure they were that smart.

He paused as if considering something and then turned toward me. "Did you watch the video of the night you buried him?"

I hesitated. "No."

"There was a blank tape in the camera." He gave me another look.

I could tell he already knew how that had come to be. I could have lied to him, but I was tired of living with lies. He, of all people, would understand. "I took it last night. When you went to get the tarp."

"And put a new tape in the camera?" The disappointment in his voice killed me. We both knew I'd done it to try to trick him.

"I'm sorry, Jed. I couldn't let you see it. I'd rather go to jail than let you see what he did to me."

"Neely Kate . . ." He pushed out a breath. "You have nothing to be ashamed of. If you just give—"

"*No*," I said, harsher than I'd intended. "If I hadn't taken it, you would have watched it last night. Otherwise, how did you know it was blank?"

A guilty look crossed his face.

I sank back into the seat. "I'm not angry." And strangely enough, I wasn't. I understood why he had looked. He was trying to make sure every shred of evidence connecting me to Pearce Manchester was destroyed. "But you can't see it, Jed. You can't." My voice broke.

He rested a hand on my leg. "I only want to protect you, Neely Kate. I want to make sure this is put to bed forever."

"I know," I said absently, staring out the window. "But I don't think you need to see it to make sure that happens."

"Where is it now?"

My shoulders stiffened as my head swung around to face him. "Are you gonna take it from me?"

"No," he said, sounding sad. He lifted a hand and lightly massaged the back of my neck. "It's your tape, NK, but I think you should destroy it. I'll even help you if you'd like."

I didn't answer. I wasn't sure what I was going to do with it yet. "What about Kate?" I asked.

"It sounds like she knows nothing beyond what she's already told you. You're safe as far as she's concerned. Your past is locked up. Even so, I'm going to look into Pearce Manchester and find out everything I can."

While I knew that was the smart thing to do, part of me wanted to forget it had ever happened. It didn't fit with my life in Henryetta. It didn't fit with Rose and Joe and my job at the landscaping business.

What about me and Jed? Did we fit together outside of Ardmore?

"What happens with the two of us?" I asked. "You're goin' back to Skeeter. I'm still married."

"I'm *not* going back to Skeeter. I'm helping him find Scooter. And while you're still technically married, the *guy*"—he said it with so much disdain, it might as well have been a swear—"abandoned you. He's not even worth considering when we look at you and me."

"What do you want to do about us when we get back?" I asked.

"I still want to keep seeing you. I care about you. I can't turn that off, and I don't want to." He turned and offered me a warm smile. "You're probably the best thing that's ever happened to me."

I leaned my head on his shoulder and wrapped my hand around his right arm. "You're one of the best things that's ever happened to me too."

He leaned over and kissed the top of my head.

"So we just tell people we're seeing each other?" I asked.

He was quiet for a moment. "No. I think we need to keep this under wraps."

While his answer wasn't a total surprise, it still stung. I slowly sat up. "Because you're ashamed of my past?"

"No," was his harsh reply; then he relaxed and said, "God, no. Because once people know I care about you, you can be used as a weapon to get to me."

I considered arguing with him, but he had a point. I'd seen that very thing happen with Rose and Skeeter.

We fell into silence for a few minutes.

"There's one thing I'm still confused about," Jed said. "How did Beasley get a DUI?"

"After we buried the body, we headed back to town. I'd handled everything just fine up until that point, but it all came crashing down on me. So I was almost to town when I started crying so hard I couldn't see. I plowed through several mailboxes and hit a parked car. I was driving Branson's car, so I freaked out. Beasley said he'd tell them he was driving and told me to leave town. Only, I hadn't counted on him still being so drunk. I sure never thought he'd get fifteen years, but he already had a few DUI convictions."

"He deserved every second of it," Jed grunted. "Don't you feel one ounce of guilt over it."

I wasn't so sure.

Chapter Twenty Four

It was well after lunchtime by the time Jed pulled into the Henryetta town square. He parked in a space on the side street next to the building that housed the RBW Landscaping office and left the engine idling. He'd offered to drop me off at the farmhouse, but I'd already missed two and a half days of work. Rose needed me.

"Why do I feel like I'm losin' you?" I asked quietly. I couldn't look at him when I said it. The whole ride home it had felt like the string tying us together was growing tauter, reaching a breaking point.

He tilted my head up to face him. "You're not, Neely Kate."

"But we're keepin' this a secret. How's it gonna work?"

"I don't know yet, but we'll figure out a way." A sexy grin spread across his face. "Besides, we're both great at keeping secrets."

My stomach cartwheeled. When he smiled like that, I practically melted.

Still, we were back home, and Jed was known for his extremely short-term *relationships*. If I was reading this wrong, I needed to know before I got hurt. "Are you sure

254

this isn't your way of giving me the brush-off?" I asked. "Because I'm a big girl, and I can—"

His mouth was on mine, his tongue parting my lips. I wrapped my arms around his neck and kissed him back. This was a kiss of promise and hope, not a goodbye.

He lifted his head with a warm smile. "We'll make it work."

I smiled back. "Yeah."

Lifting a hand to my face, he brushed the hair off my cheek as he looked into my eyes. "If you need me for anything, call straightaway."

"Okay."

His smile faded. "I'm serious, Neely Kate. With Scooter missing . . . Skeeter's not sure if he's just wandered off or if it's foul play. With the recent trouble around the necklace . . . just be careful, okay?" Worry filled his eyes.

"You're in a lot more danger than I am," I said. "You're not only lookin' for Scooter, but you're at odds with his brother."

"I can handle it." He kissed me again, a leisurely kiss that quickly warmed into a raging inferno. He put his hands on my arms and pushed back. "We need to take this slow."

I blinked. "What?"

"After . . . everything . . . I want you to know I want you for the right reasons."

Part of me wanted to protest, but outside of high school, I couldn't think of a single man I hadn't slept with soon after getting involved. Maybe there was something to his idea. "Okay."

A frown crossed his face. I wondered if he was upset with me for agreeing, but he pulled his phone out of his pocket and checked the screen. "I'm going to walk you to the office door."

He moved to get out, but I grabbed his arm. "Jed. Stop."

He turned back to face me.

"If we're keeping this secret, then we should say goodbye here. I'm not sure I'll be able to let you go without kissing you goodbye."

His grin was back. The one that lit up his eyes and made me glow with the knowledge that his smile was for *me*.

I lifted my hand to his cheek, my thumb brushing his skin. "I love your smiles. I've become addicted to them. You should smile more, although I suspect it wouldn't be as intimidating when you're trying to stare down a bad guy."

His grin spread. "You might have a point. I'll save them for you."

His promise warmed me more than it probably should have. "Go find Scooter. Then, as soon as he's back, I'm expecting you to take me to Colorado to feed the chipmunks. Maybe I'll get some cute outfits to put on 'em too. Like I do with Muffy."

Jed released a full-on belly laugh. "I really want to see that, so it's a deal."

My smile faded. "Why is this so hard?"

"It's not goodbye. I promise."

"I know. But it's hard anyway." I leaned over and gave him a quick kiss. Then I forced myself to open the door and climbed out into the Arkansas July heat.

I opened the back door and grabbed my bag and walked toward the sidewalk. I gave Jed a little wave, waggling my fingers with the hand I'd used to hold my bag.

He lifted his palm, his smile gone. Something rumbled in my guts, and it wasn't the greasy burger we'd stopped to get in Lewisville about an hour ago.

Disconcerted, I turned away and headed toward the street corner, spotting my dead car still parked in a spot on the end with a few parking tickets under the windshield wiper.

Great. I was stuck with a bunch of fines *and* car repair bills.

I turned back toward the office. As I approached the door, I saw Rose inside, talking on the phone as she sat at her computer. The feeling of disquiet grew, and I finally recognized it for what it was, the all-too-familiar feeling of being on the outside looking in.

I sighed as bitter disappointment washed over me. I had believed that confronting my past would make that feeling go away, but Pearce Manchester's body had been reduced to dust and that feeling still held sway over me. Nevertheless, I felt like the chains holding me back from feeling like I truly belonged had lost a few chinks over the last couple of days. Maybe it just took time.

Rose looked up and saw me staring through the glass. Her eyes widened, and she said something into her phone before dropping it onto the desk and running for me.

"Neely Kate!" she cried out as she burst through the door and enveloped me into a tight hug. "Oh, my God. You're really home."

Home. I'd been searching for it my whole life, and now I'd destroyed the secret that could have stolen it from me. So why did I still feel on edge?

I glanced down at my purse and knew why. The tape. I had a powerful urge to make a roaring fire in the alley behind the building and destroy the awful thing right away. It was what Jed thought I should do. But something held me back. Beasley still knew my secret, Branson wasn't to be trusted, and some unknown man had been searching for me. Right or wrong, that tape was the only record of what had really happened that night, and I needed to keep it. First chance I got, I was walking to the Henryetta Bank and putting it in a safety deposit box.

My rainy-day insurance policy.

But today I was basking in the sun of my new life. Family who loved me. My best friend who stood by me no matter what. And the man who put everything on the line to help me.

I had a lot to be thankful for, and I wasn't about to squander any of it. Because I never knew when it might be snatched away.

Read the Jed bonus chapter on the next page

For the Birds
Rose Gardner Investigations #2
July 11, 2017

BONUS CONTENT

Note from Denise:

When I started writing *Trailer Trash*, I had decided to include a few chapters in Jed's point of view. But after my editor, Angela, read the first half of the book, she told me that she thought this was Neely Kate's story to tell. Not Jed's. After a little convincing, I decided she was right.

At that point, I had two Jed chapters, so I pulled them both and rewrote the chapters from Neely Kate's point of view. The first chapter was chapter eight (the drive from Little Rock to Texarkana), and Angela and I ultimately decided it didn't necessarily contribute much more in Jed's POV. Keeping it as bonus material felt redundant. The chapter *did* feature the phone call between Skeeter and Jed at the gas station in Texarkana, but Angela suggested it might be more effective if the reader didn't know what was said during the call. We liked doling that information out slowly, letting the reader know as Neely Kate found out. Still, after I read that phone call again, I decided to break it out from the chapter and only keep Jed and Skeeter's conversation.

But we both agreed to keep Jed's chapter eleven.

Jed's version of chapter eleven is a mirror image of the chapter eleven in the book—with mostly matching dialogue. (Some may have been tweaked in the editing process.) It takes place immediately after the scene in Slick Willy's parking lot when Neely Kate walks out of the strip club. She's terrified over what Jed could be thinking about her, and she falls to pieces. Chapter eleven shows Jed's reactions to Neely Kate's reaction. It's a glimpse into his soul—the pain of losing his sister. His complicated relationship to Skeeter. The utter confusion he feels in regard to Neely Kate. It's a powerful chapter, and I was *dig-in-my-heels* reluctant to cut it until we decided to keep it as bonus material.

Bonus Scene from Chapter Eight, Jed's POV

I stopped at a truck stop in Texarkana, and while I pumped gas, Neely Kate went inside to use the bathroom. I was slightly worried she'd take off—she hadn't tried to bring her bag, and she seemed resigned to accepting my help, but she'd become more despondent after our talk about her miscarriage, and I couldn't shake the feeling she was trying to push me away. I wanted to figure out a way to make her feel better, but first I needed to face Skeeter's wrath.

He answered on the first ring, angry as a bear poked with a stick. "You better have a damn good explanation for ignoring my calls. Where are you?"

"Texarkana."

"What the *hell* are you doin' in Texarkana?"

Wasn't that the million-dollar question . . . Should I confess what I was up to? I realized I was running the risk of Skeeter sending someone to fetch me, but I was no longer that eight-year-old kid looking up to the fourteen-year-old boy who'd taken him under his protection. I didn't need his permission. "I'm takin' Neely Kate to Oklahoma."

He was quiet for several seconds, long enough that I checked the screen to make sure we were still connected. "I told you to be back for our six o'clock meeting."

"Obviously I'm not going to make it."

"You're willfully disobeying a direct order?"

"For the first time in my goddamned life I'm making a decision independent of you and what you want," I snarled through gritted teeth.

"Then you're fired!"

"You would fire me after everything I've done for you?" I asked in a tone so cold it would have frozen water within seconds.

"You have a choice," he said in an equally cold tone. "Me or *her*."

"No, you're the one forcing the choice on me. I can choose both. Just like you can choose both."

"What the fuck is that supposed to mean?" he growled.

"It means you screwed Rose over, and you know it. The sooner you suck it up and apologize to her, the better off we'll all be."

"It will be a cold day in hell before I apologize to her or anyone else."

Since I was already hanging out on a limb, I figured I might as well shimmy out the rest of the way. "You need her."

"Let's make one thing perfectly clear," he said, his voice sharp as the edge of a blade. "I don't need anyone. Not even you."

His words cut deep, but I wasn't about to let him know that. "You are such a stubborn ass; you refuse to see what's right in front of your face. I don't expect you to announce it to the world, but why can't you admit to yourself that she makes you a better leader, not to mention a better person? She makes you stop and think through the consequences."

"She's made me weak," he spat out. "I was too damn blind to see it."

"The men who are vying for your crown may see you that way, but dammit, Skeeter, once they've turn to your side they're ten times more loyal than they used to be. They know you're just and fair. It's painful now, but long term, the county will be much stronger."

"There is no room for just and fair in our world."

"You're lying to yourself, and that makes you dangerous."

"Well, you sure as shit don't need to worry about it anymore. Don't bother coming back from Oklahoma," he snapped, then hung up.

I leaned my forearm on the roof of the car, letting our conversation sink in. I wasn't necessarily surprised he'd fired me *again*, but it still stung.

"You okay?" Neely Kate asked. She stood on the other side of the car, her hair blowing into her face. She reached up a hand and brushed it away.

She'd come back.

Maybe Skeeter was too stupid to realize what he had, but I could learn from his mistakes. At this point, I had nothing to lose.

"I am now."

Chapter Eleven
Jed

If ever there was a man who ran from tears, it was me.

Maybe it was because I'd heard my sister Daisy cry herself to sleep too many nights. The helplessness had been overwhelming. We had often gone to bed bruised and hungry. I couldn't save her from the bruises except for the few times I managed to draw my father's wrath and his fists from her tiny body to my own. The hunger was easier to manage. As often as I could without raising suspicion, I would steal food from my father and sneak it to her at night. Skeeter knew she had a sweet tooth, so he'd sometimes steal cookies and small cakes from the Piggly Wiggly. I'd dole them out sparingly, trying to make them last, but some nights we gorged ourselves. Still, a belly full of sugar couldn't ease the ache in our guts. She'd climb into bed beside me in our shared room, and we'd huddle under my covers as my mattress shook with her silent sobs.

The person I'd loved most in the world had been miserable, and there was absolutely nothing I could've done to help her. I'd felt hamstrung and helpless.

Exactly the way I felt now.

One of the things I loved about Neely Kate was that she was like dynamite packed into a tiny body. She was nearly a foot shorter than me and probably half my weight, but she had presence. Her smile was infectious and her laugh . . . her laugh was like the hot chocolate Daisy and I got when we used to go Christmas caroling with the church—rich and delicious, warming every part of me as it went down. She always looked for the good in things, which I was even more in awe of after this tiny glimpse into her previous life. She was strong and loyal and had a loving heart. When she walked into a room, people noticed.

But there was no sign of that woman now. She was a broken shell, and I knew she'd only just begun this trip down memory lane. How would she handle the rest?

She'd collapsed into me, sobbing so hard I was pretty sure she was hyperventilating, yet all I knew to do was hold her. She needed to know that she wasn't in this alone, because something deep down insisted I wasn't leaving her side no matter how hard she tried to push me away.

"Let's go find a room, Neely Kate. Okay?"

She continued to cry, although the gut-wrenching sobs had quieted to labored sniffles. I guided her to the passenger door and helped her inside, shutting the door and hoping she didn't try to take off before I got behind the wheel. I had no doubt I could catch her, but I didn't want her to run. I wanted her to know we were doing this together.

I got back in the car and headed back to Ardmore. I passed a few seedy motels I would have stayed in if I'd been alone, but I wanted something better for her. Something that wasn't a reminder of the hell she'd lived through over half her life. I settled on a Motel 6— wishing I could find something nicer, knowing we'd at least have clean sheets.

After our trip to the strip club, I wasn't sure what Neely Kate had gotten into five years ago. I'd feel more prepared if I knew the rest, but why would she tell me? I suspected the only person who had ever truly been loyal to her was Rose. It should have been her husband, but I wondered how much she'd told him about her past. Had he understood how devastating the miscarriage had been for her? Probably not, but it still didn't justify him running off.

So help me God, when we were done with this trip, I was going to find that son of a bitch and rain down justice on his head. And since I apparently no longer worked for Skeeter, I had all the time in the world to complete my task.

Skeeter had a short temper, and it wasn't uncommon for him to fly off the handle. Hours later he would do damage control, or more often than not, *I* would be the one who did the damage control. But his sharp edges had softened considerably since he'd met Rose. She grounded him. The fact that I'd pointed that out to him earlier in our phone call wasn't exactly in my favor, especially since I was usually the one who did the reaching out on his behalf. I knew it might be days before he called or texted me. I'd given that man the last fourteen years of my life, working for him before I was even out of high school. He owed me more than this shitty send-off. More than the belated, inevitable demand that I return, which would be made, as always, without an apology or explanation.

But maybe it was time to do something on my own.

Truth be told, it wasn't the first time I'd had that thought. While I'd always known Skeeter had secrets— hell, I had plenty of my own—it had shocked me to find out the truth about his connection with J.R. Simmons. He'd worked for Simmons in the years he'd spent away from our hometown. Worse, he'd remained Simmons' henchman for years after returning to Henryetta, and he'd sought my help with his new enterprise without telling me.

I'd thought time would help me get over it, but months had passed and I was even angrier than before. I was Skeeter's best friend, and I'd devoted my entire life to his business, but more often than not, I felt like an employee rather than a partner. It was making me question whether I wanted something more.

Hell if I knew what that was.

I parked in front of the hotel and locked the still-despondent Neely Kate in the car, keeping an eye on her the entire time I checked in and filled out the paperwork.

I handed over my credit card—my personal one, not the one Skeeter had me use when I was traveling on *business*. Maybe it was a bad call. I felt vulnerable staying here as me and not one of the aliases I used to keep a low profile, but I didn't want to owe Skeeter any favors right now.

"Can I get a room toward the back?" I asked. "I like to be farther away from the road." The clerk gave me a strange look, so I added, "Noise. I'm a light sleeper." It would be harder for someone to sneak up on us in the back. I'd made a point of choosing a place with outside entry for the same reason.

"Must be your lucky day. Not only did you get the last room, but it's in the back." He handed me two room keys before returning to the game on his phone.

Neely Kate was quiet when I got into the car and drove us to the back of the building. I grabbed her bag and walked around to her door. She was still in the same position, so I opened the door and squatted next to her. "We're going inside now."

She lifted her mascara-smudged face to look at me but didn't say a word.

I reached for her arm as I stood, making sure she didn't hit her head. She got out next to the car, her body limp as she took a step toward the building. Our room was on the second floor, so I guided her to the stairs. She was moving slowly, so I swung her bag around to my back and swept her into my arms. When she didn't protest, part of me panicked. The woman I knew would beat me over the head for trying such a thing.

I jostled her in my arms so I could unlock the door and then flipped on the light. The room was cleaner and newer than I'd expected. I wasn't surprised to see a single king-sized bed; I already had a game plan. I could sleep in the chair in the corner. God knew I'd spent hours sleeping in worse situations.

I set her down on the bed, thankful she remained upright instead of curling up into the fetal position she'd assumed in the car.

I tossed her bag onto the dresser on my way into the bathroom. She'd feel better if she cleaned up, but she was in no position to take care of that herself. Wet washcloth in hand, I headed back out—she was in the same position I'd left her in—and sat on the edge of the bed next to her. I grabbed her chin and gently turned her face toward me.

Her eyes were downcast as I lifted the cloth to her face and began to wipe the mascara streaks.

She lifted her hand to my wrist and stopped me, still looking down. "Jed. Stop. You don't have to do that."

"I know," I said as I tugged her hand free. "When was the last time someone besides Rose took care of you?"

"Ronnie," she said, her voice breaking. "After my miscarriage. He tried, but he didn't understand."

"Didn't understand what?" I asked as I continued wiping her face. I had a pretty good idea, but I wanted her to confirm it.

"He knew I was upset over losing the babies, but he didn't get why I felt so guilty."

"Wasn't he upset too?"

"In a way, I guess. I think he was partially relieved, especially when he found out they were twins. Part of me wonders if he really wanted them. He just went along with anything I wanted." She lifted her blue eyes up to mine. "Now I wonder if he wanted any of it for himself."

"Wanted what?"

"The house. The baby. Our marriage. He wanted those things, but I think I pushed him into them a whole lot sooner than he had planned." She shrugged. "Maybe I was scared he'd see the real me and run." She took the rag from my hand and finished wiping her face.

"He must have wanted all of that if he gave in."

She shook her head. "I can be . . . insistent."

The more I heard about Ronnie Colson, the more I suspected he was a spineless jellyfish. There was no doubt that Neely Kate was a headstrong woman. She needed a man who could meet her toe-to-toe. "He was a grown-ass man, capable of saying no," I said more gruffly than intended, but I couldn't stand the thought of her taking on his mantle of guilt too.

"Maybe." She lowered the washcloth to her lap, resting it on her open palm. "I'm sorry for earlier . . . I'm humiliated beyond belief. I shouldn't have . . ." She paused. "I couldn't stand to think you thought less of me—"

"Don't you ever be ashamed of doing what you needed to do to survive."

"Still . . ." Her cheeks flushed. "I've made it weird between us. I plan to visit my old trailer park tomorrow. I'm sure I still have friends there. You don't need to come."

"I'm not leaving you, Neely Kate," I said in a firm voice, hoping to end the debate.

"I know you made Rose a promise—"

"You think I'm staying for Rose?" I asked in disbelief. "Let's get one thing perfectly clear: I'm here for me."

Her blue eyes searched my face. "Why?"

"Because you need a friend. I'm your friend." She looked down again, and I couldn't tell whether she believed me.

"But you were so angry with me . . ." she finally said. I could tell each word cost her.

I shook my head, realizing she'd misinterpreted my fury. "Not with you, Neely Kate. I was angry at the situation." I pushed back a bit, turning to look at the blank TV screen. There was no way I'd be able to put my thoughts into words if I kept my eyes on her. "Look," I said, feeling frustrated. "I could see you were hurt . . . that someone or several some*ones* had hurt you bad. You've told me next to nothing, so I don't know who the people who hurt you are or what they did . . . and then I saw you drowning your sorrows in cheap whiskey . . . talking to that lowlife you used to work for . . . and it makes me *so angry* that I can't fix this for you." I paused, trying to control my rising temper. "That's what I do, Neely Kate—I fix Skeeter's problems—and I'm damn good at it, but I'd give anything to fix this for you, and I don't even know what *this* is."

She lifted her arms to my neck and hugged me. I sat there for several seconds, holding her in my arms, and I realized I could get used to this.

I wasn't so sure that was a good thing.

"I have to do this on my own," she said quietly.

My heart jolted. "Are you going to try to ditch me again?"

She was quiet for several seconds. "No. I like having you here." Then she grinned up at me. That smile looked like the sun rising in the morning, and I'd do anything to keep it on her face. "And it's not so bad having badass backup."

"You think I'm a badass?"

She snorted and her smile spread even wider as she rolled her eyes. "Please."

"So you'll keep me around?"

She plucked at my shirt, still grinning. "You make a pretty good pillow to cry into."

"At least I have a purpose," I teased.

Her smile fell as she lifted her gaze to mine, suddenly serious. She lifted her hand to my face, her palm skimming my cheek as she searched my eyes. "You're a good man, Jed Carlisle."

It was my turn to snort. I pulled down her hand. "No. I am *not* a good man. But we'll exorcise *your* demons, Neely Kate, and then we'll bury the bones and light it all on fire. I'll make sure you're free of whatever happened here. No more running."

Her face paled. She was bothered by something I'd said, but I knew better than to press her. "Are you hungry? Thirsty? You probably have a headache after crying so hard."

She shook her head.

"Do you want anything?"

She stared at me for a moment and then opened her mouth to speak, hesitating for another moment before she asked, "Can I ask you a favor?"

I gave her a reassuring smile. "Of course."

"I'm exhausted, but I've had a lot of nightmares lately . . . Will you hold me?"

I hesitated, not because I didn't want to comply, but because I wanted her so much I wasn't sure I could sleep with her and not end up taking advantage of her . . . and that was the last thing she needed. "I was going to sleep in the chair."

Her eyes flew open. "In the chair? You paid for the doggone room. If you don't want to sleep with me, then *I'll* sleep in the chair."

My face hardened. "Like hell you will."

"How about a compromise?" she said. "You can sit at the head of the bed and hold me. Just for a few minutes. *Please.* If you'd like, you can move after I fall asleep."

I could tell it was killing her to beg for what she needed. Why was I being such an ass?

"Of course." I kicked off my shoes and scooted up on the bed, rearranging the pillows to support my back and head and stretching my legs straight in front of me. I reached out my arm toward her.

She shed her jacket and kicked off her sandals, then crawled up the bed and snuggled into my side. Her head rested on my chest, and she curled her leg over my upper thighs. Her arm draped across my chest, her hand cupping the back of my neck. Then she sank into me, as though melding her body into mine.

I sat there breathless and in awe. I'd slept with more women than I could count, but this was somehow the most intimate experience I'd ever had. We were both fully clothed, although all I had to do was move my hand, which was now resting on her hip, down several inches and tug up the hem of her dress to show me what she was wearing underneath. And while the baser part of me was aching to touch her—her impromptu attempt to seduce me in the parking lot hadn't been completely

Denise Grover Swank

ineffective—there was a deeper part of me that only wanted this . . . *needed this.*

I reached over and turned off the light, but she clung to me as if afraid I'd let her go. When I sat back upright, I lifted my hand to smooth her hair. "I'm not leaving."

Soon her breathing became shallower and her hand loosened its hold around my neck. I moved her arm down to my waist. I knew she was asleep, and I could have moved her to the other side of the bed, but if she woke up frightened, I wanted her to know I was there. At least I could do *that* for her. Still, as I drifted off, I knew I wasn't just holding her because she needed me— I needed her too.

That scared me more than anything.

For the Birds
Rose Gardner Investigations #2
July 11, 2017

272